ALSO BY DAVID BERGEN

Sitting Opposite My Brother
A Year of Lesser

SEE
THE
CHILD

A NOVEL

DAVID BERGEN

SIMON & SCHUSTER
New York London Toronto Sydney Singapore

SIMON & SCHUSTER
Rockefeller Center
1230 Avenue of the Americas
New York, NY 10020

Copyright © 1999 by David Bergen

All rights reserved, including the right of reproduction
in whole or in part in any form.

Originally published in Canada in 1999
by HarperCollins Publishers Ltd.

SIMON & SCHUSTER and colophon are registered trademarks
of Simon & Schuster Inc.

For information regarding special discounts for bulk purchases,
please contact Simon & Schuster Special Sales: 1-800-456-6798
or business@simonandschuster.com

Manufactured in the United States of America

1 3 5 7 9 10 8 6 4 2

Library of Congress Cataloging-in-Publication Data

Bergen, David, 1957–
See the child : a novel / David Bergen
p. cm.
1. Children—Death—Fiction. 2. Fathers and sons—Fiction.
3. Grief—Fiction. I. Title
PR9199.3.B413 S44 2002
813'54—dc21   2001057571

ISBN 0-7432-2925-8

The financial assistance of the Manitoba Arts Council
is gratefully acknowledged.

For Hilary, Nicolas, Luke and Levi

MANITOBA

J UST BEFORE DAWN ON A COOL MORNING, A KNOCKING at the door pulled Paul up through dark layers of sleep. He rose, confused, and looked down at his wife, Lise, saw the rise and fall of her body, caught a hint of the warm smell of her. The knocking came again, a distant tapping which was light but insistent, and Paul realized, with relief, that this would be Stephen finally coming home. Paul felt lighthearted. Forgiven. He pulled on a bathrobe and walked barefoot down the stairs and beyond the kitchen to the side door, a thin metallic taste of anticipation in his mouth. He twisted the lock, turned the knob, opened the door. Harry Kehler, the town constable on duty that night, was standing there. Harry looked down at his feet and then back at Paul and he let loose a slight moan and said, "Aww, Paul. We found your son. He was lying face down in Hiebert's field. He must have been walking home and fallen over. Drowned himself in the mud."

"Stephen?"

Harry nodded and then he said, "Should I come in?" and he took Paul's arm and guided him to the kitchen where they sat across from each other. Harry placed his big hands on his thighs and looked over at the patio door and beyond to the darkness outside. Paul shook his head. He thought of Lise and Sue upstairs, still sleeping.

"Lise is sleeping," he told Harry.

Harry looked around. Nodded. "I'm so sorry," Harry said, and he put his hands on the table and made two big fists.

Paul thought, Poor man, bringing this news. He said, "I'll make coffee. Should I make coffee?"

"If you want to. If you think so."

Paul stood by the counter and spooned coffee into the filter. He ran water into the pot and poured it into the coffeemaker. Closed the lid. Set the pot on the element and turned on the switch. He came back to the table and sat down. Objects around him stood out in relief, as if time had halted. The toaster there, Harry's head, the dark square of window, the sound of the wind in the eaves, and the hairs which grew from his own fingers. Conrad clicked across the linoleum. A wet muzzle, tongue, flop of ear.

Paul's mouth quivered. He took his hands and covered his mouth and his hands were shaking and he began to cry. Harry took Paul's arm and pulled his hand down and placed it between his own two hands. He said, "There, there." And then he said, "Sweet Jesus." Paul stopped crying and looked up. His jaw ached and he realized with sudden clarity that he wanted to know everything.

"Farley Hiebert's field?" he asked.

Harry nodded.

"Who found him?"

"Farley himself."

"When?"

"Aww, I don't know, sometime early this morning."

Paul shook his head, uncomprehending.

Harry said, "Farley wasn't sure, and I was only called an hour ago, and I went out to Farley's and there were others there." He showed his palms to the ceiling. "Then I came here."

Paul wondered who the others were. He imagined a gathering of men and doctors and dogs looking down on his dead son. He stood and took two cups down from the cabinet and he thought again, Poor Harry. He turned and said, "You want to go? You must be tired."

"I'm not tired. How could I be tired? This is no time to be tired."

Paul poured coffee and put in cream. He gave a cup to Harry and said, "How long had he been there?"

Harry shrugged, "A few days?"

Paul thought about that. He said, "He looked like himself?"

Harry shrugged again and looked away.

"Where is he?" Paul asked.

"At the hospital."

"Can I see him?"

"You don't want to. There were crows. Something. That's how Farley noticed. He saw the crows." Harry gestured helplessly at his own face.

Paul thought of crows circling and calling, wings spread, falling into the crop on Farley's field. He put his head in his hands. Smelled his own smell and found it familiar and common and he hated it, this smell of being alive.

"They did what?" Paul asked. He leaned forward, very alert now, expecting the worst.

"Farley chased them away," Harry said. "He chased them away and covered Stephen with a tarp."

That was good, Paul thought. Good for Farley. Amazing what people would do for another person.

"His eyes?" Paul asked. He wanted to know.

"No," Harry said, "He was face down."

"Lise will die," Paul said.

"No she won't," Harry said. "You're strong, both of you. You have Sue. You have each other."

As if they had raised Lise from her sleep by talking about her, the sound of her moving about upstairs drifted down to them. It was dawn now, light filtered through the blinds. The kitchen tap dripped. Paul lifted his head as if to call out and warn Lise but said nothing.

"Do you want me to stay?" Harry asked.

Paul shook his head. "You can go," he said.

At the door Harry touched Paul's shoulder. Then he hugged him and Paul thought that Harry was a good man. Paul stood outside in the new light and watched him leave. Waited until his cruiser had disappeared and then he went back inside and stood by the stairs leading up to Lise and he listened for her. He thought about what he could say. He thought about what had happened. Then he climbed the stairs.

In JUNE OF THE YEAR STEPHEN WOULD DIE, PAUL MET Nicole Forêt for the first time. She was Stephen's new girlfriend and had been invited to supper. They shook hands in the foyer. Paul said, "Hi, nice to meet you," and Nicole nodded and said, "Hello," and then Lise said, "Forêt, I know your family. Jean Paul, *ton père*."

Nicole nodded and dipped her chin.

"She speaks English, Mum," Stephen said.

"It's okay," Nicole said. "I don't mind." She leaned towards Stephen. Her eyes were nutty-coloured and sleepy. A light blue vein ran up one side of her neck. She said to Lise, "Nice," and looked around at the house. Her tongue was pierced, three studs laid out like stepping stones to the back of her throat. Silver rings of diminishing size climbed the rims of her ears. Hair cut short, bleached, she wore sandals and her toenails were painted orange. Her hand moved about, touching Stephen's arm, her own face, while the other held Stephen's waist. She went up and kissed Stephen's jaw, below his ear, then she looked at Paul and smiled.

Paul turned away and back and said, "Come," and led them out through the patio to the pool where, before supper, the young people swam while Paul and Lise prepared food and watched from the kitchen window. Their daughter Sue sat at the edge of the pool while Stephen bounced on the diving board and talked to Nicole who floated on her back near the shallow end. The day was muggy. Earlier, low dark clouds had come in from the west, thrown down some rain, and then fled past the town of Furst, and by late afternoon the sky had cleared. Paul, watching the three-some, asked Lise, "What do you think?"

"Nothing to think yet. She's pretty, and more confident than I expected."

"What'd you expect? A mouse?"

Lise went to the oven, lasagne in hand. "No, it's more the body language. Seems fairly mature."

"So you remember the family," Paul said. Earlier in the week Lise hadn't been certain who Nicole Forêt was, even though they both came from St. Pierre, a small French-speaking town twenty miles west of Furst.

She nodded now. Said she remembered Nicole as a child, the mother dying of some kind of hemorrhage, the father and daughter a peculiar pair on the streets. But nothing terribly odd. Just slightly different.

Lise was wearing a black tank top and jean shorts. Her legs were tanned. She was flushed from the frenzy of food preparation and Paul wished, at that moment, she would go up and kiss his jaw, as Nicole had done to Stephen. He ducked and smelled the top of her head. Said, "Maybe she'll make Stephen happier." The boy, in the last months, had been angry and reckless. He'd quit school and wasn't working and this worried Paul, who did not want a dull and shiftless son. The dinner had been Lise's idea; a new beginning, though Paul wasn't too hopeful.

Through the window he saw Nicole talking with Sue. Both of them were sitting on chairs now. Nicole was holding her knees with her hands. Stephen hoisted himself up beside the girls. Nicole pushed a hand through Stephen's hair, twisted her fingers round and round. Stephen ran a finger along her neck and down inside one of the cups of her bikini top. Sue was watching this. Nicole looked at Stephen and then back at Sue. Nicole spoke. Sue laughed. Stephen put his hand down at his side. The sun went behind a cloud.

They ate on the deck. Paul's parents, Jack and Beth, had joined them. The backyard was filled with the clatter of dishes and cutlery and the murmur of voices. Everyone was polite, too polite, Paul thought, and so he poured wine and offered beer and, at one point, pulled out the whisky which caused Lise to give him a studied look.

Beth wanted to know if Nicole was in school.

"Yes, grade twelve," Nicole said. She'd put on shorts and a white long-sleeved button-down shirt over her bathing suit. The wetness had come through the shorts but it was harder to see the dampness on the shirt, unless you looked carefully.

"Then what'll you do next year?" Beth asked.

Nicole shrugged. "I'll work."

Lise said, "I went to school with a Forêt. Bernadette."

"That's my aunt," Nicole offered. Beyond the pool, out on the golf course, a twosome passed by. Nicole lifted her head and watched them disappear. "It's beautiful," she said. "The view, the pool, the golf course. It's beautiful. And innocent."

"Innocent?" Paul's father asked. "What's that?"

Nicole's hand went up to her hair as if deflecting something. Stephen said, "She means we're rich."

"No," Nicole started, but Jack jumped in, "Of course, we're rich. There's nothing wrong with rich."

"If you're poor, there is, Dad." This was Lise, who seemed to have placed herself out of the fray, as if observing from above.

"That's jealousy," Jack said. "Pure jealousy."

"Grandpa," Stephen said, "you don't know that." He'd put his hand on Nicole's neck. Left it there as a form of protection.

"I don't mean rich," Nicole said. "I mean innocent, as if this is how it was, is, and always will be. It's all you know."

Sue, who was listening and taking sips from Paul's beer and picking the feta out of the salad, said, "That's true, that's true. I feel that sometimes."

"I remember," Lise said, "when I married Paul and moved here, I thought how simple everything was. It's not true, of course."

"I didn't mean simple, I meant innocent," Nicole said.

"They're the same, aren't they?" Lise turned to Paul.

He said, sensing a trap, "Can be, sometimes. Unless you mean blameless instead of innocent, then they're different."

"Yeah, blameless," Sue agreed, still trying to help Nicole. "That's what I would say. We think we are, anyways," and this time she turned red and stopped talking, sensing that she had blundered in some way. Paul squeezed her leg under the table. Looked over at Lise, who asked Nicole, "Where in St. Pierre do you live?"

"Behind Le Routier. My mother worked there and then she died and my father kept the house. It's small." She looked over at Paul's father and said, "We're poor," and then she laughed.

Jack laughed with her briefly and then said, "I'm sorry about your mother."

"Oh, don't be," Nicole said, "I was only three." She said the word "three" as if it held some significance.

Lise said, "Your father was a magician. I remember that."

"Still is," Nicole said. "His favourite trick is pulling caps off of beer bottles. All day."

Stephen smiled. Paul's mother had a pained look, as if things had gotten completely out of control. Lise said, "I remember my father. Gaston. You've probably seen him around town, Nicole. I remember him lining up bottles on bricks and shooting them with his rifle. Except he only shot one bottle at a time and only after he'd made love to my mother."

Paul said, "You never told me that."

Lise looked at him. She said, "One morning he was yelling and then he shot all the bottles at once. It turned out he was angry and had threatened my mum with no more sex."

Beth laughed. Nicole leaned her head towards Stephen. Lise said, "My mother was not upset, of course."

"Of course," Jack said.

"Is that true?" Paul asked.

"Oh, Daddy," Sue said, and she clutched his elbow.

Later, after dessert and coffee, they played water polo, Lise and Paul against the three young people, while Jack and Beth watched from the deck. Paul and Lise chose the shallow end so they could attack and rest. Nicole treaded water at the deep end, protecting the goal, an old plastic hockey net. Paul loved the physical contact, the scrambling for the ball, the frothing water, sliding under and rising, sucking for air, to seek out the elusive ball. Once, he received a long pass from Lise and in one motion snapped the ball towards the net. Nicole rose out of the water, the white slip of bikini like a thin strip of tape, her arms akimbo, Sue beside her, all limbs and hair, and Paul was startled by the possibility of family and love.

He swam underwater back to Lise who clutched his chin and drew him upwards and kissed him on the mouth and said, "There." And that night in bed she repeated that same move, "There," and Paul, sloping to take her left breast in his mouth, thought of Nicole and the gully of her belly button and the way her mouth moved when she said *innocent* and he wondered if Stephen understood Nicole, if he was in any way her equal. All these thoughts faded as Lise pushed him lower and his ears felt the comfort of her thighs.

In the night he woke to a cry. He opened his eyes and turned to Lise, who was still sleeping. He heard again a voice, laughter, another cry, and a splash. He climbed out of bed, went to the window, and looked out. Saw the outline of the trees and the fence. A figure at the edge of the pool. Paul put on his bathrobe and went down the hallway, downstairs, through the kitchen, out the patio door, and walked towards the pool. At the gate he stopped. Nicole was jumping up and down on the diving board. He could not see her properly but he heard her voice. She called out, "Nickel, nickel," and giggled.

Paul saw Stephen's head rise out of the water, his fist in the air. Nicole leaned forward and with a gasp and a scream she fell forward.

Both heads surfaced now. Stephen said, "Quiet."

Nicole laughed and pushed him under. He came up. Called out, "You're gonna drown me," and then Nicole pushed him under again. Stephen resurfaced, gasping, "Jesus, Nicole." Nicole went soft and said, "Here," and she helped him float. She swam under him. Treaded water and kissed him for a long time. Paul hadn't moved from the gate entrance but as Nicole and Stephen moved to the shallow end, he stepped back. Lifted his hand as if to say something, then lowered it.

Nicole drew her leg up and held her foot. Put it down again and said, "Ready." Stephen kissed her, then dived and stayed under. Nicole giggled. Her head went back briefly, her throat a dark silhouette. Stephen surfaced and held up his hand, triumphant. "There," he said, and she took what he had, threw it, and said, "Fetch." Stephen disappeared. Nicole turned and hoisted herself from the pool. She stood and walked towards the gate and as she drew near to Paul he saw that she was naked. She stopped and picked up a towel from the ground and, in rising, she turned her head and saw Paul. She did not seem surprised. She did not startle or draw the towel across her body. She looked at him and he looked at her. He saw the ends of wet hair at her shoulders and her long arms, hands at her bare hips, vague patch at her crotch, breasts which were small and dark in the shadows. She angled her head and appeared to laugh and it was Paul finally who turned away and walked quickly back to the house.

Later, when he'd regained the bedroom, he went to the window and looked down to where Nicole now sat at the pool's edge, one leg pulled towards her chest, knee pointed at the sky, and Stephen below her, in the water still, whispering and reaching with one hand to touch Nicole's mouth. Her head was tilted slightly and Paul imagined her gaze moving upwards to where he stood and he experienced a curious mixture of jealousy and anger. The jealousy surprised him and he shut the window and the curtains and sat at the edge of the bed. He waited, and when their voices carried up to him, he went again and parted the curtain and looked out at the pool. Nicole and Stephen were on the grass now. A flash of a bright limb. Her hair. The shadows. He thought he should go down, or wake up Lise, but he did neither. It would be much later, long after

Stephen's death, when he would understand that it was Nicole, and not Stephen, who had kept him from acting. Finally, perhaps an hour later, he heard the sound of Stephen's car. Headlights passed across the window, and then they were gone.

When he woke in the morning, it was late. He got out of bed and showered and then, crossing the room to the window, he opened the blind and looked out onto the pool. Lise was swimming laps. Sue and a friend were eating at the table beneath the shade of the plum tree. The setting was serene. Unremarkable. Paul thought perhaps he had imagined the scene from the night before, though it was still vivid, especially Stephen's head being pushed underwater, and the shape of Nicole, her light giggles, the angle of her head as she stood before Paul and divined his presence. It seemed, now, a strange and predetermined event, as if Nicole had wanted him to watch.

Paul turned from the window. Dressed and walked down the hallway to Stephen's room. Knocked, got no answer, and entered. The bed had not been slept in. He crossed over, sat down, and surveyed the room. There were some trophies from Stephen's earlier years when he played soccer and baseball. There were banners of hockey teams and posters of rock stars, some now dead. In the corner sat Stephen's violin. He stood, lifted the case onto the bed, and opened it. Removed the bow. Tightened it. Then took out the violin. It was a half-size. Stephen had stopped playing at the age of ten. Paul had studied the violin with him and they had practised downstairs, beside the piano, Paul standing slightly behind and to the right of Stephen so as to give him room and to be able to observe his bowing and fingering. He had loved the way Stephen's face drew inward as he played. How easily the boy produced music, one shoulder hunched slightly, though for this he was reprimanded by his teacher, an older man named Horch, who had deep black grooves on the middle and index fingers of his left hand, and who spoke gruffly and had little patience for children. Still, Paul and

Stephen persevered and by the second winter of lessons they were giving small concerts to grandparents and unsuspecting company, who were forced to sit through versions of Bach's minuets or Paganini's theme from "Witches' Dance."

Paul replaced the violin and crossed over to the window from where he could see that Lise had finished doing her laps and was now standing by the girls and talking. He went downstairs, poured himself coffee, sat at the dining-room table, and looked at the newspaper before him. He read the headlines and found no reason to read further. Lise came in from the outside. Her hair was wet and hung to her shoulders and water dripped from the ends of her hair and onto her black bathing suit where it disappeared. She had a white towel wrapped around her waist. She poured herself coffee and sat across from Paul and said, "You slept in. That's not like you."

"Bad night," Paul said.

Lise looked at him and then she looked at the paper. She turned it around so she could read. She said, "What was wrong?"

"Stephen didn't come home for the night."

"He went to St. Pierre," Lise said. "He stayed with my parents. I thought I told you."

"You're sure he was there?"

"Yes. I called this morning. He was still in bed."

"You slept fine."

Lise patted Paul's hand and said, "I always sleep well after sex. You know that." She pulled at the ends of her wet hair. It squeaked. She had brought with her into the room the smell of chlorine. Her nipples showed through her bathing suit. Paul looked at her hands; one of them held the coffee mug now, the other lay flat on the paper. The tips of her fingers were pruned from swimming. They were like Stephen's hands, nails neatly clipped, fingers long.

Paul said, "What'd you think? Of Nicole?"

Lise stood and put some bread in the toaster. Pushed it down and turned back to Paul. "Well, she's not innocent. Which we are, according to her."

"You didn't like that," Paul said.

"It was like she'd planned all along to tell us our faults. This morning I asked Sue what she thought and she hummed and hawed. Though she did seem to want to please Nicole." Lise paused, then said, "There was this girl I knew in high school. Georgette Ferland. She was amoral. It was act first and then deal later with the consequences. Needless to say, there were consequences. Nicole reminds me of her."

"That's not amoral," Paul said. "Just greedy."

"Either way it's bad if your son is going to get hurt," Lise said. "And I'd say she'll break his heart."

"I hope not," Paul said. He stood and buttered Lise's toast. Put it on a plate and handed it to her. Pushed down two slices for himself. He said, "Was that true? That story about your father?"

"Sort of."

"You didn't have to tell it."

"She needed some help. Seemed that way to me, anyway."

"Maybe she wanted to talk about her father. Maybe she wanted us to know the man's a drunk."

"I don't know," Lise said, and she bent to her toast as if they'd discussed Nicole long enough. Beyond Lise's head, past the window, Paul could see Sue sitting cross-legged by the pool. She was facing him and was bent over the bare back of her friend, applying lotion. Her hand circled the shoulder blades and slid down to the lower back. She talked and moved her hands up her friend's spine. She looked up at one point and studied the sky through her dark glasses and then she faced her friend again and said something. The friend turned onto her back and shielded her eyes with a hand. Paul thought about arms and feet and elbows and a leg bent so that the knee pointed at the sky. He thought about Nicole's shoulders and the colour of her breasts. He thought about Stephen's head going under and coming up and, later, dipping towards Nicole's thigh. The sum of so many parts, the trick of the mind. He watched his daughter Sue go onto her knees, toss her head, and flip her hair over her shoulders. "Hot," she said. He didn't hear it. He saw her mouth say it. He thought about Lise and himself. He remembered their courtship as brief and inevitable. Paul had gone off to college and returned in spring, brimming with assurance, planning to continue his studies the following year. However, this was not to be; Lise became pregnant, and by the end of summer they were married and Paul was working in his father's furniture store. The books on philosophy and linguistics to which, for a season, he so lovingly referred, were relegated to a drawer and eventually ended up in a box in the attic, beside a collection of pressed leaves and goldenrod that Lise had a fondness for in the first years of marriage.

A week passed. On Sunday, well before dawn, Paul drove out ten miles east of Furst to his land near La Broquerie, where he kept bees. And as he drove he remembered when Stephen was three or four and would come out to the bee farm. The straight strip of road, the rich landscape disappearing. The soil sandier, the trees scrubby and twisted, rocks growing out of the fields. Stephen would stand on the seat in the cab of the half-ton and look at the land sliding past. The boy was like a small bird, mouth open, head lifted, eyes wide. Later, walking among the hives, Paul pointed at the sorrel, clover, stinkweed, and wild roses, and called out their names to Stephen. He crouched before a willow blossom and held Stephen close and said, "Look, there, the bee. Its mouth is like a tiny straw. Sucks up the nectar and brings it back to the hive."

One night, driving home late, the boy fell asleep and Paul saw that children were so easy to love. He wondered if his own father had loved him as a child as deeply as Paul loved Stephen at that moment. Paul could not imagine that. He had no memory of his father's love other than the bungled swimming lessons and the occasional golf game that descended into disarray because Paul was more interested in wading out into the creek in search of lost balls than golfing. He supposed his father walked him to sleep as an infant but this he could not remember. He himself had walked many a night holding Stephen, treading a path across the rug, the child sucking on the crook of Paul's arm, perfectly calm until Paul stopped, and then Stephen howled, and Paul walked again.

He wished it were easier to love Stephen these days. Since last weekend Paul had seen little of him. One night he had found Nicole and Stephen sitting in the dark of the TV room. He entered, turned on the light, and saw that Nicole was crying and Stephen was leaning forward and looking at the floor. Nicole's obvious sorrow, Stephen's helplessness, this surprised Paul. All week he had imagined talking to Stephen but he had not done that; the boy's sullenness scared him. An impossible petulance.

La Broquerie appeared on Paul's left. A fog hung over the fields and the roads, a spotty brume that made the air damper, the dark darker. He arrived at his farm where he loaded seven hives and moved them four miles south, setting them up close to the Avery place beside a field of canola. Moving hives in the dark was easier because the temperature was lower and at night the bees were in the hive. Paul used a dolly and walked the hives up a ramp onto the back of the half-ton. Conrad ran out in the yard, barking at shadows and the night animals. They drove slowly out to the canola field, the hives swaying in the truck box. Conrad hung his head out the window and squinted into the sky which was threatening dawn. Paul unloaded the hives, spacing them six feet apart, in the protection of a windbreak, with the entrances facing away from each other. Each entrance was coloured, black, white, yellow, or blue, so the bees could see the hives. When Paul was done, the fog had lifted. A few stars remained in the sky. He drove home and the sun rose behind him and came through the rear window onto the back of his neck and head.

When he got back he washed beeswax from his fingers and showered. And then, falling into bed naked, he saw himself briefly as a man out of prehistory who was beating back the shadows from the cave. When Lise woke they made love and then he fed her breakfast in bed. The morning was infinite, time stood still, a raspberry seed clung to Lise's lower lip. Paul worked at home throughout the day, walked over to his mother and father's, drank lemon tea, talked about the store and the death of his mother's aunt, and then he came home to a cold supper in front of the TV. He went to bed with a sense of gratitude; for what, he was not sure.

That night Paul was lifted from a dream in which he was giving a speech to the local Chamber of Commerce. He broke through the ceiling of his dream and discovered the gentle prodding of Lise and her groans, "Phone, Paul, phone." She fell asleep again, one hand resting between the pillow and her cheek as if it were a precious leaf and required pressing.

He answered. It was Harry Kehler. "Paul, I'm sorry but you'll have to come down here. To your store."

"Why?"

"I caught someone breaking in."

"There? You have them there?" Paul's feet touched the floor. "Who?"

"Can you come? Now?"

Then, in the background, a voice, not Harry's. Harry hung up.

Lise was still sleeping. Paul found his clothes, knocked through the kitchen, worked his feet into boots, slid into a jacket, and stepped outside. A train whistled, miles away, near Giroux. The air carried the sound tight and clean. He drove to the highway, crossed the median and pulled into the store lot. The lights were on. Paul went through the front door, walked past the showroom and down the hall into the storage area where he found Harry taking pictures of the smashed-in door.

Harry took Paul by the arm and led him into the coffee room and nodded over at Stephen who was handcuffed to the door of the fridge. The boy had his head bowed.

Paul looked at Stephen, at Harry, back at Stephen. Then he said, "What the hell?"

He turned to Harry and asked, "Are you serious?"

Harry dipped his head. Lifted it. Said, "Yes."

"Son of a bitch," Paul said. He walked away to look at the door. Saw Stephen's car. The rear end had been slammed into the door. He re-entered the coffee room, went to Stephen, stood over him and said, "What are you doing?"

Stephen turned away.

"Look at me," Paul said. Stephen lifted his chin. His face ovaled whitely around his mouth.

"Hey," Harry said.

Paul asked, "Why is he handcuffed?"

"He tried to run."

"Great." Paul was looking at Stephen's head, the two ropes of tendon at the back of the neck, the short hair revealing the crown. He thought he might draw his finger along the gully between the two ropes. He didn't. He motioned to Harry and they walked out into the showroom. Stood by the front window and looked out into the night.

"What are we gonna do?" Paul asked.

"Not much choice. It's a break and enter. I have to charge him."

"What if you weren't here?" Paul asked. "What if I had found him?"

"You didn't," Harry said.

"I was wondering," Paul said, "if we should leave this between us. Not report it. Let me handle Stephen."

"I can see that's what you're thinking."

"It's only the door. He's scared."

"He's guilty."

"Well, sure, of course."

"I'd get fired."

"Nobody'll know."

Harry stared out at the rain which fell heavier now and with more force, so that it no longer all ran off into the gutter but stayed put and began to build its own depth.

"It's the truth, nobody'll know," Paul pushed.

Harry said, "You're my friend and that's the only reason I'll say this. I'm going to leave. I'll take the cuffs and walk away. I'll destroy the film. I never knew about this, I didn't phone you, I didn't talk to you. Okay?"

"Okay, that's good. Good."

Harry walked back through the hall and into the coffee room. Bent over Stephen. The key went *snick* in the cuffs. The claws separated. Harry stepped back. Stephen rubbed his wrists.

"I'm for sure an idiot," Harry said. He pointed at Stephen, finger like a big bone. "And you're an idiot."

"Everything'll be fine. Just fine," Paul chanted.

He boarded up the back door with a sheet of plywood retrieved from the back room. Found several bent nails, a hammer in the rear of his half-ton, and strapped the plywood with lengths of two-by-four. In the darkness he flailed at the slippery nails and hit his thumb. By the time he was finished the job he was sweating and thirsty. He circled around to the front door, entered and walked back to the coffee room where Stephen still sat.

"So?" Paul said.

Stephen looked at the floor.

"You gonna talk to me? Give me a reason?"

Stephen gave no indication he had heard.

Paul wanted to hit him. "Look at me," he said.

Stephen refused.

There was a lunch bag on the table with two oranges in it. Paul took out an orange and threw it at the wall. Stephen jumped and looked up, first at the wall and then over at his father, who had picked up the other orange and was rolling it in his hands like he was looking for the seams in a baseball. Stephen looked away and Paul said, "Jesus Christ," and he pitched again, lower this time, and the second orange hit and stuck on a nail protruding from the wall. Mounted, it looked permanent, like a quirk of design or the impaled head of a small animal.

"I'm angry," Paul said. "You understand that?"

Stephen looked up at his father finally. Then he turned away.

"Look at you," Paul said. "You show no remorse. None. Absolutely none. You drive into my store, using the car I bought you, and you try to rob me?"

Stephen shrugged.

"You've gotta talk. You can't not talk."

Stephen looked up and faced Paul again. Stared at him for a long

time. Then he raised his hand to his pocket and took out a cigarette. He was going to put it in his mouth when Paul reached over
and knocked it away. "No smoking," he said. "You know I don't like
you smoking."

"I know," Stephen said. He took out another cigarette. His
hands were shaking. He had trouble lighting the match but he
succeeded and lit his cigarette. Paul let him.

Stephen said, "I know what you like and what you don't like."

For a brief moment Paul thought that he might be in the wrong
here; it felt as if he had broken into the store, that he was the crim-
inal. He shook his head and looked around. The orange remained
stuck to the nail. There was nothing left to throw, so he said, "I saw
you and Nicole. The other night. At the pool."

Stephen held his cigarette midpoint between his lap and his
mouth. He appeared to study his hand, then he laid the cigarette
down at the edge of the table and he sat up and looked over at his
father and he said, "I know, Nicole said you were watching us."

"What are you talking about?" Paul asked.

"Like I said. You were watching. Nicole said you were watching.
You didn't tell us you were there, you just watched." Stephen's
voice fell away. Fright perhaps. Paul couldn't tell anymore.

Paul said, "I woke up and there you were. Frolicking like you'd
discovered your own little Eden. Grow up, Stephen, I couldn't
help but hear you. Like no one else existed. I'm sure the Courts
heard you. And the Huberts. Everyone." Paul sucked a quick
breath and leaned forward and his voice dropped to a whisper.
"How do you dare have sex with a girl in front of the whole neigh-
bourhood, on my property? And Nicole. Who is she? What does
she want?"

"You don't like her, do you?" Stephen's head was still bowed but
he lifted it to say this.

"That's not it. Not at all. It's you. You think you have the right
to take whatever comes your way. Look at you. You break into my
store. For who? For her? You think she's sweet and innocent."

"She's not sweet and innocent. I know that."

"What do you mean?"

"You've met her. You know."

"And she loves you?"

"I didn't say that. You always do that. Make up things I said when I didn't."

Paul wondered if that was true. He thought it wasn't. He said, "Well, you're sure willing to give up a lot for her." He was waving his hands now. This was not a good sign. He laid them out on the table and looked at the knuckles, the veins which formed an *M* near his left wrist.

"Can I go?" Stephen asked.

"No, you can't. Besides, where would you go?"

"Home."

"Oh, so you'd go home. And everything would be forgotten and we'd never ever talk about this again and I'd fix the car and you'd drive it and ask me for money and then you'd have sex with Nicole on the ping-pong table or wherever you bloody well pleased, maybe our bed, hey, and then what? Hey? Where's the remorse? Where's the punishment? The forgiveness?"

Stephen looked as if he was going to cry and Paul saw hope in that possibility. Then Stephen said, "You were watching us. That's sick, Dad. You're sick." He was working his mouth. Paul saw that he was trying to grow a moustache but it was just a trace of something, like mould. Seeing this, Paul felt a great ache for his boy. He wanted to say, "I love you," but Stephen stood up and asked for his keys. He said, "I'm going. I won't go home. That's what you want, isn't it?"

Paul gave him the car keys. He kept the house keys. He looked up, hoping that Stephen would be crying, but he wasn't. Paul said, "Fine, go."

After Stephen had left, Paul cleaned up the coffee room. He threw the split oranges in the garbage and wiped the walls. He turned off the lights, locked the front door, and stood and looked out over the parking lot to the highway. A tractor trailer hauling chickens geared up, heading north. Flashes of white fowl, squawks. The air was warm and sticky after the rain. A half-moon balanced in the eastern sky. Paul climbed into his half-ton and drove home. The house stood dark and silent. He entered, went into the kitchen, and brewed a pot of coffee. He imagined Stephen limping around town with his beaten-up Mazda, trying to find a place to sleep, perhaps even becoming aware of his wrongs. It was important to reflect on your actions, on motivation, on consequence.

Paul stood by the patio door, holding his coffee, and he looked at the yard and seeing the pool he thought of Stephen accusing him of watching, as if he were sick, rather than a father who had stumbled upon his teenage son and girlfriend. Blame was not to be laid at his feet. Paul felt again the rage he'd experienced at the store, throwing oranges at the wall and listening to the absurdity of Stephen's reasoning.

From where he stood in the gloaming of the sitting room, Paul saw Stephen's car pull into the driveway, headlights panning the trees and the backyard. Stephen killed the engine, climbed out of his car, and approached the back door. He searched his pockets for his keys. Paul, watching him, touched his own pockets where Stephen's house keys sat. Stephen tried the door, jiggled it, tried again. He put his hands in his pockets and went down the stairs and across the lawn towards Paul and the patio door. Paul stepped back. He heard his own breathing, felt the smooth enamel of his coffee cup on his palm. Stephen pulled at the door. "Fuck," he said. Then he walked around the side of the house and Paul lost sight of him, heard him eventually at the front door. Rattling. Stephen gave the door a kick and Paul jumped. He suddenly saw himself as trapped. Still, he did not move, and it was not until Stephen climbed back into the Mazda and the one undamaged taillight disappeared that Paul opened the patio door to stand and listen for the whine of Stephen's car. But he was already gone.

Conrad, who had heard the commotion, came down from Sue's room and shuffled out onto the patio and sniffed Paul's leg. "Hey, boy," Paul said. He reached down and scratched his ears. After a bit he went inside and closed the patio door. He did not lock it. Heaviness had settled in like a sudden fog; he felt thick and lost.

Later, in bed beside Lise, Paul rubbed her back through her nightgown. Brought her back to consciousness. His hand slid down her bum. "Hey," he whispered.

"You," Lise mumbled, "you fine?" and then she went back to sleep.

Paul didn't answer, though he believed deep down that he was fine, that the world he knew would exist tomorrow as always, that morning would find him whole again, drained of heaviness. He fell asleep with his chin pressed into Lise's head. Later, her heat began to suffocate him so he turned and searched for a new hollow. For a moment he saw Stephen; he was standing all alone and kicking at the body of a large dead animal. Then Stephen disappeared and Paul recaptured his sleep just before dawn touched at the window above his head.

At breakfast he told Lise about the break-in, about Harry and Stephen and about Stephen's car. He told her about his rage and about throwing oranges against the wall. He said that Stephen had been unrepentant, had seemed to think life should go on as usual. "He was in handcuffs when I got there," Paul said. "Harry, the over-zealous constable. He was going to charge him but I convinced him to let me deal with it."

"What do you mean?" Lise had been planning to eat but with this news her spoon went down and she looked across at Paul who wondered if he had told this story all wrong.

"I thought Stephen might see the kindness in that act," Paul said. "Did he?"

"No. I tried to talk to him but he wouldn't listen. Took his keys and left."

"And you let him go?" Lise's voice had risen. She had two little red dots on her cheeks. "This is incredible," she said. "Why didn't you wake me? Call me down to the store? He listens to me these days. We talk, I listen to him, and he listens to me. Where is he now?"

"I don't know."

"Jesus, Paul. You don't know?"

"No." There was more to tell but he wasn't going to tell it now. He said, "He probably went to Nicole's."

"That girl's trouble," Lise said. "I'll call her."

"He was angry, Lise. He doesn't want to be chased around the countryside."

"I don't care what he wants," she said, and she turned away to look out the window. Paul watched her and suddenly hated her meddling, her need to know everything. He wanted to tell her that knowing everything would not make her any happier. She walked over to the dishwasher and took out a coffee mug and Paul saw, as if through a warped glass, his wife forty years into the future, an old woman, dwindled, her neck bowed from the weight of living, surprise in her eyes as if what she had become was both unexpected and undeserved.

Lise called Nicole's house and got no answer. After she hung up she said, "I'm going to St. Pierre. You want to come?"

Paul shook his head. Said he was going to work. But when Lise returned three hours later Paul was still home; he had not dressed for work, and had no more intention of going.

Lise looked at him and said, "They weren't there. I talked to Monsieur Forêt and he said Nicole and Stephen were out. Didn't know where. Just out. So I left Stephen a note. Told him to call." She lifted her shoulders. Her eyes were red as if she'd been crying. She came over to Paul and put her head against his chest and folded her hands at her stomach. "Poor Stephen," she said.

That evening Paul called the Forêt house. When Nicole answered she didn't seem surprised to hear him. She said, "Stephen's not here."

Paul could hear the TV in the background. A man's voice, perhaps her father. "Could you have him call me," he said.

"I'll tell him."

"I'd like to talk to him."

"For sure, he's your boy."

"Yes, he is," Paul said, and as he hung up he was aware of how close and familiar Nicole's voice was and how, hearing her tongue dip into *boy*, he again saw her standing before him at the pool, the lift of her head, the dark, her mouth opening as if she were laughing at him.

The following morning Paul went to work. The heavy spring rains had subsided enough for gardens to be planted and fields to be seeded but now more rain had fallen and continued to fall and the sky was grey and the world was soggy and sloppy. Children in brightly coloured splash suits puddled along the edges of the ditches, poking sticks into the dirty water, testing the depth, spearing frogs. A six-year-old boy had nearly drowned when he fell into a ditch near the high school. A passing teenager pulled him from the water and breathed life back into him. The boy's mother was hysterical with relief. There was a picture in the Furst *Clarion* of the mother holding her son. Beside them stood the teenager. He appeared sheepish, as if surprised by this sudden christening as saviour.

Paul was at the store, on lunch break, when he came across the photo and story, written by Emily Wish. He was surprised by the mother, Gladys Dirks, who was homelier and fatter than he remembered. She was the daughter of a beet farmer and in high school flirted with the athletes and drove the younger boys around in her father's half-ton. Paul, generously, believed it was grief that had made her photo so unflattering. He wondered if his son Stephen knew this heroic teenager.

He folded the paper and looked out through his window which gave out onto the sales floor. The store was quiet. Lise was out. She had said she was going back to St. Pierre and Paul did not argue. There was a young couple looking at a leather sectional. Jill Falk, one of the salespeople, was talking to them. Wendy, the secretary, was talking on the phone, doodling as she spoke, twisting the phone cord around an index finger.

Paul saw Nicole enter the store. Perhaps she had brought Stephen, who would be waiting outside in the car. Paul began to stand and then, uncertain, sat again. He felt the weight of Stephen, as if he were a stone planted in his heart, a stone he could neither polish nor throw away. Nicole approached Wendy, spoke, and leaned over the counter. Wendy hung up the phone and came into Paul's office. She said, "There's a girl here who wants to see you. Nicole Forêt."

Paul said he knew Nicole and that Wendy could send her in. She entered and sat. Across the expanse of Paul's shiny desk her eyes were still dun-coloured and sleepy. She was modestly dressed, a knee-length skirt and a long-sleeved shirt. No make-up. She tucked her shirt under her bum, crossed her legs, and said, "Hello, Mr. Unger."

Paul nodded. Said, "Hi, Nicole." Then, he said, "So," and he waited.

Nicole folded her hands on her lap. "You don't know why I'm here?"

Paul shook his head.

"Stephen didn't tell you?"

"Nooo," Paul said. How strange this was, talking here, Nicole fully clothed, Paul behind his big desk. In her attempt at modesty she seemed suddenly vulnerable. Plainness suited her, made her more attractive.

Nicole's hand went to her hair. Pushed it around. "He said he had. Last night after you called, I asked him. He said he'd talked to you."

"I believe you've seen him lately. I haven't."

"That's a fuck-up," Nicole said. She sucked in a breath and blew out through her nose. Her nostrils, elongated, went out and in. A dryness at the corners of her nose, perhaps the effects of a cold. She had, Paul noted, the kind of skin that offered a faint webbing of veins.

"He's angry, I guess," Paul said. Even as he spoke he heard the weakness of this confession.

Nicole laughed. Her mouth dropped open and presented the three studs bevelled across her tongue. She said, "I'm going to have a baby." Her hand flicked upwards as if to ward off a blow, then resettled on her thigh. She looked at Paul and then looked away. She continued talking and as she did she stared off through the window out onto the sales floor where the TVs were showing a multiple image of a surfer riding a large wave. She said that Stephen made her really happy and she really liked Paul and Lise and Sue and being asked for supper. That was great. She usually didn't get to do things like that. She said she'd known families like the Ungers but she'd never been a part of one and now, with Stephen, she felt that there was a chance. "Though, now," she said, and she stopped talking and looked down at her hands. Cupped a bare knee. Looked up. Her top lip stuck to her teeth briefly, then slipped away, stretching ever so briefly as it went.

"Stephen's still a child, barely eighteen," Paul said.

"Old enough to get me pregnant."

Paul pressed on, in his heart a vision of his son manacled to this girl. "If you wish, I'll pay for it. You know?" The meaning was there and as he spoke he experienced a sensation very much like shame and this surprised him.

Nicole sloped her head, closed her eyes. She did not move for some time and Paul was about to speak when she opened her eyes and said, "I couldn't do that. Like the fetus was a bug or an ant and I just push down with my thumb and squash it. You know? Pop?" She stopped, then said, "Anyway, I'm too far along."

Paul felt chastised, wondered if he hadn't misjudged Nicole. He recalled the pool and the shadows and wondered now if he hadn't seen a slight swelling of the belly. He asked, "How far?"

Nicole counted with her fingers. Clasping her small finger, she looked up and said she wasn't sure.

"Certainly more than a few months," Paul said.

"Four." Nicole's mouth twisted.

Paul said, "You think because I saw you and Stephen having sex that that makes this baby his. Then you make me out to be a pervert. Tell Stephen I was watching."

"That's wrong, Mr. Unger. I didn't plan for you to wake up and find us. The baby's his. I don't sleep around. Ask Stephen. He'll tell you."

"Well, he didn't tell me, did he? Tried to drive his car through the store instead." Paul stopped. His breath fifed at the back of his throat. He asked, careless now in his haste to have this girl leave, "What do you want from me then?"

"Money."

Paul lifted a hand. Waved it as if refusing an offer.

Nicole's voice became tighter, more edgy. "It's Stephen's, too. He doesn't have money. You do. I'll need money. Every month. That's what he was supposed to talk to you about."

Beyond the office window, out on the floor, Paul could see a male customer talking to Wendy. The customer leaned towards Wendy and whispered in her ear. Wendy smiled. Paul said, looking back at Nicole, "Maybe, but I want to talk to Stephen first. Is he okay? Lise is worried."

"Yeah," Nicole said. "He's okay. He's staying at our house."

Paul noticed again her transparent skin with the blue veins. He said, "Could you tell him I'm sorry."

"Sure, sure I could do that. That's awfully sweet of you." She meant this.

Paul said, motioning at her stomach, "And we'll see the baby after it's born?"

"Oh, don't worry, Mr. Unger. There'll be a baby."

And there would be. She would come to him five months later, carrying an infant, and sit in that same office and ask, "You want to hold him? His name's Sky." Paul would take that child and note the size of the head and the long fingers and he would remember Stephen as an infant, gumming Paul's knuckles, and then he would hand him back, the baby squalling now so that Nicole had to feed him, pushing him up against a swollen breast, looking up and saying, as if it were a slogan, "It's the best for him. Better than formula." And Paul, both awed and troubled by the sight of his grandchild at Nicole's breast, would usher her from the office and let her disappear from his life.

He called Harry Kehler, found him at home, and said, "Can we go for a ride?" Harry picked him up at the store and they drove to Marchand where they stopped at the hotel and seated themselves in the lounge. Harry had a beer, Paul drank rye and Coke. They hadn't talked much on the way out, just odds and ends about the town, about Harry's work, Bunny, Lise. But now, holding his glass, the rye guttering in his throat, Paul said he had more news. About Stephen.

"His girlfriend Nicole came to see me today. She walked into the store at noon, sat down in my office, and announced that she was pregnant. The baby is Stephen's."

"Oh boy."

"Uh-huh."

"Today?"

"That's right."

"Gonna have a baby?"

"That's what she said."

"How do you know?"

"What do you mean?"

"Well, did she lift up her top and show you? And even so, how do you know it's Stephen's?"

"She said, though I don't really know."

"Of course you don't. Have you asked Stephen?"

"No, haven't had the chance."

"That'd be a start."

"He won't tell me the truth."

"Well, then you've got trouble. What did she want? The girl-friend."

"Money. She wanted me to pay child support."

"Oh boy."

"The thing is," Paul said, "I will. If it's Stephen's, I'll pay."

"Does Lise know?" Harry asked.

Paul shook his head. The lounge was filling up. Hydro workers, a couple of farmers, an older man who talked loudly of welding and carburettors. Two strippers appeared on the stage. One blonde, one redhead. Music started up. Harry and Paul watched for a bit. The redhead had a flashlight, handled it like a baton. Shone it out at the men, then back on herself. She wore a gold stud through her belly button.

Driving home later, Harry said, "I'm going to dream of that redhead. Like holding dynamite."

Then he asked, "Did you tell anybody about the other night?"

"I told Lise about the door, and Stephen, and you."

"Shit, I wasn't even there."

"I thought about that. The phone rang. It was you. Lise knew that."

Harry pondered this. Nodded finally and said, "I figure he was looking for money. The pregnancy and all. He was scared."

"Nicole said he was supposed to talk to me about money. He never did."

Harry lifted an eyebrow. Grunted. The clouds beyond Harry's windshield were wild and dark. They told of a storm, though Paul thought they might mean nothing, just a bit of a threat and then they'd move on.

It rained Wednesday, a constant rain brought in by a low, heavy sky. Paul made a trip out to La Broquerie to check the hives and Lise came along, which was unusual, as she disliked the bees and the old buildings and the general disarray. While Paul worked in the honey house Lise walked around the yard in a yellow slicker and oversized high-tops and picked wildflowers and looked at the drowned garden and then she poked around inside the house. She joined Paul later in the honey house. Stood dripping water down onto the cement, holding a sorry collection of chickweed and catchfly. She said, "I think she's lying."

Paul was sitting on a stool and peeling propolis from the brood frames. His hands were sticky. He said, "Maybe, but I doubt it. And besides, if Stephen thinks it's true, it's true."

Yesterday he had told Lise about Nicole and about the money. She had accepted the news carefully, waiting, and finally said, "Why does she talk to you and not me?"

When she had driven out to St. Pierre on Monday she hadn't found Stephen. She had talked to Monsieur Forêt who asked her in and told her a long story about a bull and a cow. Lise had come home distraught and tired. The last few nights she had not slept well, and last night she had shaken Paul and said, "I hear him. There's someone at the door." Paul had descended the stairs and opened the door and looked out at the driveway and the sky. The night. Wild clouds. A strong wind blew through the trees. A branch clattered against the eaves. He poured a glass of milk and warmed it in the microwave. When it was done the clock glowed blue: 3:10. He brought the milk up to Lise. Said, "Just the wind knocking things." She drank and then he went to sleep and when he woke in the morning he found Lise sleeping in Stephen's bed, a thin sheet covering her.

Now, hearing Lise say that Nicole was a liar, Paul was not surprised. The complexities here, the twisting of relations, the knowledge not shared, his own secrecy, all this had ceased to surprise him. "I'm tired," he told Lise.

Lise seemed to accept this claim. She turned and walked outside and when he came out of the honey house to drive home she was sitting in the half-ton, the flowers wilted in her hand, the windows fogged up from her own heat.

On Wednesday afternoon Paul called the Forêt house. He hoped, strangely, that Nicole would answer, that he could again hear her voice dipping and rising, but her father answered and told him, in broken English, that Nicole wasn't around and neither was Stephen. Paul tried again on Thursday morning and this time nobody answered. He thought he might drive out that evening.

Thursday afternoon, Lise, who had been working at home, called him at the office and told him the police had located

Stephen's car. Her voice was low and tight. She'd been crying and her words were bent and hard to understand. When she'd finished she breathed quickly as if she'd run a long distance to give him this news. Then she began to cry again.

"What do you mean, found?" Paul asked. "It was never lost."

"In Tacoma. Washington. The state," Lise said.

A quick fall. A relocation. "What about Stephen?"

"The police say the car was stolen. Two guys from Winnipeg were driving it. They claim to know nothing about Stephen. They were at a party near here. At Lawrence Isaac's farm. That's where they got the car."

"What about Stephen?" Out on the floor, through the glass window, Paul saw Jill's hands flying as she talked to a customer. She was wearing a black jacket and skirt. White boots. Her hair was pulled up tight so her neck was revealed.

"They don't know where he is," Lise said.

"Have you phoned Nicole?"

"She saw him two days ago. At that party. That was Tuesday night."

"And he was there all evening?"

"Nicole said he left without her. She didn't want to talk about it. I told her Stephen was missing. 'So?' she said."

"That's what she said?"

"And I called Harry. Then the Winnipeg Police. They consider him a runaway. Harry says they may be right."

"You think all that was necessary?"

"Necessary? What do you think? Stephen's missing. He's vanished."

Paul listened for her, thought he heard a moan, then he said, "I'll find him."

"I'm scared, Paul."

He said again, "I'll find him."

Out on the floor Jill had finished with the customer. She turned. Looked over. Paul was still holding the phone. There was the sense that he had lost something, that he was spinning wildly, that what

was safe and right and his was sliding away from him. He resock-
eted the phone, stood, tapped a sleeping foot against the floor, and
pulled on his nylon jacket. He walked across the store, waved at Jill,
then he stepped outside. The wind came from the north and
chilled him. He sat inside his half-ton and held the steering wheel.

Paul turned on the wipers. Then he pulled out, crossed the
median, and drove north two miles and then another three east.
Paul watched the fields, the roads, passing vehicles, even the sky, as
if expecting his son to suddenly appear, to step out from some
water-logged ditch, or to drop from heaven. The world out here
was flat and fully available and empty of surprises. A man walking
down a gravel road could be seen at three miles distance. Groves of
trees were few, the horizon disappeared in a puddle of mirage. Paul,
who usually liked the flat earth, found himself despising its lack of
difficulty, its dearth of hiding places. The fields were lakes of grain,
the occasional one lying fallow and dotted with brown muddy
islands. A hawk circled in the sky. A tractor was parked on a side
road. Waiting. A clutch of crows lifted and fell far away to the south.

Isaac's place wasn't really a farm. More a receptacle for cast-off
cars and rusted seeders and old roofless granaries and discarded
tires. In the middle of this rubble was a house, two and a half stories
with weathered clapboard and cracked windows. Paul parked his
half-ton beside a dull-coloured truck whose windshield was missing. A limping collie approached. "Good boy," Paul said through
his open window. He got out and walked towards the front stairs
and knocked on the door.

He knew the man who answered. Mr. Isaac. Had seen him at the
store. He must have been sleeping; his eyes were pink, he blinked
and squinted into the light.

"Yeah?" he said.

Paul introduced himself. Shook the man's hand. Talked about
his son. The party.

"There was a party," Mr. Isaac said. "I was gone that night.
Came home the next morning, found a mess and thrashed my boy."

Paul wondered what constituted a mess in this man's mind. He shifted on the porch, looked around, avoided the man's thick face, kept thinking he'd see something of Stephen's, a shoe maybe, or a jacket. Paul heard a curse, a yelp from the dog, and Lawrence, the boy, appeared. He came out from around one of the doomed granaries. He approached slowly. He stopped and looked up at Paul and said, "Stephen's not here."

"Watch your mouth," the old man said.

"Was he here that night?" Paul asked.

"He was," Lawrence said. "Was drunk, too." He looked up at the roof of the veranda as if expecting it to fall. "He met a girl here. Shiny boots. Smelled real pretty. They went off together." Lawrence smiled.

Paul's fingers tingled. Absurd. "What girl?"

"I don't know. Some girl from Winnipeg. Older."

"Nicole? You know Nicole?"

"Not Nicole. She was pissed at him."

"Watch your mouth." The old man stuck out his chin as he said this.

"Did Stephen come back?" Paul asked.

"Never saw him."

"How about his car?"

"It was here." Lawrence pointed out at the driveway. He was sullen now, tired of talking.

"In the morning, too?"

"Don't know."

"And you haven't seen him since?"

"No."

The old man must have been moved by something because he took Paul's arm and said, "You want coffee, a drink?"

"No," Paul said. He pulled away.

"He'll show," Mr. Isaac said. "They always come back."

Paul wasn't listening. He walked out to his half-ton. The mud pushed up and over the rims of his soles. He scraped at his feet with a stick he'd retrieved from the ground. Back in the truck he looked out over the yard at the old man and his son who stood under the eaves, watching him. Then he left, drove out to the mile road, looked right, left, and straight ahead. Then, after a time, he turned south, his eyes lifting to a pale sky. As he drove he talked to himself and by the time he arrived home he was convinced that his son was fine, that he had probably run off with that girl.

Lise was in the garden, raking leaves and branches through the mud. She turned and leaned against the rake handle. Her face from this distance was a white spot floating above her red squall jacket. Her hair was thicker, messier because of the wet and the rain. Paul, before he climbed out of the car, watched her watching him and he thought she had a bruised appearance; lips like plums, dark eyes, one side of her face in shadows. Then the rain on the windshield blurred the image.

Paul got out and went over and stood by the edge of the garden. Lise waited. Paul shook his head, lifted his shoulders. Lise turned away. Then she stepped out of the garden, her rubber boots sucking mud. Paul followed her inside where they sat at the kitchen table and Paul told her about Mr. Isaac, about Lawrence, about the girl.

"Stephen's dead," Lise said. "Isn't he?"

"Don't be silly. He's run away. Trying to scare us."

Lise's mouth was open slightly. A darkness there, beyond those white teeth. She had teeth like Stephen, small with little gaps. Her mouth closed.

"We don't know all of Stephen's friends," Paul said.

"I know my son," Lise said. "He wouldn't be so foolish to run off with some strange girl."

"It'd be easier if his car hadn't turned up. Then he'd be safe," Paul said. And it was true, the possibilities of Stephen lying in a ditch, or stuffed in a garbage bag, were greater now. Because of the car.

"Other kids at the party must know who this girl is," Lise said.

Paul nodded. Said, "I'll talk to some of them tomorrow morning. I'll do that. And if we can't locate him that way, we'll get everybody looking. We'll search for him."

Early the following morning Paul was woken by a banging at the door. It pulled him from a vivid dream in which Lise was bent over her little pile of raked and naked twigs and she was trying to light a fire but the wind kept snuffing the flame. The garden became littered with charred matchsticks that appeared to have grown chaotically out of the puddle that encircled her. The odd thing was Lise was crying, then she turned and called for help. Paul only recalled this dream a few days later; it came to him from another life, and by then any significance it might have had was unimportant, because the person at the door was not, as Paul imagined, Stephen returning home, but Harry Kehler. Harry looked at his feet and back at Paul and then he spoke, the words a litany.

THE WEDDING RECEPTION FOR SUE AND DANIEL WAS held on a Saturday in late June at the groom's parents' house near St. Pierre where the wide lawn sloped to the bank of the Rat River. A large circus tent had been erected and beneath it tables were spread with potato salads and ham sandwiches and cakes and the odd Asian dish which Hélène, Daniel's mother, had fallen in love with on a three-week trip to Thailand the previous fall. She had prepared them herself, insisting that folks would adore the four basic ingredients: hot, sour, sweet, and salty. However, the spiciness had driven most revellers over to the drink table, where wine and beer and Orange Crush and gin and ice and Canada Dry and scotch and various mixes loosened tongues and produced love and joy.

The stage for the band was set up near the house and as the instruments were tuned the older folks gathered on the screened-in deck to talk about cataracts, golf, and cancer while the young gathered close to the river where the girls with their coltish bare legs folded themselves into the large jackets and sweaters of boys they hardly knew, making promises they could not keep.

Early on, before the light faded and the party became more serious and the children fell asleep at the feet of their parents, Sue danced with her father. They swung out across the grass. Sue was barefoot and wore a bone-coloured dress that came to mid-calf. Buttons up the back. Collar and cuffs of pale satin. A yellow-and-mauve sash, gathered in a bow at the back, near the base of her spine. The moaning fiddle, the thump of the bass viol, the last light of the sun falling through her hair, all this made Paul nostalgic and for a moment he believed Sue was still a small child who needed attending to rather than a woman he had just handed over to a nineteen-year-old boy.

Paul was already a little drunk, the top of his head tingled and Sue's back against his hand felt both familiar and odd. His fingers doodled her buttons. His chest expanded. He looked down at his daughter and said, "Hi."

She smiled.

"You're happy," he said.

"Yes, Daddy." She went up on tiptoe and kissed his cheek.

He felt the perfection of her crown and said, "Daniel's a lucky man."

"I love him."

"I should hope so. I want happiness to chase you," he said.

The song ended. Sue pecked at him and slid through the crowd like ether. Paul sought out another drink. Found himself beside Gaston, who was seated near the tent and already drunk, just as he had been twenty years ago at Paul and Lise's wedding; a hardware store clerk who wept and drank and danced and sang.

Gaston was remembering that earlier wedding. Said, "At least these two don't have to get married. *Hé?* Though that wouldn't be so bad. Make me a great-grandfather. At sixty. *Merde.* The family is doomed to have teenage weddings. It's a bumpier road now than when I got married." He leaned forward so that the setting sun shone off his brow. His hair was grey, thick. "And you?" he asked. "And Lise?" He slurred his daughter's name. Lifted a hopeful eye.

Paul shrugged.

"She's stubborn," Gaston said. "Like an old cork."

Paul thought the image suited himself better. He was bobbing in a swollen river with no means to reach the other side. Though these days he took comfort in simple things, like his hives, his bees, their business, the thick protective anger of the little animals.

Then, like a bee herself, Lise appeared. She bent to kiss Gaston.

Paul. A light sting. She sat on Paul's knee, wrapped an arm around his neck.

"Isn't this wonderful?" she said. "Look, my feet are green." And they were. Her bare soles had acquired the colour of the damp grass. Paul touched one. Dragged a finger along the whorl of instep that remained unblemished.

"Come," she said, and she pulled Paul upwards and together they turned onto the lawn, leaving Gaston who unwittingly teetered at the edge of the crowd as the legs of his chair sank slowly into the earth.

Lise was familiar and easy. Paul smelled her head, adjusted the jumble in his mind, registered briefly the touch of her breasts against his rib cage. As it had always been she guided him with a careful pressure on his back. He saw, over the top of her head, the trees that lined the river, their dark shapes cut out against the sky. He recalled skating on that river one winter day long ago, holding Lise's mittened hand. They had skated beyond a bend in the river where, hidden from the Leblanc family, he had pressed his bulky parka against Lise and kissed her cold cheeks. Back then Paul saw girls as houses into which he would never gain entry. Houses with locked doors and windows; in his experience a shutter might be thrown aside, but then just as hastily closed again. Lise, however, was an open house. She left Paul wide-eyed and grateful.

He had found her one summer among a swarm of French girls at the edge of the man-made lake in St. Malo. During a heat wave in July of that year he'd gone camping with three other boys from Furst. During the day they lolled and strutted on the beach, the girls in their coloured bikinis, the baby fat still evident at the rim of their bums, the boys in too short shorts, their newly hairy legs turning blonde from the sun, bare chests dark and smooth and thin. Lise chose Paul. She lay on her stomach in the sand and told him that she was a volleyball player from St. Pierre, Most Valuable Player, and she stood, sand sticking to her sweaty stomach, and they looped and volleyed a ball between them. When Lise dived and rolled for an errant pass her legs scissored and pedalled: a quick glimpse of her crotch, the bright green cloth of her bikini bottom hiding her centre.

That night, on the beach, they kissed and Lise, coming up for air, said, "That was good, thank God."

Paul knocked his head against her chest, body stretched with desire. "Lise," he said, and he said it like she did, with a long *eeee* ending in a curt *zzz*. Lise.

Now, dancing on the lawn by this familiar river, the band playing "Contessa Waltz," she asked, "Are you okay?" He realized that he was clutching her. A drowning man. His mother swooped past, grabbed his elbow and let go and moved on.

"What I hate," he said, "is the silence. Only three years and it's like he never existed."

Lise's chin pushed up. The pipe of her throat. The dull light of dusk fell on her shoulders. "What do you want? A banner with his name on it?"

"Why should a dog, a horse, a rat, have life? I'd like to hear his name sometimes."

"Stephen," she said. "Stephen."

"You're drunk," he said.

"A little."

Hélène whispered by. She was dancing with Harry Kehler.

"Hi, Harry," Paul said.

Harry nodded, looked at Lise, said, "Paul," and fell away.

"Who invited him?" Paul asked, and even as he spoke he heard the foolishness of the question, and knew the answer, which arrived with the lilt of Lise's voice.

"Everybody's here."

Paul's neck tightened. He remembered last Sunday and the flash of Lise's bare knee, her shoulder, her hip, breast in his mouth, and the familiar just-showered smell of her: armpits, neck, crotch. "I was thinking," he said, "we should elope. Run away."

Lise leaned back and knocked at a crumb of cake on Paul's shoulder. "I do love you, sometimes," she said. "Anyways, we're still married even though you live out on the farm." She tucked her small head into Paul's neck. "Know what I was wondering? How you do that. Just walk away from Harry. He was your friend."

"There are things you don't know."

"That's the saddest part. You not telling. He was just the messenger, he didn't kill Stephen."

Paul did not answer. Words tired him out. They began to resemble the flux Conrad produced when he had eaten something bad.

"You're both so stubborn, you and Harry," Lise continued.

"What do you know about him? He talks to you?"

Lise shrugged as if to avoid the question, then suddenly pulled her head back and said, "I can talk to him if I like. He's my friend, too."

"And Bunny? You talk to her?"

Lise didn't like this question. Her body reacted; shoulder blades moved under Paul's hand. "Ahh," he said. He smelled Lise's black hair. Closed his eyes, rested his chin on Lise's head.

"Don't be glum," she said. "This is Sue's night."

"I won't. We already danced. She's beautiful. Frightens me."

"You're like two potatoes in the dark," Lise said. "She worries about you."

Paul was pleased. "Does she? That's silly."

"That's what I told her." Lise's hand dropped to Paul's chest.

Paul wondered what part of her brain, that complex coil, made her love him, then hate him. She didn't mind him these days. Perhaps she was grateful for the small measure of joy produced by the wedding. His hand splayed her back. In the distance a child shrieked. Happily. The band played on.

Last Sunday Lise had phoned him at his bee farm in La Broquerie and asked, "Can you come over?" Her voice fed across the wires into his ear. The prospect of something, a hint in her voice. He drove to Furst and found her in her kitchen, at the table. She was looking through photos taken years earlier, when Stephen and Sue were toddlers. "See here," Lise said, and she pointed at a photograph of Stephen on Paul's back. "He looks bigger than three. I wrote on the back he was three."

Paul studied the photo but didn't really recognize himself or Stephen, whose head seemed much too large. He looked for something familiar in the picture and saw the same chair he was sitting on right now. A small comfort in this. He slid the album back around to Lise. Re-entering this house defeated him. The well-known smell, the trail worn in the hardwood from kitchen to dining room, the nap of the rug in the corners, the felicity of the smooth banister, the geraniums in the kitchen window, the chipped kettle, Lise at this table, her mouth and nose in profile against the window, the bones of her knuckles.

Lise closed the album. Put her hand to her throat, then her chest, then took his fingers and played with them. She said, "I was wondering. You know? If we could possibly have sex?" She exhaled. Quickly. Then pulled air back in through her nostrils and lifted her head, looked right at Paul and smiled weakly.

"Now?" Paul asked.

"Yes. Yes. If that would be okay?"

"Well, you've got me, haven't you?" Paul said. "I'll try my best."

He followed her out of the kitchen and up the short flight of worn stairs to the hallway and down to the bedroom where they used to sleep, night after night after night, until they had each hollowed out a place in the mattress. He followed her feet, socked in grey, her jeans, tight at the calves, the push of her bum against denim, the short light shirt with long sleeves, pale yellow. He smelled Stephen's room as he passed and his forehead itched. He closed his eyes and opened them again, focusing on Lise's face as she turned and sat on the edge of the bed and undressed. Her flesh appeared. "Take off your clothes," she said. She smiled and it seemed a simper, as if this were a trick and once Paul were undressed she would laugh and walk away.

Paul ignored his own doubt and said, "I like that, say that again."

"What?"

"That line. That was nice."

"Take off your clothes," she whispered.

"That's so nice," Paul said.

She stood and watched him remove his shoes, his socks, his pants. He pulled his T-shirt over his head; Lise disappearing and reappearing. He took off his underwear and faced Lise, aware of his own obvious delight. He showed her his palms as if to prove he came in peace. "See," he said. They had not touched yet. Lise placed a finger on his mouth. "Shhh," she said. She seemed flatter: a disappointed look to her breasts. He leaned forward and touched. Remembered.

He lay on the bed. She fell onto him. It seemed both that they had never known each other and that they had been together forever. Paul nosed her belly. She rutted above him and offered him first one breast, then the other. The taste of the past. The beginning of bristles in her armpits scraped lightly at his tongue and he tore at her and raised her up and she did things which surprised him and "Oh my," he said. Only later would he consider the origin of her knowledge, and wonder, and then push the wonder aside.

After, they lay side by side, not touching, studying the ceiling as if it were a summer sky and she said, "I woke this morning with an empty cup for a heart. I waited for it to go away but it didn't, so I called you."

"And now?" Paul asked.

"The cup is full."

He put his hand on her hip. The bone there. A dip. She dragged a rumpled T-shirt off the floor, covered herself.

"How long has it been?" he asked.

"Don't get too hopeful, okay?"

"Of course not."

While she dressed he watched and she let him and he took this as a sign, a balancing of favours, and he thought of his house darkening in the bush, and he realized that Lise had passed on the empty cup to him. For his heart, as he left her, felt hollow.

Lise danced with Harry Kehler. A slow one so that she needed to wrap her arms around his neck. Paul watched and when the song was done Lise kissed Harry's cheek and walked away. Paul sat on a chair by the fire which had just been lit, and he drank a raft of gin with a little tonic thrown in. At some point he went into the house to find the bathroom and when he returned he attempted to walk the garden hose which snaked along the side of the house. He failed. He sat down again and surveyed the crowd. Resorted to sipping warm 7Up. Mrs. Wish, the doctor's wife, swayed past. Her baby had died during the winter, just stopped breathing. Paul thought they'd have something to say to each other. When he believed he had regained control of his body he ducked through the crowd to discover Hélène standing by the food table in the tent, picking at the radishes and celery, dipping, ferrying them to her mouth.

"Paul," she said.

Hélène had thin bare shoulders browned by the summer. Her dress was white and sleeveless. Her husband Don was playing in the band. Bass fiddle. Sang, too. Paul could hear him now, calling out the next song, "Point au Pic."

"It's a success, I think," Hélène said. "They're beautiful together."

It was Hélène who had wanted a wedding in the local parish, as did Lise. That was fine, Paul thought, let the women organize. His preference would have been a smaller wedding, less rigmarole. During the wedding the priest had used a word that Paul remembered now. He leaned towards Hélène and muttered, "Cleave. Isn't that strange? Can go both ways."

Hélène didn't understand. She dabbed at some dip that was stuck to her lip. Paul wanted to pursue the subject but Hélène wouldn't let him. She looked at him with black eyes. Perhaps she thought he was stupid. Paul wondered if Hélène, like Lise, simply lacked curiosity, or maybe it was a symptom of their long friendship. Blindly accepted what was given them, even when they suffered. Lise did it quickly and quietly, meandered her way through the valley and believed she would eventually exit. That's why Paul had been surprised last Sunday morning. It wasn't like her.

He told Hélène now, "I saw Lise last week."

"She said."

"Really?" Paul wondered why Lise would talk about that. In her mind it would be like admitting failure.

"I think the wedding was throwing her. She panicked."

"Huh."

Hélène blundered on, "The loneliness frightens her. She's thinking of asking Sue and Daniel to live with her. They can't really afford their own place, with Sue in school and Daniel just beginning at the store. Which reminds me, thanks."

"Sure," Paul said. He'd hired Daniel a couple of weeks ago. He figured there wasn't much choice, son-in-law and all. "He'll do fine," Paul said. He was thinking about Daniel and Sue and Lise all under one roof. A cloister.

"Don't you get lonely? Way out there? Lise says it's cozy, but."

"Sure. Sometimes." Paul let this dangle. It had been his decision to move out to La Broquerie after Stephen's death. And Lise had let him go. He'd expected more of a battle but she just said, "Fine, maybe it'll be better."

And it was, though there was still this knowledge that what came before had not been finished, that he and Lise were still running and that now Sue was running too, especially with this marriage. And they were merely children. Ridiculous. From where Paul and Hélène stood they could see Lise go up to Harry Kehler and ask him to dance.

Hélène touched Paul's arm as if she knew but didn't want to tell. Paul said, "That's Harry, an old friend of mine. That's the third time he's danced with my wife."

In fact, when the song was over and Harry and Lise had fallen away from each other, Paul pulled Harry over to the fire and they sat and bent towards the flames and watched the shapes and shadows and Paul said, "Lise says that it's time we talked."

"That's just what she told me."

"She's a peacemaker."

"Yes, she is."

"Why is that?"

"What?"

"Why don't we see each other?"

Harry looked up at the sky.

"You like her?" Paul asked. Nodded over at Lise, whose arm was looped over Hélène's shoulder. They whispered and swayed.

"Lise?" Harry laughed, too easily. "She's your wife, Paul. You know the rules, 'Thou shalt not covet.'"

"I don't live with her. Not anymore."

"True."

"So?"

Harry shook his head. Turned to seek out Bunny, his wife, who was holding a sleeping baby under the tent.

"Shit," Paul said. "No law says you can't have her. You want her? Here." He rose and lifted a hand to call out to Lise, but Harry pulled him back into his chair.

"Don't be an ass," Harry said. "You're drunk."

Paul could feel Harry's big hand on his neck. He'd forgotten how large a man Harry was. Beef farmer turned cop, calluses on his fingertips. "Okay," Paul said. "Let go."

When he was released, Paul drew with his finger through the air. "Like a series of steps. Going downwards. One step, two step."

"Ahh, you gotta forgive yourself."

Paul sensed a distance suddenly, as if Harry were more interested in the darkness which began at the edge of the circle that the bright lights had created in the night. The band played a reel. "That's nice," Harry said, and he squeezed Paul's shoulder and walked out across the lawn. Danced by himself, a large shadow, until Lise joined him. She took his thick hands, looked up at him, said a few words, and Harry nodded. As if they'd known each other forever.

It was Pastor Herb who, after Stephen's death, suggested they have breakfast every Tuesday morning. "You need to talk," he said, and though Paul was wary, he liked Herb's manner, the habit he had of asking questions and then listening to the answer. Paul said once that he was so angry he wanted to hit Lise with a hammer. "Smash her skull," he said.

"Is that right?" Herb asked. He seemed unsurprised, as if this were natural and even good.

"She's always cleaning. Washing sheets. On her hands and knees, scrubbing floors. Taking a knife to all the nooks and crannies. The house is a bloody dentist's office."

"Have you ever tried to understand this?"

"Not pretty these days. Her and me." Paul held up his empty palms. "I'm guilty."

"You didn't kill Stephen," Herb said. "He went to a party, walked out into a wet field, fell over drunk and drowned."

Paul looked at Herb as if this was the first time he'd heard this news. He tilted his head and nodded. Listened to Herb breathe through his mouth. He had the urge to lean forward and confess, to whisper, "But, there is more." Instead, he touched his temple tenderly and said, "It's the enormity of it. Almost as if there were an infallible order in the world. An awful symmetry and there's nothing anyone can do to stop it."

"What about now?" Herb asked, "You can't rearrange the order of your life?"

"I have no more courage," Paul said. "I find I lose my way. Become short of breath. Panicky. Not fearful, but it's almost as if I were falling behind in a race that was too long and too hard."

Herb pounced on this as if it were an invitation into philosophy. "The fact that you are sitting before me means you haven't despaired. This breathlessness is like a phantom that comes and goes. It has no clear outline at which we can point a finger and say, 'There, there, there it is.' It is fear, distress, dread. Things we must face. With Stephen, you have to remember him. Hold on to him."

The last time they'd met was the Tuesday before the weekend of the wedding. Paul talked about Sue and how happy she seemed. He explained he'd hired Daniel. He said what was saving him these days was his daughter. And his hives. The bees.

"Smart animals," he said. "I'd like to do that full-time. Let Lise take care of the store. My heart's not in it."

Herb read a few verses from the Psalms and then whispered a brief prayer for the Unger family. Paul listened and studied the coffee in his mug and found there a dim reflection of his eye.

Daniel and Sue wanted to leave. They intended to drive back to Winnipeg for the night but before they left there were speeches to be made. Hélène took the mike and said, "Oh, I'm so sad. But happy, too. Oh. I think Sue is a wonderful girl and this was a beautiful wedding and you were good guests and there's still food to eat. Daniel, my boy. Oh." Don set his bass viol on the stand and walked over and put his arm around Hélène. She angled the mike at his face. He said, "Thanks," and pushed her hand away.

Then Gaston got up and took the mike and said, "I was thinking. About weddings and love and how I love weddings. Because they remind me of when I was young and could get it up every hour. *Hé. C'est une farce.*" He shrugged his shoulders. Hélène tried to take the mike but Gaston pulled it back. He said, "When I was young, marriage was there so we could fool around in the open. You know. I'll climb onto you if you'll climb onto me and we can do it one, two, three. In the open. In the first year it happened every day, and then later, on Sunday afternoons while the children slept, and finally, on birthdays. Well, you see, love is wonderful." He paused, licked his lips, said, "*Bonne chance, Daniel et Sue,*" and then he bowed, as if this were his own wedding, and everybody clapped.

Paul's mother, Beth, came onstage. She took the mike from Gaston, who kissed her on the mouth. The crowd clapped. Gaston did a jig. Beth turned her back on Gaston and looked down on Sue and Daniel who were holding each other. She said, "There are two people who aren't here tonight. My husband Jack and my grandson

Stephen. We miss them." She paused, then said, "Love is like an onion. Layered and complex and you have to pull away the layers to get at the heart. Sue and Daniel, I hope you take all your lives to pull away the layers. Take your time. Be patient. Enjoy the moment. I love you." She began to cry. Gaston stepped up from the shadows and put his arm around her. She let him. He was shorter than Beth, smaller all over and this made him look child-like. He was pleased with himself as he led Beth offstage. His wife, Marie, watched this and nodded at the people around her as if all this were good and right.

Then Paul was called up. He found himself standing next to Don, who rested his chin on the scroll of the bass fiddle. Paul shuffled his feet. "Hey," he said. "Funny. I remember when Sue told us she was getting married, I asked, 'To who?' Not as if there were boys boys boys, it's just I never expected. I'm always the last to know, I guess.

"The thing is, with children, they're born and immediately they get under the skin, into the blood system, work their way up to the heart which is what blood does, doesn't it? Goes to the heart. Then they go away.

"Welcome to the family, Daniel. Our small family, anyway. May all your children be brilliant. Here's to making children." He lifted his glass. Saw it was empty. Said, "My glass is empty." He continued, "Sue, come up here. Daniel, you, too."

After they were standing beside him Paul squeezed Sue and said, "You're beautiful. And, Daniel, you keep her that way." He kissed Sue. She was crying. Lise came over and hugged Sue. Took Paul's hand. Don kissed Sue on the mouth. Quite a long time. Sue looked surprised. Daniel took her then and the band started up a slow foxtrot. "Faded Love," Don called out, and Daniel rested his cheek against the top of Sue's head and the newlyweds danced a last tune, sliding out across the grass and down the slope towards the river, where they huddled alone, no longer dancing, their mouths locked.

Paul didn't go out to the front of the house to wave off Daniel and Sue. He let Lise do that. Instead, he came upon Mrs. Wish and he said, "Would you?" She looked over at her husband who was leaning into and talking with Sue's former German teacher. "Yes," she said.

Mrs. Wish, in Paul's arms, felt very different from Sue or Lise or Hélène or any of the other women he had danced with throughout the evening. With the others there was a sense of haste, as if they were looking beyond him, or seeking an escape. Mrs. Wish was slower. Paul thought if he were to whisper in her ear, she would wait several seconds before reacting, offer him her wide mouth and nod. She was thick-waisted, her bum and legs chubby. Perhaps grief had filled her out. She was also younger than Lise or him. Her neck and the backs of her arms offered a smoothness that reminded Paul of the girls in high school. He wondered at her age.

She said, after a while, "That was nice. Your speech. You love your daughter."

Paul didn't answer. He wondered what this woman did when she found her baby. Howl? He had never howled. Though he had wanted to.

"You raise bees," she said.

"Keep. I keep bees. How did you know?"

"Your hands. Your clothes. They carry the scent of wax."

"Naww." Paul freed a hand. Sniffed. "Well, I can't tell."

"It's there." She lifted her nose. "Actually, someone told me."

"Gossip."

"Buzz, buzz."

"And you're a journalist," Paul said.

"Yes."

"I see your articles. Maybe you should do a piece on beekeepers."

"Mr. Unger?"

"Or someone. I like the way you say what you say."

"That right?"

"You don't have a mission."

"I don't?"

"Doesn't seem so."

They were quiet until the song ended and Don called out, "That was 'Thanks to Emma.'"

"Thank you," she said.

"Another?" Paul asked.

"No. Thank you." She walked away, towards her husband, who waited in the shadows. Dr. Wish leaned and whispered in his wife's ear. She shook her head. Turned away. Paul found an empty chair further from the crowd, close to the fire which ate a hole in the darkness. He went back to drinking gin and tonic. At one point, across the lawn, he saw the doctor and his wife leave. A flash of her round face, then gone. People passed by. His mother approached and asked, "Are you happy?"

He shook his head, no.

"Good," she said, misunderstanding, spinning away.

Doug Frohm, the cheese factory manager, was talking with Lise's mother. They laughed. Touched hands. The night passed and the sky was brightening before Don called out, "Last dance." The air was cooler, the grass wet with dew, and the river began to change colour with the new light. Paul was still sitting by a dying fire. He had been watching Lise dance with various men. Mostly Harry though. Harry's wife Bunny was sleeping over by the food table now, her head in her arms, baby wrapped up in a blanket and sleeping at her feet, another child curled around the legs of the chair. For the last dance Lise found Harry again. The wet grass had buffed her bare feet and so it seemed her white heels, as they slipped into view, were waving at Paul. This made Paul want to wave back. He lifted his hand and made a little gesture, the kind of motion a generous man makes to a waiter who is returning change; as if to say, I do not mind losing something of value.

On a Friday, two weeks following the wedding, Lise showed up at Paul's bee farm with breakfast in hand. He was in the out yard smoking a hive when she called through a gap in the honeysuckle hedge. She was afraid of the bees and refused to approach. She yelled and he looked up, waved, replaced a top on a hive, collected his tools, and walked to the house. His clothes carried the smell of the grass smouldering in his smoker. Lise was in the kitchen cutting cheese and cantaloupe. She was dressed for a hot day: shorts, a thin top, runners, no socks. Paul stood in the porch and shook off his gloves. An ache in his chest. Lise turned, licked a finger, and smiled.

"Breakfast," she said.

Paul went to the sink, washed his hands and looked over at Lise. She had lifted her hair into a bun with a black clasp. Her shoulders were brown, arms, too. Paul took a slice of cantaloupe, ran water into the kettle, set the element, and organized the coffee in the filter on the pot. Everything was second-hand, borrowed and begged. This was his mother's kettle, the table and chairs came from the store. The stove and fridge he supplied himself. Brand new, though they were a mismatch. Their gleam didn't fit the carelessness of the house.

Lise sat. She rested her elbows on the table, chin in her hands, and watched Paul. He knew she was watching. He rubbed his face and thought he should have shaved. Maybe she would want to kiss him again. He ran the boiled water through the filter and said, "Was attempting to re-queen a colony. Tricky stuff. Rules say you should introduce a new queen in the second year so the colony doesn't swarm."

Lise lifted her head and nodded, though Paul thought she didn't really care. Still, he said, "When the new queen hatches out she'll get to meet the boys, lay her eggs and get her support. By August I'll arrange for her to meet the old queen." He paused, poured two mugs of coffee. Sat across from Lise. "At that point," he said, "nature dictates that the new queen will kill the old queen and the two colonies will unite."

"Kill the old queen?" Lise said.

"Yup."

"How?"

"Backs herself into the cell and stings the other queen to death."

"Well."

"Right now I'm just hoping it'll work," Paul said. "You make these?" He took a cinnamon bun. Buttered it.

"You're like a child," Lise said. "Playing with the animals. And that little muzzled tin that smokes. What's that?"

"Calms the bees. I'll show you. After this." Paul envisioned for a moment Lise and him living here together. Rebuilding this kitchen. Her painting walls, him rewiring. Beam here, open ceiling there. Huddling together like this over coffee.

"No thanks," she said. Her hand went up to her mouth, a flicker of knuckle and polish. Finest bones he had ever seen. Sue shared that fineness, as did Stephen. "They scare me," she continued. "I got stung once as a girl. On my foot. Golfing with my dad. I've told you that." She looked down at the floor as if the result were still there. Paul saw the part in her hair, a fine line of scalp. Her eyes reappeared and she shrugged. His vision floated away.

"Did *I* leave you?" he asked.

"You did."

"Wonder why."

Lise took his hand. Squeezed, then let go. "I think of you out here sometimes and I wonder if you're okay or lonely. What do you do?"

"I'm fine," Paul said. "Had the Leclair family over for a barbecue and baseball game last week. They've got five boys. One girl. Didn't have enough dishes. Ellen had to haul some this way."

"I've asked Daniel and Sue to live with me," Lise said. She looked at a spot above and behind Paul's head. Her chin had the tiniest cleft. Age was drawing her mouth downwards.

"I heard," Paul said.

"Who said?"

"Hélène."

"Okay."

"Is that what Sue wants? I mean, is it healthy?"

"Those are two different questions."

"Are they?"

Lise ignored him. "Sue's terribly young. She could use some help."

"You wanted the marriage."

Lise didn't respond so Paul continued. "I mean, it would have made more sense to let them experiment. Live together, maybe. Check it out."

"And she gets pregnant?

"Yeah, well, either way it can happen."

"Yes, *we* know that."

Paul thought of Sue. Like Lise, she was forever hopeful, and Paul missed her now. Daniel didn't deserve her, had done nothing to earn the right. He was a doltish boy bedding his daughter.

"They back yet?" Paul asked. The newlyweds had flown to Las Vegas for their honeymoon. Paul had paid the bill.

"Came back on Monday. Sue seemed tired, a little lost, so maybe you're right, marriage is not what she expected. You should go see her."

"Is she at the house?"

"She was when I left. Had settled in by the pool. Daniel started working at the store."

"I guess we'll see how he manages."

"And where have you been?" Lise asked. "Is this an early retirement?"

"Things falling apart?"

"Not at all. I guess I'd like to know who's in charge. Jill fancies herself a bit of a queen."

"Does she?" Paul had always been intending to make Jill Falk the manager of the store. Just never got around to it. She was smart and understood the rubbery quality of the market, how something sold one month and then was out of favour the next. Lise, on the other hand, liked the numbers. Paul imagined the two women hissing at each other every morning. He said, "Go ahead, you can take it over."

"I don't want to," Lise said. "And besides, you're collecting the big cheque."

"Am I? Well, look at the name on the front of the building. There it is: UNGER. That's me."

"Easy to pretend you're poor, living out here, flowers and bees, this run-down little house. Still, you have that trough of money in town. Bit of a hypocrite, I'd say. You always wanted everything."

"Bitter?"

Lise waved him away, lifted her nose.

He said, "I'll come by the store tomorrow and talk to Jill. Arrange something."

"One other thing," Lise said. "Nicole's back. She's in St. Pierre for the summer. With Sky."

Paul sat and waited. Felt his legs go weak. "Where's she staying?" he managed.

"With her father. Supposedly ran out of money. Surprise, surprise."

"You've seen her?"

"No. St. Pierre's out there. Furst's here. Besides, I don't want to see her."

Paul nodded. "Yes," he said. "Maybe she'll just leave again." This news had left him resonant and wayward. Still he liked the idea, the notion of her being near, of Sky toddling about, fumbling his way in and out of bed, grasping a spoon in his fist. Paul's scalp went funny.

Lise had no time for this nonsense. "She's lying. Always has been. You just don't want to see it."

Paul didn't answer. He wanted to smile.

"I've gotta go," Lise said. "I want to get some new bedding for Sue and Daniel."

Paul rose and followed Lise out to her car. She paused at one point and turned to take his hand. They walked on in that fashion. The sun was higher and had warmed the air. Heat lifted off the fields. The Leclairs were running a generator over on their land and the chugging of the motor floated through the air.

Lise's little red sports car crouched on the gravel driveway. Paul ran a hand along its round flank, lifted up a line of dust. Lise slid in, a slender foot into a red shoe. Her bottom half disappeared into the darkness. She palmed the gearshift. Paul leaned forward, smelled the leather. The light fell through the windshield onto Lise's hands. It was the perfect vehicle for her: easy, quick, clean, rich. She loved what she could touch. She reached up now and touched his cheek.

"Know what?" he said, surprised by the sudden fierceness of his heart. "I love you."

She kissed him. Made as if to shake her head, but stopped. She lifted her eyebrows, and then she was gone. A burst of dust, then more dust rising, a cloud against the blue sky.

After Lise had left, Paul cleaned up the kitchen and took Conrad and drove to Furst to visit Sue. Approaching town from the east like this, he was struck by the sleepiness of the streets, the perfection and cleanliness, the sense of nothing being wrong. The new suburbs and rows of shrubs on both sides of road, the dark glass-fronted Credit Union building, the recently installed median with its red oaks and potted geraniums. This side of town was dozier than the west where Unger's Furniture was located between the Dairy Queen and the new Canadian Tire. Lise's house, which had been Lise and Paul's, and before that Paul's parents', was in a more established area, where trees were taller, and the landscaping was less than perfect, and the sidewalks had grown cracks. The house was flattened by the bright sun and the heat. Someone, Lise perhaps, had planted pansies along the sidewalk. Paul parked the half-ton on the street and walked down the driveway towards the house. He sent Conrad around to the back and entered through the front door. Called out Sue's name. Nothing. The interior was cool and quiet, the fridge hummed, the air-conditioning was on.

Through the patio doors Paul could see the pool and beyond that the golf course. A foursome was finishing up on the thirteenth green. Two couples. The women wore matching white skirts and sleeveless tops. One bent to retrieve her ball from the cup and her bum flared. When Stephen was thirteen or fourteen he used to sell cold drinks—beer, wine coolers, Cokes, orange juice—to the golfers as they passed by. He made large amounts of cash and Paul recalled praising him, standing above him and holding his warm thin neck and looking down at his head and saying, "Wonderful. A businessman just like your grandpa."

Paul slid the patio door and stepped outside. Walked towards the pool and opened the gate. Conrad scrabbled through and clicked over to the water and drank. Sue had been here, her towel lay by the deep end. A glass of something pink, an upside-down book. Paul sat in a chair beneath the overhanging plum tree. Removed his shoes and socks, wiggled his toes, and listened to the foursome, the *lap lap* of the water in the pool, a killdeer in the sky.

He looked up at Sue and Daniel's bedroom window. Wondered if Sue was up there. Showering. Sleeping. He told Conrad to stay and walked through the gate and beyond to the patio door. He entered the house. The cool air was easy to breathe. He climbed the stairs and walked down the hall to Sue and Daniel's door. Knocked and called out. No answer. He pushed the door open but did not enter. The unmade bed, a pair of Sue's panties on the floor as if she'd just stepped out of them, coins and business cards on the dresser, half-full suitcases at the end of the bed, the morning light coming through the window and falling on flowered sheets, Daniel's jeans crumpled by the closet, all of this was common and domestic and sexual. Paul felt like a prowler. He considered leaving but then stepped across the room to the bed where he sat and looked down into the contents of the suitcase. Sue's toiletries, an electric shaver, an open box with a new pair of shoes, a package of condoms. He wondered if Sue enjoyed sex, if Daniel helped her, let her take her time. Young people were arrogant in love. Thought they knew it all. Like Stephen and Nicole, who seemed to think sex was made for them alone, reckless and obvious. That distinct well-worn memory of Nicole's laugh, a gurgle, as she turned and saw Paul standing by the pool gate and the fierceness of her gaze, the absolute shamelessness, and her silence as Paul stepped back, out of sight, just before Stephen surfaced from the pool bottom. Diving for nickels stuck between Nicole's toes.

Paul lay on the bed and studied the ceiling and the corner shadows and the sunlight on the far wall. He was suddenly tired; breakfast with Lise had worn him out, or these recollections, the sinuous and often false movement backwards. Perhaps he slept, because he heard, as if from a great distance, Conrad barking and Sue's voice, and he rose from the bed quickly and went to the window to look down on the pool where Sue was bent over Conrad, rubbing his ears and talking to him, and even from this distance Paul could see her vertebrae curving to the base of her spine. And then Daniel appeared, through the gate, and Paul realized Sue had not been talking to Conrad. Daniel approached Sue and held her from behind. Swivelled her so they were facing and they kissed. Daniel was a tall boy and so Sue had to go up on tiptoes. Daniel put his hands on Sue's bum and pulled her in. She ground her hips against his and hung on to his shirt with her fists. This was surprising to Paul and somehow wrong, but he kept watching and Sue kept hanging on, as if she were being buffeted by a strong wind and Daniel was there to save her. Sue was too thin; she seemed diminished by Daniel who was large and clumsy and seemed to need a lot of attention. Paul turned and left the room and descended the stairs and exited the patio doors to come upon Sue and Daniel in another embrace. He called out, "Hey," and Sue slipped away from Daniel, lifting a hand in greeting as she said, "Daddy."

She came to him and Paul held her and noted her fragility. He said, "Welcome back." He released Sue and shook Daniel's hand. Daniel's face was dark from too much sun. His eyes were black, his manner sheepish. He said, "I'm on coffee break, Mr. Unger," and Paul realized that Daniel must have been skipping out of work. He looked at the boy. Daniel was tall enough for Paul to have to look up to. He was trying to grow a beard and it was scraggy on one side. He was wearing runners and jeans and he needed a haircut. He had a rough edge, and Paul understood, standing there, the attraction Sue must have felt for him. He offered the prospect of something wild and Sue seemed to want that.

Paul asked, "How was it? The honeymoon?"

"Great," Sue said. "Swam a lot. Gambled. Saw the shows. Got back Sunday."

"Yeah," Daniel said. He was fidgety. Must be strange, Paul

figured, living in this town now, sleeping and eating in your mother-in-law's house, working for your father-in-law.

To put him at ease, or perhaps to threaten him, Paul asked, "When did you start work?"

"Yesterday. I started yesterday."

"Good. Good. That's good." Paul didn't really care but he found it strange that the boy would be skipping out already. Maybe it was Sue's idea.

Daniel said, his voice verging on a whine, "They've got me unpacking boxes in the back. That's okay, still I hope there's a chance for sales."

"Sales isn't easy," Paul said. "Customers trust experience. They look for dependability."

"Oh, I know. And I'll learn that, I will."

Sue leaned up against Daniel. Wrapped her arms around him and went up on tiptoe to kiss his ear. "Daniel's great with people," she said. "You should have seen him in Las Vegas. At the tables. In the restaurants. On the streets. People loved him. In fact, one guy gave us his card after he heard Daniel do this comic routine for our breakfast table. Some other couples we met ate with us." Here Sue slid her hand along Daniel's bum to his wallet. "Show him the card," she said.

"Naww." Daniel pushed at Sue. She fell back and returned, like a tightly bound coil.

Paul shook his head. "That's great, Daniel. The vaudeville life. Just don't run away and join a circus."

"That's mean, Daddy."

"No, I'm sorry. Listen, I'll ask Lise about the sales floor. She's making the decisions these days at work."

"No, she isn't," Sue said. "Jill is."

"Really?"

"Yeah, Jill said Mum's never there."

Paul looked down at her, preferred not to consider that information. Daniel ducked his big head and said he should go, and Sue patted him off, gave him a peck, and then he was gone and Sue stood before Paul, her bare feet pigeon-toed, and she took his hand

and he thought about how pretty she was. The skin tight over the forehead. The shape of her mouth. Amazing really, the frailty of the human body. An expanse of neurons and skin and bones and blood. How random it seemed that this was his daughter. It was a miracle to have her alive and talking to him. Life bristled with miracles.

He said, "Mum said Nicole's around. In St. Pierre. With Sky."

Sue looked up at him. Let go of his hand and walked over to her towel and lay down on her back and looked up at Paul who stood over her now, the sun on the back of his head. She said, "Good or bad?"

"Good," Paul said.

"I'd say bad."

"Why?"

"I don't know." Her shoulders went up and down. The symmetry of her rib cage. "What good things has she brought to our house?"

"Sky."

"You've seen him once, Daddy, and then he was a few weeks old. It could've been anybody's baby."

Paul listened to her talk. Heard the words and nodded and looked at his hands and waited for a long time when Sue was finished.

Finally he said, "You're too thin."

"Daniel likes me like this."

Paul took the chair under the tree. Slid it around so he was close to Sue. "He's a big boy," he said. "I'd forgotten."

"He is," Sue said. "Big people get more attention. I saw that on our honeymoon. People liked him. Especially the women. Not that there was anything wrong or bad, he's just liked."

Paul asked, "Was it good then, really? The honeymoon?"

Sue nodded.

"You happy?" Paul asked.

"Sure, Daddy."

"Good."

They sat, not talking but not uncomfortable with the silence, and

Paul looked out onto the golf course and put his shoes back on while Sue laid her head back against the towel and closed her eyes to the sun. After a bit Paul stood and looked down on his daughter and said, "I'll go then."

Sue opened her eyes and said, "Bye, Daddy," and then she closed them again and Paul thought she might be sad but he didn't want to ask her more questions so he left her there, by the pool, a lone figure laid out against the white cement encircling the water which appeared as a brilliant blue eye from above.

July and into early August is a busy time for a beekeeper. The bees are collecting nectar and producing honey. At night the bees create a hum as they fan nectar in order to evaporate moisture. A persistent drone, like the whine from hydro lines, fills the air. Later in the evening of the day he had seen Lise and Sue, Paul walked to his hives in the out yard. If he held his hand by the cracks or entrances of the hives, he could feel wet air being pushed out. In the west, lightning fell. Paul was in shorts and a T-shirt. Barefoot. Mosquitoes breathed on his arms and legs. He swatted them away but was eventually forced back into the house where he sat in the screened-in porch. The animal, a weasel perhaps, who had made a home under the porch, snuffled and foraged in the dark. Paul went to bed late. Woke early and made coffee. The rain had passed by to the south during the night. Lots of thunder, distant muffled growls that Paul had heard at the edge of sleep.

After breakfast Paul ironed a shirt and put on clean jeans. He took the half-ton and drove out of La Broquerie, through Furst and along the Number 52 west. At the junction which would take him to St. Pierre, he passed a hobby farm, horses fenced in, a small barn for chickens and sheep. A Vietnamese pot-belly pig rooted in the mud of the horse pen. A young boy straddled the fence, throwing rocks at the pig. Off the back porch a thin woman in dark hair was hanging laundry. Happy family, hopeful, a languor at the supper table, the smell of horseshit, talk of tomorrow. That's what

Paul missed. The anticipation of tomorrow. Eventually, he found himself in St. Pierre, across from the Forêts' house. It was located in the middle of town, just behind the local restaurant, a block off the main highway. A sprinkler fed back and forth on the scrubby front yard. A little boy ran a muddy circle around the falling water. Paul stepped out of the half-ton and walked towards the boy. He stopped on the driveway and waited. Didn't want to scare him. When the boy saw Paul he slowed down, tipped his head, and made a hoop with his bare toe. Paul waved. The boy dropped his head. Paul squatted. Said, "Hiya. I'm Paul." He waited, then said, "You're Sky. Is your mummy home?"

The boy looked at the house. Back again.

"Inside?" Paul asked. "Fine. Are you getting wet?"

"Mummy said no."

"Well. We'll listen to Mummy then, won't we?" The boy had hair the colour of mud. Eyes blue or green, it was hard to say in that light. His nose was burned, freckled. Should have been wearing sunscreen. There was a scrawniness to him, twig-like. His bare legs were spattered with scrapes. Paul moved closer now and patted the child's head. The boy looked up and grinned. Paul heard a voice calling.

"Mummy's coming," the boy said.

She slid from around the corner of the house, hefting a lawn chair, balancing a cup of coffee. She didn't stop when she saw Paul, just kept coming. Set down the mug on the driveway, snapped open the chair, sat down, shook out a cigarette, lit it, and finally looked up. She shielded her eyes and said, "Mr. Unger."

"Hello, Nicole," Paul said.

"Speed of light," Nicole said, snapping her finger. "News."

Paul didn't respond. There was a clarity to Nicole that took his own breath away. The centre of the world. Sky was touching his knee. Paul felt a fuzziness in his head that on other occasions he'd have labelled happiness. He had no reason to be happy, but it seemed he was. He touched Sky's head again and said, as if revealing a secret, "Sky."

"That's him," Nicole said. She drew on her cigarette and looked at her boy. She still had a brazen elasticity to her body that reminded Paul of his own daughter.

He said now, "My daughter Sue, she got married."

"I heard. Daniel Leblanc. I knew him from school."

"Sue and Daniel are living with Lise. In the same house," Paul said. He bumbled on, charged by the current flowing from Sky's head into his fingers. "Daniel's working at the store and Sue's going to school in fall, which is good because she's still terribly young. How long you staying?"

Nicole looked out across the street. She flipped open a pair of sunglasses and slid them on. Her too-blonde hair was permed or something because it was wavy. Sweat gathered in that space between her nose and upper lip. A minute dip. A hum of bees in Paul's head, millions of transparent wings. "I was thinking of settling down," Nicole said. "Buying a house. Maybe work up at the Pic-a-Pop. Five flavours!" She stopped. Shook her head.

Paul looked down at Sky, who was singing to himself and walking around Paul as if he were a post or a tree. The boy's hands fanned across Paul's pants. "I could offer you work at the store." Paul didn't know why he was saying this, he had no idea if Nicole was dependable or even good. Nicole's eyebrows went up and this made Paul continue.

"Could use a clerk, someone at the front desk. Or in the back. Inventory."

"Really?"

Paul couldn't see her eyes so he didn't know what her mood was, though it seemed she was mocking him. Still, he continued, "Even if you're not staying, I'd like you to come out to my land. My house. Supper, maybe? Or just a quick visit." He added, as if this were unimportant, "I keep bees. Always did, but I've been expanding."

Nicole pushed her dark glasses up onto her forehead and said, "Hey?"

"For the honey."

"I'm not allergic," Nicole said. "Neither's Sky. We both got stung at the lake last year. Was at my boyfriend's cabin and Sky found a hive under the porch." She punched a finger against her forearm and let go. Did it again. "Two times."

Sky wandered over and knocked on Nicole's knee. "I'm hungry," he said.

"He's hungry," Paul told Nicole.

"We're always hungry," Nicole said. "I'll just get him some crackers." She heaved upward. The lawn chair's webbing had tattooed the backs of her bare thighs. She was barefoot and her feet were careful on the gravel.

After she was gone Paul dug in a pant pocket and produced a piece of gum. Lemon flavoured. He held it out to Sky. "You like gum?"

"I like gum," Sky said. He unwrapped the gift carefully. The paper floated to the ground. The gum disappeared. Sky's cheeks went in and out.

"Whose house is this?" Paul asked, pointing behind Sky.

"This is Grandpa's house. Grandpa is Mummy's dad. This house has a bathtub and it is blue." The boy was precise, loquacious for a boy who was almost three. He walked to the edge of the spotty lawn. Stood on one foot. Hopped. Navigated the sprinkler and came back. His feet were wet now, bits of grass clippings and dirt between his toes.

"Grandpa who?" Paul asked.

Sky was confused. "Grandpa."

Paul nodded. Tousled the boy's head. Of course, Mr. Forêt looked like a grandfather. Older, probably had that smell. And why would Nicole talk about him, Grandpa Unger? He was only forty-four and he didn't mean anything, hadn't been a part of life other than the monthly cheques deposited in Nicole's account. You'd think that would give him some credibility, but not a word. Didn't matter though. Crouching now beside the boy, that was enough. Paul's heart swelled as he smelled Sky's head. Nicole appeared and he drew back, stood and smiled weakly. Realized he had little reason to stay longer but didn't want to leave.

Sky took the crackers. He fished the gum from his mouth and held it out for Paul who accepted and held it gently. Nested it in the palm of his hand.

"Do you want to come and see my place?" Paul said. "Now. Are you busy?"

"Aren't you working?" Nicole asked.

"Not much these days. Lise is in charge. Her and the manager, Jill Falk."

"I guess," Nicole said. "Nothing else to do. I just gotta change Sky." She scooped Sky up, held him so he was dangling with his belly across her arm. Bare feet poking backwards, heels like mushrooms. Nubs for toes. Crackers going in the other end.

Paul went to the half-ton and waited, realized he was still holding Sky's gum. He balled it up and set it on the dash, swept off the passenger seat. Dust and bits of gravel, an old newspaper, a book, a novel he read when he was fishing.

Nicole returned. She had changed Sky's shirt. Her own, too. Both T-shirts now offered the word "YO" in thin black script. Paul nodded at Sky and went, "Yo."

Nicole ignored this. She settled Sky on her lap and said, "Okay, let's go, farmer."

"Wanna buckle him up?" Paul asked.

"No," Sky said. Nicole rolled down her window and while Paul drove she let Sky push his head out and gulp the wind.

Paul drove slowly, imagining Sky tumbling, bouncing along the highway.

"It's weird, being back again," Nicole said. The wind took her words and tossed them about the truck so that Paul had to lean towards her and decipher.

"The same," Nicole said.

"Of course," Paul answered. "On the surface."

"My father." Her finger did a few spirals to indicate mock excitement. She was still so young, though the hardness, the veneer she used to have, was gone now. It was as if the last three years had defeated her in some way.

Paul asked, "What did you do? This last while?"

She was thinking. Holding Sky who was balanced on her lap. She turned, pushed up her nose. Opened her mouth but closed it again. She said finally, "Lots of stupid things."

Paul nodded, as if this were clear to him. "So, what now?"

"Don't know. I'm begging. My boyfriend left. Took my money. My father'll let me live with him. Don't know if I want that."

Paul didn't answer. He thought what this girl needed was for someone to sit her down and hold up a mirror to her so she could see what she had become.

"I had a friend once," he said, "who thought he had to do everything before he turned twenty."

"And did he?"

"He's dead."

Nicole rolled her eyes, licked her lips. The wind snapped at her short hair. Sky had fallen asleep, his head rolled against Nicole's chest. They drove east towards La Broquerie and then took the gravel road south to Paul's farm. As the half-ton turned onto Paul's driveway, Nicole said, "Happiness isn't something I see a lot of. In my father, the people around me. I'd guess even you, Mr. Unger. Sky's happy. Most of the time. Maybe children have a secret we've all had at some time, it's just we throw that secret away."

"Happiness doesn't mean much," Paul said. He pulled up under the shade of an apple tree. "Lay the boy down on the seat."

Nicole did that. Sky's cheek held the imprint of one of her buttons. His hair was damp. He curled up, opened an eye, shuddered, and slept on. Paul left a window open for air flow, then he and Nicole walked to the house. While he prepared sandwiches and took out beer, she wandered the main floor. He could hear her in the living room. The rocker groaned, books shuffled, a light clicked. She returned holding a book on bees. Sat at the table, fanned the pages, and said, "I was taking correspondence. Trying to finish calculus and English. Never managed."

"I'm good at neither," Paul said.

"I didn't know bees couldn't hear," Nicole said.

They had lunch in the screened-in porch. From here the half-ton was visible. Paul ate slowly, watched Nicole gobble her food. She was quick with her beer, too. He didn't offer more, just watched her lick her fingers, wipe them on her shorts. "Mind if I smoke?" she asked.

"Okay."

She lit up. Closed her eyes. Sky had her nose and chin. Paul had looked but hadn't seen anything of Stephen in the boy. Maybe the ears. He said, "Does Sky know me? Who I am?"

Nicole held her cigarette like a pointer. Ashed into her plate. She said, "You want that?"

"Why not?"

"Kids are funny."

"I'd think they're pretty obvious," Paul said. "Take what you give them."

"I can tell him," she said. She was lazy. Her bare foot doodled the porch floor. She described an arc with her hand and landed it on her thigh. She said, "I like it out here. I was thinking I should take up meditation, Tai Chi or something. But maybe this'd be just as good."

Then, without asking she stood, went into the kitchen, and found another beer. She returned with two and gave Paul one. He remembered the supper on the deck and Nicole announcing that the Unger family was innocent and how harsh that had seemed, and he recalled Nicole putting her hand on Stephen's cheek after the meal and he remembered the pool that night and Nicole standing and staring at him, and now, thinking about this, he was ashamed of himself.

"You ever think about Stephen?" Paul heard his voice beyond the thick drumming of his ears. Someone else's words.

"No," Nicole said. Then, seeing Paul was shaken, she continued, "It was nothing, Mr. Unger. I mean, not nothing, but we were young. A sport, that's all. You know. I don't think I loved him, or if I did, it wasn't enough. We were seventeen." She stopped, looked at Paul and said, "He wasn't perfect. He could be mean."

"Sure," Paul said. "Sure."

She said, "He got me pregnant. Didn't want to use a condom. Said it'd be fine. Do that *interruptus* thing." Here Nicole leaned towards Paul and whispered, "It's okay, I'll pull it out."

Paul recoiled at this intimacy. Shook his head. Turned away and imagined his son's young body bucking into this girl's. There were nights when Paul had entered Stephen's room as he slept, turned on the lamp and leaned over his son, studied his body. Limbs, sweat, a sweet ripple of skin over the ribs, dirty nails, purple nipple. Careless youth. Two children lunging through the night.

He said now, understanding that he was throwing out pearls, "I still ache. In fact, it is unusual not to ache."

Nicole looked out across the lawn towards the half-ton. A cry and Sky's head appeared, then dropped away. "It's Sky," Nicole said. She seemed relieved to be able to escape this conversation. She walked out to the half-ton, arms swinging, elbows thin. She pulled Sky from the seat, held him to her chest, whispered in his ear, and walked back to Paul. Sky's head was wet with sweat. Paul stood, fetched orange juice from the kitchen, and pushed it at Sky. The boy turned away. "He's gotta wake up," Nicole said. "He's slow."

They sat then and Paul talked about how bees work. While he talked Sky became more alert, curious now about Paul, the porch, the yard beyond.

"I was going to show you my hives," Paul said. "But we'll wait. Safer without Sky."

"You wear all that stuff? The net and gloves?"

"Uh-uh. I use the smoker. I get stung sometimes but you build up an immunity. Like mosquitoes."

Nicole mimicked him, "Like mosquitoes." She said to Sky, "Your grandpa's tough, isn't he?"

Sky ignored her. He had discovered Conrad lying under Paul's chair. He climbed off Nicole's knee and crouched before Conrad. "God," he said, and moaned with delight.

"He loves dogs," Nicole said.

Paul was not focusing. He was still glowing from the "grandpa" reference. Him. Odd. It allowed him a new dimension, as if he were more solid suddenly. Not just a cranky guy who had run away from his family. Paul stooped and touched Sky's head. Let his hand rest there a while, felt the sweaty perfection. Little precious ball.

The beer had made Paul sleepy. This was nice, sitting here now, with Sky muttering at his feet and Nicole over there, everything sliding into the afternoon shadows. The girl here, the boy below, they were like gifts thrown his way. And he would open his arms to catch them.

The remainder of the day was unoccupied and slow. While Paul took care of Sky, Nicole slept. She lay on the couch in the porch, one arm under her head, the other thrown across the back of the couch. Her chest rose and fell. Her mouth was open slightly. Her ankles and calves were thin, too thin to be beautiful, Paul thought. She had a bruise on her shin; fall on a stair perhaps. Her face as she slept was calmer, it revealed a hidden core that suggested peace. Her moodiness was gone. Her eyelashes, blonde and spare, flattened and disappeared against her skin.

Paul lay on the floor and let Sky climb over him. He said, "I'm your grandpa."

Sky shook his head, no.

"I'm your grandpa," Paul said again.

"My grandpa has a blue bathtub." The boy's fluency was studied, the careful and methodical laying out of words as if they were fragile and shouldn't be mistreated. Though there were moments when he missed, like when he had upended a simple word like "dog."

"Every boy has two grandpas." Paul held up two fingers.

Sky touched them and asked, "Do you have a blue bathtub?"

"I don't have any bathtub."

Sky considered this. Began to unbutton Paul's shirt. When he had loosened all the buttons, he put them back together. He did this again.

"I'll get you a bathtub," Paul said.

Sky nodded. A serious gaze. A question: "Blue?"

"Of course." He hugged the boy, wanted to kiss him. The boy spun away. Came back and sat on Paul's head. He tickled Sky. Giggles rising. Nicole turned on her back, a wraith of bones and flesh and blood, her chest flat now. Could have been a boy herself except for the fineness of her neck, pallor like the milk flowing from a broken dandelion stem. Sky wandered off to find Conrad. Paul looked at the ceiling.

He fell asleep for a moment. And then he was sitting up listening for Sky. Nothing. A memory, faint but still there, of the screen door squeaking. Paul rose, gave a quick glance across the lawn. He stepped out onto the stairs, the sun lower now though still hot. "Sky," he called softly, not to wake Nicole. The front yard was empty. Beyond the yard was the hedge and then the field holding the hives. If there was danger, it was there. Paul ran towards the hedge and through. In the distance were the harmless grey boxes sprouting from the grass and flowers and weeds. Paul wished he had cut the field. If the boy was here, he'd be swallowed by the sheer height of the growth. A bark. Paul saw the dog leaping. Yelping. Over by the farthest hive. He ran, his ankles picking up weeds, tripping now. Sky's head appeared. He was standing beside the hive, pushing against it, fitting his fingers into the entrance, pulling them out. Purposeful. No panic there. Paul approached quietly and said, "Sky."

The boy swivelled his head. Two points of blue. A grin. "All the bees."

"Come," Paul said. He took Sky's hand. Brushed bees from his hair. Arms. The guard bees weren't unhappy, just a little confused by this intruder. Paul walked him away. Picked him up. "Where's Conrad?"

A hand pointing. A nod. The smell of heat on his neck. Stem like his mother. Paul kissed him. "Thirsty?" he asked.

Another nod.

"Come."

They walked back through the honeysuckle hedge, across the

lawn and up the path to the porch stairs where Nicole waited, a cat newly woken, standing in the sun. Light bled through her white shirt.

"Where were you?" she asked.

"Exploring," Paul said. He carried Sky inside, held him with one arm as he poured a glass of juice. And the child drank. Came up for air, his tongue pushed out, working his teeth in the way he would a breast.

"Another," the boy said. Drank again and then slithered away. Paul watched him, wary now.

Nicole was restless. She wanted to leave. She sat on her hands and her eyes followed Sky. She smoked. Opened another beer. Paul, afraid he would not see them again, gave Nicole the keys to the Camino. "Here," he said. "I have the half-ton. No use for both vehicles."

Nicole looked at the keys. Then she plucked them like a fruit from Paul's fingers. "Neat," she said. They went then, Sky bouncing on the seat, the heel of Nicole's hand against the purple steering wheel.

"Watch him," Paul said.

Nicole swung the Camino around on the drive, small behind the wheel. A child. "Thanks," she called out and then they were gone, away across the prairie and beyond the trees, leaving a hole in Paul's evening. An evening during which he cleaned up the kitchen, washed the dishes, drank the remains of Nicole's beer and imagined the taste of her, made a pot of tea and a batch of macaroni that he ate with ketchup and sliced cheese. In his mind, the images of Sky and Nicole, one asleep, a wafer on the couch, the other holding out his arms, full of bees. Paul swept them away.

On Thursday night Paul played slo-pitch and after the game Gladys Frohm invited some folks over for drinks. Paul decided to go. Harry Kehler's wife Bunny showed up at the house. She was wearing a sleeveless sundress and it was obvious she had gone out of her way to fix her hair and face. She sat beside Harry and talked loudly about how Harry caught the Lazlo boy stealing gas from the Petro Can.

"Chased him all the way up Dead End Road. Lazlo ended up in the field. Broke both arms." Bunny patted Harry on the back. Lit a cigarette and said, "Area's first high-speed chase. Constable Harry Kehler. Here he is."

"Come on, Bunny." Harry pushed her hand away. Looked at the grass.

"Great fire," Jake Krist said to Gladys. She had piled logs in the outdoor fireplace, poured on some gasoline and lit the bundle, singeing Jake's forearms.

"Doug taught me," Gladys announced. Her legs were long. Shorts too short. Paul could see the round white rim of her bum in the glow of the fire. He sat and watched the fire, glanced once in a while at Harry and Bunny. Bunny was drinking too quickly and Harry was telling her to slow down.

"Fuck off," Bunny mouthed at Harry, her thin lips pushing into an *O* and then her large front teeth clipping down to the dip above her chin. She *was* a bunny. Paul watched Harry. Thought how he missed spending time with him. They had just fallen away from each other after Harry showed up at Paul's door that morning and announced Stephen's death. Perhaps it was inevitable. And now any return to a friendship was impossible with Harry sleeping with Lise.

Daniel and Sue, who had played slo-pitch, hadn't come to Gladys's. Too young for this crowd. Paul had talked to Sue at the end of the game, asked her about Lise.

"Oh," she said, "I don't know."

"It okay, living with her?"

"All right."

"Harry ever come by?"

Sue was thoughtful. Then she said, "Yeah. You okay, Daddy? I'm sorry."

"Aww, don't worry about me."

"I do."

"Come visit. We'll fish or something."

"I hate fishing."

"Right. Still, we can visit."

"I will."

Sweet and protective, she still loved him.

Paul finished a beer and went inside to find the bathroom. He sat on the toilet, his shorts at his knees, and through the open window he could hear Earl Wright talk about his new air seeder. One hundred thousand dollars. Gladys laughed at something. Deeply, from her chest. Earl asked, "What's the difference between a husband and a lover?"

Then he said, before anybody could answer, "Forty-five minutes."

Harry laughed the loudest. On his way back outside Paul passed through the dark kitchen and he found Bunny at the sink. She was running water but just standing there. He came up beside her. "Hey," he said. She started. Tucked her chin and turned away. Paul touched her shoulder and Bunny leaned towards him as if he were pulling at a string. She wrapped her arms around his neck, pushed her mouth against his chest. The scent of gin floated upwards. Paul held her and thought, Okay. Fine. She was a warm mass; where he would have expected sharp angles he discovered a soft pliancy, a boozy willingness.

Now, beyond her breathing, he heard steps on the stairs and Bunny heard this, too, but she didn't seem to care, and Paul, pushing gently at first, had to shove at her to free himself. She fell backwards against the countertop. Stumbled. Her ankle rolled and she hissed past her big teeth. The footsteps that worried Paul turned back and disappeared. Bunny supported herself on the counter.

"I'm sorry," Paul said.

"Oh, no. Don't. I'm a bit crazy. Harry says." She could, Paul thought, charge at him.

"I'm sorry," he said again.

"Well, we can't stop them, can we?" Bunny said. She had removed her shoe and was rubbing her ankle. She looked up at Paul as if she were begging. Her eyes were moist.

"People do what they want."

"You're a good man, Paul. I've always known that. When you'd come over and talk to Harry, he was a better person for it. It's awful what he's doing, taking his best friend's wife."

"We're not best friends. You know that."

"You were. It's like you're reaching out your hand to help him and he's cutting it off."

Paul didn't think that was a great example. It didn't make sense. But then Bunny wasn't very bright. "I don't know," Paul said. "I don't think I ever tried to help him."

"Oh, you did." Bunny paused and held her hand in the air, as if there was more. But there wasn't.

She said finally, "I'm sorry for attacking you here. Now."

Paul waved her away. "That's okay."

"I get lonely. Harry comes home, but that's all. You know?"

Paul looked away. Thought people deserved what they got.

"But you're good, Paul. I like you."

Paul wanted to go home now. He was tired. He nodded at Bunny, said, "Bye," and then he walked out the front door to his old half-ton. Voices and laughter rose and floated over the house and down onto the front lawn. The sky was black. He started the truck and drove through Furst. Thought of Nicole in St. Pierre. The Camino huddling on the driveway. A light shining from a bedroom. "Sky," he whispered. He drove on, out of town, past the fairgrounds, and down the back roads to his home.

Sunday noon Paul picked his mother up from church and drove her home.

His mother, looking around inside the dirty half-ton, asked, "Where's your car?"

"Nicole's using it."

"Nicole? Forêt? Why?"

Paul shrugged. His mother would make too much of this, would think he was grasping.

"Oh, don't get caught up in her net," she said.

"Sky's got your blood, too, Mum. Anyways, Nicole's older now. She's more focused."

"All I remember is the funeral and her walking in wearing that nothing top that showed off her belly. At least if she'd been dressed in black."

"She was over on Monday. With Sky. We spent the afternoon together. You really should see Sky, he's got Stephen's ears."

"Big then. She'll want something. Isn't it enough that you're giving her money? Lise'll have a fit."

"Lise still doesn't believe that's her grandson."

"She's stubborn."

"Nicole's harmless."

"What was she doing? These last three years?"

"Living in Winnipeg. Going to school."

"By herself?"

"Yeah," Paul lied. "Her and Sky."

"Well, I'm surprised."

"I told you she was older. More focused."

"I guess it can't be easy. Poor girl's gotta raise a child."

"Sky uses some big words," Paul said.

"Remember Stephen?" his mother answered. "He was precocious. Sky must have got it from him."

Paul nodded. He could not recall specifics. Going back in time was like entering a dark and troubling tunnel. He had a faint memory of driving home late after a trip to the bee farm, with Stephen asleep, the dim light from the dash falling onto his hair and forehead and chin. Paul touched Stephen's cheek and told him of the things they had done and the things they would do and of the baby sister he had, beautiful girl, and then he traced Stephen's eyebrow and imagined it as the gossamer wing of a bee and tried to imagine his father having this much love for him when he was a boy. He couldn't. The overwhelming desire to eat the child, to suck on his arms, bite the neck, the cheeks.

Perhaps this memory was not real; it may have been something he wished he had done. Paul wasn't sure, though he knew he loved his son. The smell of him, the firm flesh, the weight of him on his shoulders, in his arms.

They arrived at his mother's house. Paul exited the car and walked around to release his mother. They entered through the front door; it was cool inside. A picture of Paul's father hung on the foyer wall. Beside that was a photo of Stephen wearing a baseball cap. Taken just before he died. Paul didn't like looking at this particular photo; it was as if time had stopped. But it hadn't. There's my son, he thought, that's him, forever and ever.

Paul made coffee while his mother fried rice and vegetables. They ate at the small table in the dining room. The TV was on and tuned to a religious program. A man in a red suit exhorted them to fall on their knees.

"Achhh," Paul said, and reached over to turn it off.

His mother said, "I saw Lise last week. Riding around with Harry."

Paul looked up.

His mother continued, "She should be more careful." She stood and poured coffee.

"I can live with it," Paul said.

"Perhaps if you cared more, she wouldn't be stealing another woman's husband."

"I would think Harry had some say."

"And so it's okay then? Bring another marriage down with your own? Poor Bunny."

"Yes, poor Bunny." And he felt this. Bunny was in some way innocent. A bland figure who floated outside the business of lust and desire; even her desperate push at him the other night was flat and ineffective. That was probably why Harry went for Lise.

His mother, returning with two cups of coffee, wouldn't stop. "Lise was always too interested in sex."

"Was she?"

"Oh, Paul, of course. It's that French-Catholic thing. They're either prudes or nymphomaniacs."

"Don't be ridiculous."

"Look at all the local boys running after French girls. Why, the summer you got married there were at least three other weddings." She grabbed her fingers and wanted to list them but time had erased their names. Confused now, she rattled a cup, spilled and said, "Oh, look."

"Funny," Paul said, helping her out, "but Lise is quite happy these days."

"Well, happiness. It's everybody's right, I suppose."

"The fact is," Paul admitted, "I'm not certain I love Lise anymore. Maybe that's an awful thing to say, but it's like she's drifted away and I'm okay with that. In a way, I'm happy for her."

His mother shook her head. Said with a muttered finality, "Love isn't something you shuck off like an old coat."

Paul ignored this. Thought about how he had felt this past week since Sky and Nicole showed up. Happy. At peace was perhaps more fitting. As if there were a chance of something. Paul wondered if his mother would understand or even remember the wormy quality of a three-year-old. He wondered if she would ever admit to failure or if she knew love in a completely different way from him.

After lunch Paul's mother went to her bedroom for a nap while Paul did dishes. When he was finished he left the house, drove home and found the Camino parked in the yard. Nicole was feeding crackers and peanut butter to Sky in the kitchen.

"It's us," Nicole said.

Sky looked up, nose tipped with peanut butter. Looked away.

"Good," Paul said. "Good."

Nicole licked the knife. Her tongue was thin and sharp. Paul sat opposite Sky, kitty-corner to Nicole. "Good thing I like peanut butter," he said.

Nicole scooped up some more. Said through a mouthful, "Sky's favourite."

"You've been busy," Paul said.

"Uh-uh," Nicole answered. She lifted her hip slightly and out of her pocket appeared a flattened pack of cigarettes. She found one in reasonable shape and lit it. Inhaled. Her nose went up and down. She said, "I went to your store yesterday. Filled out an application form. Gave it to some woman. She was wearing a suit."

"That would be Jill. Did you tell her I sent you?"

"No."

"Why not?"

"She wasn't very helpful."

"Of course."

"Said, 'We're not hiring, but you can fill out this.' I filled it out. Said, 'Thank you, ma'am.'"

"I'll talk to her," Paul said.

"That's okay. I don't need work. It's not why I came here. Wanted to ask you a favour."

"Yeah?"

Nicole dipped a finger in the peanut butter now. A claw going in. She alternated between the cigarette and finger.

"My father's gone tonight and I gotta go to Winnipeg. Meet Romel, he's the guy who ran off with my life, my money. Anyway, I was wondering if you could look after Sky. Just tonight. I'll be back late."

"Sure." Then he asked, "You explained this to Sky?"

"Sort of. He likes you."

Sky looked up. "Conrad?"

"In the porch," Paul said. Sky rolled out of his chair and tiptoed to the porch, whispering, "Conrad, Conrad."

"He loves it here," Nicole said.

"He doesn't know any better."

"Sure he does."

Paul suffered a ripple across his chest. Protective suddenly of Nicole. "You wouldn't do anything stupid. With this Romel guy."

"Whaddya mean?"

"Is he dangerous?"

Nicole laughed. "Only to himself."

Paul shook his head. Nicole's collarbone made her skin bluish and the column of her neck moved as she swallowed the beer Paul had handed her, and her eyes were surprisingly bright in the dimness of the kitchen. Paul imagined a wire stretched tight from top to bottom running the length of this girl. Through the centre.

"And," she said now, as if this were a thought, just arrived, "I'll need the Camino again."

"Sure," Paul said.

Nicole had left nothing for Sky. Paul thought there should be a baby bag with clothes, pyjamas, books, toys. But, nothing. Sky was wearing coveralls and a T-shirt, runners and socks. He had a soother he pulled out every now and then from his pocket. He sucked it once or twice to verify its existence, then tucked it back. "This is my soother. I like it," he said. Paul considered that the boy was too old for a soother. Made him look foolish. There were certain things that Nicole didn't understand about children.

Sky niggled on, discovering an ant behind the door, the broom, a drill and bits that he clattered across the living-room floor leaving scars in the soft pine. Paul didn't mind. He watched from his chair. How easy, he thought, to care for a child.

Sky had finished exploring. He began to whimper and looked around for Nicole. Came to Paul, beat a fist on his leg and said, "Mummy." He descended into a wail suddenly, inexplicably, as if he had caught his hand in a door. Paul hoisted him and asked, "What is it?"

Sky cried on.

"There's nothing wrong," Paul explained, but the child didn't want logic.

Paul walked with Sky to the porch. Pointed out at the yard. "Look," he said.

Sky stopped. Said, "What? What?" His cheeks were wet. What utter sorrow he felt. This was surprising. So unexpected.

"Conrad," Paul said. "Did you hear him bark? Woof, woof."

"God?" Fatigue twisted Sky's mouth.

"Yes, out there. Conrad."

"Conrad?"

"Yes."

"What? What?"

"The dog. He was barking."

"Out there?"

"Yes."

"Ohhh."

And then he cried again, a wail produced from some deep and ancient inner core, an oh-so-terrible sadness that pushed its way out of that round black hole of his mouth.

"Stop it," Paul said.

Louder now. Harder.

"Here," Paul said, and he walked to the kitchen. Took a piece of bread and pushed it at Sky. Rejection. More crying.

"Well, go on then," Paul said, and he found the rocker and held Sky's head against his chest. He held him till the crying stopped, till all that was left were stuttered sobs.

"There, there," Paul said. A soaking of relief. A satisfaction that he had come through this. "I was thinking we should make some pancakes. Do you like pancakes?"

And that was what they did. Together they measured out flour, cracked eggs, spilled in milk, measured baking soda. Heated the pan, poured in oil, and spooned out the batter. Sky's busy little fists.

At the table Sky ate greedily, dribbling syrup. Paul swiped at him with a wet rag. He gave the boy a glass of milk: a tumbler too big, full of white froth. Sky spilled and began to whimper again. "Don't," Paul said, impatient now, tired.

He put Sky to bed early, lay down with him on the king-size mattress that sat frameless in the centre of the bedroom. He sang lullabies, pulled them up rusty and weak from long ago and found that his memory worked. The words slid out and Sky fell asleep.

At dusk, in order to allow himself to work, he carried a sleeping Sky out to the half-ton and laid him on the bench seat, covering him with a blanket. Then he loaded up hives from the yard and drove to the surrounding fields and planted the hives close to flowering crops of canola and sunflower and alfalfa. The bees, in order to produce, required a large quantity of nectar and pollen and they would find it there. Paul worked late into the night. Sky slept unaware on the seat as Paul went out and returned and went out again. The air was heavy. Rain was coming. By midnight he had moved thirty hives. At one point he stumbled and almost dropped a hive. He was tired. The sky began to spit. He drove home, carried Sky back to the mattress, showered, and lay down again beside the child. Faced him in the darkness and listened to him breathe. His back ached. He thought of Nicole and he fell asleep.

He woke several times during the night. Sky slept crucified, on his back, arms and legs spread. Both Paul and Sky were naked; it was hot and humid and a fan waved the sheet which covered them. At five in the morning the thunderstorm finally arrived and Sky woke with a gasp, wide-eyed and fearful. Paul shushed him, said, "Don't worry," and held him, aware now of the frailty of the boy. He smelled Sky's head and said, "There, there."

Conrad huddled beside the mattress, whimpering.

"Conrad?" Sky said.

"Yes."

"Oh. Thunder?"

"Yes."

"Oh."

It rained then and a driving wind wanted to pick up the house. Paul held Sky and imagined water rising and swallowing the world. His bare arms stuck to Sky's skinny chest. It was hard to breathe. They both fell asleep again and when Paul woke the room was full of light and Sky was watching him. He put a finger in Paul's mouth. Tapped at his tooth. Nicole there in those pale eyes, the slant and shape. Her mouth now, open a little, concentrating, pouting, the slippery bottom lip.

"Jewels," Sky said. "There." He forced a finger in, touched a back molar.

Paul bit down on Sky's finger. Hard enough to keep him there.

"Ouch, Grandpa."

Paul sucked Sky's finger. Slid it out. Growled.

"Again," Sky said.

Paul obeyed. Closed his eyes. The taste of him.

They ate cold cereal in the front porch where the rainfall had left puddles on the floor. Sky, still naked, splashed and stomped. He peed into a puddle and looked up proudly. Paul tossed a towel down and wiped at it with his bare foot. He was thinking about work that needed doing and how with Sky here it wouldn't get done. He wondered when Nicole would return. Perhaps she wouldn't. That could happen. Perhaps she had simply run. He missed her, had been listening for her. For all her simplicity, she had become this tricky shape that floated and dipped at a spot somewhere near his chest and throat. He worried that she would be either harmed by herself or by some angry young man. Her lack of respect for her own life was sobering. Sorrow drifted through her, a damaging misery, selfish and unreconciled, not unlike his own. He imagined her in the arms of some boy and this saddened him. He wondered if sex meant anything to her, or if it was simply a form of barter, or perhaps a fleeting hope. Boys at that age could be greedy and she must have been easy; the push of that lip, a hard hand at her throat. What was it, Paul wondered, that made the young so careless?

After breakfast, Paul dressed Sky in his dirty coveralls, put on his socks and shoes, and took him out to the honey shed where the supers stood row on row, ten high, waiting to be cleaned. While Sky played, Paul scraped wax from the brood frames and the boxes and laid the ready supers off to the side. In a week or two he would need to use these as the bees produced their honey. In a good hive, the bees required a new super every other day and so the hive began to take on the look of a skyscraper.

Sky loved the wax. He crouched and collected the tailings, rolling them into balls, squeezing them, smelling what remained on his fingers. The wax was soft and tacky. Easy to work with. The tool Paul used was flat, about the width of two fingers, and sharpened at one end; it resembled a thin spatula with a hook. It was like a third arm to Paul. He always carried it in his back pocket, even when driving to town.

The propolis came off easily, though after several hours of this work Paul's wrist began to ache. When Sky became fussy, Paul halted, made a sandwich for him, changed and washed, then drove to Furst. There was a glee in this, coasting down Main Street, Sky's chin plunk on the base of the open window, the glance of a passerby, Paul's heart singing, "See here, see here." He drove past the store, thought he should go in and show off Sky, but the truck kept going, through Furst and all the way into Winnipeg where he went to Wal-Mart. Plopped Sky in a cart and cruised the aisles. He bought a plastic bucket and shovel, a pink ball the size of Sky's head, a green wagon. And finally, a swing set: blue metal with a glider, two swings and a slide. A clerk in a red shirt and a ponytail helped him load the boxed swing set on the half-ton while Sky sat in the cart and pressed the ball to his chest.

"Some playthings for my grandson," Paul told the clerk, who looked barely old enough to be working for money. Boys like that always surprised Paul in some way, their vigour perhaps, the sense they gave of definitely being someone's son.

Back in the truck, Paul drove over to order at a drive-thru, chicken sandwich for himself, fries, hamburger, and milk for Sky. Only Sky didn't want the milk. He insisted on having Paul's drink, an unwieldy sweating cup clamped between his legs. "Don't spill it," Paul warned. And later, back on the highway, he told Sky, "That clerk, that boy who helped us, he was like your dad. Not his looks so much, more the way he walked and talked. Both."

Sky looked up suddenly. Said, as if they were peers, "Where's Nicole?"

"At home."

"Home?"

"Yeah."

"I like her," Sky said.

"Yes, you do."

Sky went back to his fries and drink. Sucked hard at the straw so that Paul, watching him, thought the child resembled a bee bending to the flower, sucking nectar through a yellow straw.

"Buzz, buzz," he whispered and these two words become an echo from the wedding, a taste of gin, music, Don's voice grinding upwards from the stage, and there, yes, of course, Mrs. Wish, the thickness of her, swish of her hair across the back of his hand, wetness of the dark grass, grief that floated near her shoulders. A signal from a far shore, distant, far off. If she were unattached and not the wife of Furst's best doctor, then yes, perhaps, but not like this. He had chosen a kind of exile. A lonely place from where he could keen loudly. And that was what he had done, until Nicole arrived, bringing with her this boy, this babble of want and hunger and fear and joy and urgency. And wonder, that too. Paul looked over at him. He was sleeping now, lulled by the hum of the wheels, slumped over his still-full bag of food. Paul pushed at his head, gently, and lowered him to the seat. There. Took the drink. The fries spilled off his lap and onto the floor beside the pink ball the size of his head.

That night Paul moved the remaining hives. Nicole had not yet returned and Sky, wide awake after a long afternoon nap, remained Paul's responsibility. So Paul took him along, told him to stay in the cab of the half-ton. Let him watch through the windshield as Paul worked in the glare of the headlights, stepping in and out of the bright tunnel knocked out of the darkness. Driving, Paul talked to Sky, told him all about bees. "They're in the hives now," he said. "So this is the best time to move them. In the morning when they wake up they'll be surprised by their new home but not worried. They'll look around and figure it out and each new flight will send them a bit further. They're smart animals. Smarter than people in some ways."

"Animals," Sky said. The darkness of the cab with its dull light from the dash sedated him, made him softer and less needy. He was not afraid. Even when Paul left him he accepted the solitude. Trusted Paul to return.

In the bush west of the creek, bordering an alfalfa crop, Paul set up twelve hives and staked out an electric fence. Skunks and the occasional bear liked this area and both animals could devastate a hive. Skunks killed and then ate the bees. They didn't touch the honey. Bears smashed the hives and ate everything—bees, honey, brood, wax, pollen, and even some wood. Paul hammered in the plastic posts. Strung the wire at four levels. He off-loaded a car battery from the half-ton. Set it inside the enclosure and hooked up the cables. Tested the voltage with a piece of wet grass, got a jolt and was satisfied. Coming back to the truck he saw Sky leaning into the dash, the interior light made the top of his head glow. His eyes were animal-like, half hidden by the shadows. Paul climbed into the cab, rubbed the boy's head, bent to kiss the crown where the light hit hardest.

"Sleepy?" he asked.

"No." He yawned.

"Put your head on my lap," Paul said, and patted his knee, encouraging Sky.

The boy shook his head. "Scary," he said, lifting his nose.

"Where?"

The nose shivered delicately.

"Don't worry," Paul said. "You're safe."

Sky bit his lip. Lay back against the seat. "Nicole," he said.

"Nicole will come home tomorrow," Paul said. "In the morning." He didn't believe this. Just wanted to comfort the boy. Nicole, he thought, had run away and left him with her son. So easily done. The probability didn't bother him, in fact he was pleased to imagine raising Sky. He believed he could give the child a good life, better than Nicole.

The night before he had awakened and listened for her. Thought he'd heard a door slam. But it was the wind, a loose board caught in a gust and thrown against the porch. He'd lain in bed then and listened to the wind and Sky's soft breathing. He'd wondered about Nicole. Thought that when she came home he'd ask, "Who are you?" and then see if she knew the answer, or even understood the question.

Sometimes Paul didn't know who *he* was. He thought, if pressed, he'd say, "I am Paul Unger, father of two children, one dead. I have left my wife. I live alone. I am a beekeeper." And that was all. Reciting these facts, butting up against them, made Paul realize he should be lonely. But he wasn't. Solitude was not a bad thing, though it tended to narrow the mind; other people quickly became fools. In bed later, before he fell asleep, Paul felt that his own body had the texture and fineness of a bee's wing; he was a mere membrane, delicate and wonderfully futile, fleeting.

At some point during the night he sat up, as if startled by a fearful dream. He listened and heard the pop of tires on the gravel driveway, the sigh of an engine as it died. Recognized the dieseling of the Camino and waited for Nicole's approach. Conrad growled nearby. Paul shushed him. The Camino door opened and was shut poorly. Was shut again. The moan of an animal in pain floated through the night. Paul got up and walked in shorts to the porch. He stood by the screen door and listened. Conrad brushed against his ankles. Paul looked out at the darkness. Heard a snuffling, a sob. He went down the stairs and walked towards the shadow of the Camino. He found Nicole sitting on the ground, her back up against the front wheel. She had her knees at her chest and had tucked her face downwards. She might have been sleeping except her shoulders stuttered and when Paul touched her head she cried out. Looked up.

"Jesus Christ," Nicole said, and ducked her head again.

"Hey." Paul took her chin and lifted gently. "You okay?"

"Great." Her voice came up as if from under water.

"You drunk?"

"Am I?" She laughed. Began to shake again.

"Here." Paul pulled her up. Made her stand. She teetered and leaned against him. He held her and walked her towards the house, up the stairs and into the porch. Sat her down. There, in the bright light, he discovered the damage to her face.

"Look at you."

One eye was swollen shut. Her top lip puffy, almost split. He went into the kitchen and ran warm water into a bowl. Took a clean cloth. Came back to Nicole and swabbed at her eye, her mouth.

"Ouch," she said. Grabbed his wrist and squeezed.

"Nothing's open," he said. "You're lucky."

She stank. She had thrown up on her blouse and skirt. Made a poor attempt to scrape the vomit away. He said, "I'll run you a shower. Come." He guided her to the washroom, started the shower, and left her standing, stupid, by the toilet. "I'll put some clean clothes by the door," he said. He rummaged among his own clothes and came up with sweatpants and a T-shirt. He laid these outside the bathroom door and went into the kitchen where he prepared a pot of coffee. Then he sat down and read fitfully, listening for Nicole. She finally appeared. Her hair was wet and combed back. Her good eye watched Paul. She sat down at the table and said, "I look awful."

Paul poured coffee. Handed her a mug.

"Thank you," she said. She looked around, focused on the far doorway, and said, "Sky?"

"Sleeping."

She nodded.

Paul watched her.

Finally, she said, "You must think I'm an awful person. Look at me. Am I? Awful?"

Paul shook his head.

"It was Romel," she said. "We were at this party and he was making it with this chick. So, I bit a chunk out of his neck. He hit me." She touched her tongue at her lip. "Can still taste him," she said.

Paul didn't speak. He imagined Nicole surfacing with Romel's flesh between her teeth.

"Don't even remember leaving the party," she said. "Driving home." She stopped. "Sky?"

Paul nodded at the living-room.

Nicole stood. Wobbled and held the chair. "Oh, my," she said. Giggled. Her head dipped, came up. "Do I surprise you?" And then, not waiting, she added, "I like it here. Feels lucky." She paused, swallowed, drifted a hand through the air, and said, "I think I'll just throw up one more time." She went then, walking as if someone important were watching, through the door, and Paul could hear her emptying herself into the toilet.

He waited but she didn't return. Much later he went and found her sleeping on his bed, hands pressed between her legs, knees drawn up. Her mouth was open. She seemed flattened, by the dim light, the shadows, by her own inconsequence. Paul covered her with a blanket and she disappeared. Only her wounds, darker now, seemed significant.

Paul closed the back door. Went to the bathroom and rinsed out Nicole's clothes. Her white shirt, her blue skirt, her panties, her bra. He left them soaking in the tub. He turned out the lights, crept to Sky's bed, slid in, and found sleep easily.

In the morning he woke to find that Nicole had come to the bed during the night. She lay on the other side of Sky. Paul was surprised by this intimacy, the immediate awareness of Nicole at rest, there, the mother of his grandson, a bare arm facing him, her T-shirt twisted and mangled during the night, pulled upwards now and revealing her belly and a few ribs. He looked away. Lay there and compared the breathing of the two bodies beside him, one quick and almost startled, the other more prolonged, deeper, settled. In a move that surprised him, Paul held a palm close to Nicole's nose: two dots of warmth. He pulled his hand away. A knocking in his skull. He rose then, a hasty scrambling escape that roused Sky, who, opening his eyes, saw Paul, felt Nicole, and turned to locate her head. He touched her mouth, her nose. "Nicole," he said.

Nicole opened one eye. Moaned and turned away. Sky crawled over her. A movement of bared vertebrae, toes stretching. Paul, looking down, sensed a removal, a drawing away.

"God," she said. She turned. Discovered Paul. "Oh," she said. Then she took Sky and said, "Sweetie, how are you? Did you miss me? Mummy's bad, isn't she?" She asked this question so boldly, so happily, that Paul imagined he was being addressed or perhaps that Nicole was deflecting any possible anger resulting from her absence. She turned and yawned and offered him the ribbing of her mouth, her tongue, a quick and illicit glimpse into the darkness.

"My head hurts," she said.

"I'll make coffee," Paul said, and he left Sky and Nicole, passed through to the kitchen, and doing so, felt the easy slide into domesticity, the muttering of Sky, Nicole's low drawl, the water ascending to a boil, the dustiness of the morning light, the bubble in his chest.

She did not intend to leave. This was obvious to Paul, and so on the third day after her return when she said at breakfast, "Can we stay? Here?" he was not surprised and answered from the stove where he was making breakfast, "Yes," and as he said this he could see the way before him, a dark pool to immerse the rock of happiness in him.

"I'll work for you," Nicole said.

"You will?"

"Yes. There must be something I can do. I'd like to learn about bees."

"Taking care of Sky would help. It's not easy moving hives or catching a swarm with a three-year-old around."

Nicole forked the yolk of her egg. Allowed the yellow to seep to the edge of her toast. She was pouting.

Paul sat across from her and said, "It's not exciting work. Very simple. Often back-breaking."

"I could sew a little suit for Sky. He could follow. Stay out of the way. He listens."

"Yes," Paul said, "he listens. In any case, he's still three and children of three do stray, they're impetuous."

Nicole remained quiet, then she said, "If you're angry with me, just say."

"Am I?"

She didn't answer.

Paul said, "You could've called. Said, 'I'm not coming back, could you take care of Sky?' A simple courtesy. Anyways, I'm not angry."

"Don't be," she said. "I couldn't stand it."

Paul understood this as a vague threat and he realized that Nicole was an intricate web of knowledge and cunning and greed and deceit and goodness. He could see the goodness in the way she stroked Sky's ear now as he laid his head on her lap. What he feared was her greed. He wanted to say now, "Stay. Forever. Always. Don't leave," but instead he composed himself and said, "I'll make a room for you and Sky. Put in a bathtub. I've been meaning to do that and this gives me good reason."

Nicole kissed Sky's head and said, "Would you like to live with Grandpa, sweetie? Here, with the bees and the flowers and the dog and the creek?" She didn't wait for an answer but fanned a hand at the far window which gave out to the driveway and the road and the fields.

"I'm hungry," Sky said.

Paul got up and took an egg from the carton. He took out the pan, heated the element, and turned back to the table and said to Nicole, "Why here?"

She seemed surprised by this question, as if it were unnecessary or even new. "It's good," she said. "For Sky. And me. Like I said, it's safe."

"You'll get lonely," Paul said. "Not Sky. You."

"Really?" This too seemed novel, though she said, "I grew up in a small town. I know the feelings of Sunday afternoons. I'm not afraid of lonely."

"Could you give me some warning," Paul said. "Before you leave?"

She smiled, bunched her nose and closed her eyes.

"What will you tell your father?" Paul asked.

Nicole's eyes went bright with the clarity of her answer. "That I'm living at Paul Unger's. Sky's grandpa. You are that, aren't you?"

Nicole took the Camino to St. Pierre. Sky went with her. She returned late in the afternoon with boxes of clothes, wine, beer, cereal, cigarettes, and a bottle of scotch. She made supper: potato salad, Kool-Aid, bread, cheese. She called Paul from the honey house and they ate forming a triangle around the oval table. Nicole poured wine and drank more than she ate. She was talkative, excited.

"I stopped for butter in town and saw Sue grocery shopping. We talked a bit."

"You did?" Paul had not seen Sue for a while, not since the fairgrounds, the baseball game.

"Yes," Nicole said. "I told her I was living here with Sky. She seemed surprised."

"That's too bad. I was hoping to tell her, ease it out, you know?"

"I'm sorry," Nicole said, but she didn't seem it. She said, "Sue was buying supper, too. It was funny. Her and me doing this little family thing." Nicole giggled. Lit a cigarette.

Paul felt protective of his daughter. Experienced a slight shock at Nicole's perception of where she sat in this unfolding life, as if they were playing house now, for however long she wanted, until she'd quit and move on. It would not be easy, he saw, to thwart this girl. He missed Sue now, her softness, her forgiveness. She didn't demand much, not like Nicole here, whose hard voice filled the kitchen.

Sky climbed off his stool, bread in hand, and wound his way out to the swing set. The glider squeaked minutely and Paul thought this was good, a signal of sorts.

"She said she was going to school in fall," Nicole continued. "University. I said, 'Great.' She said Daniel wants her to work. Make some money."

"She should go to school. They don't need money."

"You like handing out money, don't you, Mr. Unger?"

"Do I?" He hated the Mr. Unger, though he said nothing. Around Sky he was Grandpa. But with Nicole he went mostly nameless, as if she was uncertain. The habit had become one of her seeking him out, physically approaching and beginning a conversation in flight, with no nomenclature attached, so that sentences arrived headless, somewhat bloodied and full of surprises. Sometimes she offered prologues like, "You know what?" or "I was thinking," but these were shouted from a distance, another room, or from house to yard. Or "well," she liked "well." She used it now.

"Well, you're rich and you're generous."

"Rich people are seldom generous."

"You are."

Paul was amused. Perhaps by the naivety, perhaps by the way Nicole topped off his glass of wine, even though he was not wanting any. She toddled away at her own glass, slid down in her chair. Patted her belly. Said, "I ate too much."

"You eat too fast. I've noticed that."

"My father says I'm greedy."

"You are."

Now it was her turn to query. "Am I?"

"Yes."

"I'm poor, and the poor need to be greedy."

"You're not poor. Don't even joke about that."

Nicole dipped a finger into her wine. Came back to him and said, "But why do you like to hand out money?"

"You tell me," Paul said. "You obviously know."

"Guilt," she said. She laid a hand on the table, palm down, cupped, as if she had captured something.

Paul was not surprised. Lise had proclaimed this fact through the years. He wasted money because of the guilt of having too much.

"Maybe I just don't care," he said.

"But you do."

"What did your father say about this?" Paul spun a finger around the room. "About you living here."

"Oh," Nicole said, "he didn't ask. Some people don't care how things look. He's one of them. How about you?" Nicole asked. "Do you care?"

Paul shook his head. Said, "Doesn't matter." And it didn't. It was enough to have Sky near. What other people made of this was inconsequential. Sky was everything.

After supper Paul loaded empty supers on the half-ton and left Nicole with the dishes and Sky, and drove out to the hives which sat in the scrubby bush east of the creek. The light was failing when he arrived and the mosquitoes were cruel. He freed the electric fence and climbed in to check the hives. He lifted the lids to see how full they were. Out of the twenty hives here, fifteen required another super. More room, more honey. Paul worked quickly, stacking the boxes, marking the poor producers and reclamping the fence. He walked around the enclosure before he left and found some ripped-up saplings and scuffle marks in the dirt. Bear. Not a big one, judging by the prints, but it could be a nuisance.

He drove home in the dark and arrived to find Sky asleep and Nicole smoking in the front porch. He joined her. Said, "Saw bear tracks up by the creek enclosure. East of here."

Nicole's cigarette glowed. "Is that bad?" she asked.

"Just is."

Nicole said, "Well, bears like honey, don't they?"

"A bear doesn't know there's all that honey in the hives. She gets a scent, is curious, rips the box apart, and surprise, surprise. She can make a real mess then."

Nicole stubbed her cigarette and said, "I'm gonna read. Do you mind?" Paul waved. She stood and went into the living-room and sat on the couch by the orange-shaded lamp. Opened her book. Paul could see, beyond the doorjamb, her knee, rounded and pale. He stood and called out, "I'm going down to the creek."

Nicole looked up briefly, tilted her head as if surprised to see him standing before her, smiled absently, and nodded. She looked away, back at her book. Bit her nails as she read. It was a book she had found among his meagre offerings. A mystery.

He took Conrad and walked down the driveway to the gravel road and then followed the path through the bush to the creek. The moon was a thin wedge; the night was dark. Conrad beat through the scrub and returned in a rush now and then to verify Paul's presence.

"Hush," Paul said, or "Stay," but Conrad didn't listen.

At the creek Conrad bit the water and slid in. Paddled out to the middle, turned, and came back. Paul sat in the dirt. A small animal snuffled in the bush. Conrad's wet ears went up. "What is it?" Paul whispered. He touched the dog's nose. A car passed, far away. Paul missed Lise tonight. And Sue. But mostly he wanted the familiarity Sue brought, a stability, the safety.

There was a tightness in his throat and chest. His teeth hurt. He closed his eyes. The ferocity of the mosquitoes drove him back up the path, over the road and on to his house where Nicole sat, still reading. And coming upon her, lotus-like on the couch, head bowed, oblivious to his entrance, she could easily have been Lise or Sue or even his dead son, but Paul was suddenly thankful that she was none of these people. What she brought to the house was an unpredictable and headlong light.

She looked up now. Saw him and said, "Hey."

"I was thinking tomorrow I'd drive you out to the clover field," Paul said. "Gotta start somewhere."

"Goody," she said, and touched her nose.

"Night, then."

"Okay, yeah."

He fell asleep quickly. He was tired. He dreamed first of Sky swinging on his new set. Nicole was pushing him. Then Lise was swinging and Paul was giving her underducks. Lise was wearing a skirt and Paul could see her white panties. Her mouth was open as if she were laughing or screaming, but Paul understood that she was crying, and her face became that of Mrs. Wish and Mrs. Wish was laughing and holding a baby. They were swinging together in the glider. "Emily," he said, "may I?" And he went to take the baby and in doing so the baby crumbled, powder at their feet.

Paul woke and stared at the dark ceiling. The light still shone from the living-room. He rose and went to find Nicole asleep on the couch. She had curled up around her book. Her back faced Paul. He shook her awake. "Come," he said.

She jolted upwards, frightened. "Shhh," he said, "it's me. Time for bed."

She rose. Her legs were weak. Paul held her elbow, felt the bone between thumb and forefinger. The book tumbled, its cover bent.

"I have to pee," she said. She left him then, found the wash-room, shut the door, and after a while Paul heard the spray of her against the toilet water. He went out into the kitchen. Lit a candle. He heard Nicole exit the washroom and feel her way to her and Sky's bed. Silence then.

Paul sat in the waving light of the candle by the front porch-screen. He sat with his hands on the arms of the rocker and he stared out into the night. He thought about being dead. Such a final word that. You're dead. He's dead. I'll be dead by then. *Died* was better. An action word. Bit of a sing-song. As if the word itself were hopeful. As if the boy had some choice: *I'm going to die now.*

It wasn't true.

Paul's father had been afraid of dying. He did not practise any formal religion, as did many in the town of Furst, other than perhaps the religion of work which carried him out each morning and released him late at night and left him little time with his wife and only child, a boy to whom he confessed once in a botched effort to comfort him after a nightmare, "I, too, am afraid of the dark."

Paul was young when he first heard that confession but it remained a tender recollection. Another was the smell of his father as he settled into his chair after work. Suit jacket off, tie loosened, doffed shoes beside the chair, and Paul would crawl into his father's lap and dig through his pockets and smell cigar smoke, Dentyne, and the residue of the office, which consisted of a mixture of new furniture, coffee grinds, and the ink on his fingers. The deepest and most penetrating smell was the body itself, the human odour of sweat and slightly sour breath and the tang of fatigue, the stink. Not until after Paul was married and had his own children did he realize that his father, in his awkward attempt to console him that night, had meant, "I, too, am afraid of death."

An infant, a baby, a young child, did not carry the odour of decay and rot and it was this possibility of immortality that made Paul aware of the singularity of life: his father's, his son's, his own. From his father he had acquired the feminine jaw, the detached earlobes, a pigeon-toed gait, a shyness often mistaken for vanity, and the habit of scraping together crumbs after a meal and making neat piles on the tablecloth, as if order could be created out of something so simple as scraps. However, Paul had no inordinate fear of dying. Like Beth, his mother, he had settled on a fatalistic hope, living generously, observing that a man like his father, who constantly fended off death, was like a snail who curled into itself and rarely advanced.

Nature deceived. It offered a sense of cycle and order, hope even, and then madly, without purpose, it took away, and when Stephen fell over drunk and drowned in a puddle on that summer night three years earlier, nature leapfrogged backwards over Paul and his father and did what it should not have done.

Paul remembered his father arriving at the house during a downpour on the morning after Stephen's death, and standing in the doorway, water dripping from his nose and ears and mixing with his tears, and whispering, "This is not right, this is not right." He himself would die in his sleep four months later and this quick soft death seemed to Paul to be an acknowledgement of blame, as if he had chased death from his own threshold to that of his grandson.

"The dead don't care." This was what the undertaker who

prepared Stephen's body, a meaty-looking fellow in smooth black, had said. He was trying to be helpful in an odd sort of way.

"The living care," he continued, mopping up the obvious mess he had left on Paul's soul. The thick man touched Paul's arm and said, "You must take care of his memory."

And of course the dead didn't care. Someone had told Paul that Emily Wish had held her baby for twelve hours after it died. Paul wished he could have done that with Stephen. Held him, felt the waterlogged flesh, kissed his eyes, his mouth where the mud had entered, smelled him before he had been transformed by the blood being drained from him, washed him, spoken words into his ears. Paul thought that those who were poorer than him, those who lived in countries where family burial was allowed and necessary, were fortunate to be able to prepare their own dead. What absolute care and love.

Stephen's funeral had taken place on a warm day at the end of June. Lise wore a grey suit, skirt just below her knees. Paul recalled absurd details. The undertaker's knuckles, Stephen's clipped nails and short hair, Sue's leg pressing his, the beautiful shape of her bare knee and him thinking how girls becoming women have legs to be lined up and admired and how lucky they are, and her holding his wrist, Lise crying silently, with control, and later, at the grave site, Paul looking up and finding a single cloud, and wondering how that was possible.

Nicole had been there. A strangely curious presence. What she wore was provocative and shameless, as if she didn't know better. Nobody spoke to her. She came and went, and as she left the church Paul saw a flash of her by the coatracks, her arm reaching up for her purse, the wink of her midriff revealing once again that she was, indeed, going to have a baby.

The autopsy proved that Stephen had drowned. Sucked the water from the puddle up into his mouth and down into his lungs. An easy death. As if death were an exam, a needle's eye to be passed through. In death he was laid out beneath the earth. But, knowing this, Paul had come to understand that what lay in the coffin had ceased to be Stephen. It was something else. What Stephen became then, from that moment until this, Paul sitting here beside the candle, was a consequence: he had become the hollowness of Paul's heart, the tennis racquets hanging from a wall in the basement, the empty chair at the table, the lack, the lack, and then, miraculously, he returned, bits and pieces, in the creases of Sue's smile, the child at the edge of the sprinkler, those ears, and there was the hope, too, that Nicole still carried him in some way, a trace, perhaps a word, a gesture, thought, touch; Stephen springing up sudden and unbidden from the depths of the girl who slept as if dead in the far room of the house.

The jumble of midnight thoughts. What was extreme clarity would seem vapid and twisted with the coming of morning. Still, the brain pushed against the darkness, enjoyed the freedom, the erratic leaps, the nonsense and fear. He recalled the smell of her that night she had come home beaten and bruised. The bleachy sweet stink of sex. How shocking it was; though he knew she must have a lover, a man, a boy, many perhaps, the idea had been neatly closeted in Paul's brain. A fact without context or location. But then, holding Nicole's head, wiping her eye, her mouth, cleaning her cuts, he discovered her carnality and was dismayed. He had an image of Nicole servicing various men: standing up, lying down, bending over, on her knees. Nicole, a hole to be filled up. Still, Paul felt a curious affection for her. She was brazen and unrepentant. He saw in her a path back to his son. The affection, then, was also selfish. Nicole led him back to Stephen, and this, too, was why the smell of sex on her was both intriguing and disappointing. Stephen, one of obviously many, was disappearing. From her mind. From her body. A careless erasure.

Paul rubbed a hand across his face. It was still dark. Conrad groaned at his feet. Some dream fogging his dog brain. Paul thought of Lise asleep in her bed. Was Harry there, or was he out patrolling the streets? Saving the good people. Harry and Lise. And Sue now, lying beside her doltish husband. Had she discovered yet the slipperiness of love, waking beside Daniel, aware that the boy-barely-man who rubbed up against her was less than she wanted or desired or even deserved?

Paul remembered his own youth, spiralling downwards into the arms of Glenda Dent, Linda Peck, and Dorothy Penner. Of these three, Dorothy came back to him brightest and clearest, perhaps because their relationship was hidden and illicit. Paul's parents, genteel and clean, would not have approved. Dorothy had lived with her sick father and wayward mother in a run-down house three miles east of town: a plot of land overgrown with thistle and quackgrass, sprouting a rusted tractor, an abandoned car. She was fierce and untethered, Paul an anchor she clung to. Her mother brought home strange men and kept them in the room next to the husband's, a man whose presence was only intimated: half-empty plates of food outside his closed door, large trousers and undershirts on the wash line. And then, as quickly as they came together, Dorothy and Paul fell apart. His own vision for her was as narrow as the gap between her thighs when in summer she wore shorts and leaned against the shingled wall of her house or bent over the rhubarb patch. She had pale eyes the lightest blue, lighter than the shell of a robin's egg, and when Paul remembered Dorothy now he thought of eggs and birds. He had seen her years later in Winnipeg. They passed each other on the street. Paul was with Lise, and Dorothy walked hand-in-hand with a tall, thick-necked man. They stopped and talked a while. Dorothy said she was a secretary at Dominion Bridge on Logan. "You escaped," Paul said, and as he spoke of running his father's business, he rediscovered her eyes, still a pale, pale blue. Nicole resembled Dorothy in an obscure way. The lightness perhaps, the sense that escape was both necessary and impending, and the self-possession, the "here I am" quality, as if there were nothing better to have in the world than that moment, that space, that narrow gap.

He did not sleep. He watched as the light began to wash away the night. The distant shed, the trees, the swing set, rose up as if out of water. Dew, a bit of brume, touched the trees and the grass. The grass needed mowing, which was something he'd been wanting Nicole to do, but her goodwill did not extend to yard work.

That had been Stephen's job as a child. The image was still there of a thin-limbed adolescent pushing the mower back and forth across the expanse of lawn, as if it were some ancient ritual every child must be taught. And, after, he entered the house, grass clippings on his bare shins, hands smelling of gasoline and oil, and he stooped to the innards of the fridge, rising with a glass of milk. Paul, coming upon him, was struck by the frailty of his own child, all sinew and filament and bone.

Paul was weary. He made coffee. Strong. Drank it standing up and staring east over the tree line, at the bloody rim of a brightening bowl. He finished his coffee and went out to the shed. He carried supers from the shed to his half-ton. Stacked them five high, four deep, two rows. He drove out past La Broquerie to the Farrell farm, their eastern section, and added to the supers on the hives that sat at the corner of a field of clover. The hives were getting heavy. One hive stood seven supers high and Paul required the stepladder from the back of his truck. Finished, he stood and looked out across the perfect crop and beyond to another field, and beyond that, so the sense was that silence and nature went on forever. Conrad rustled through the clover, chasing a mouse. A hawk hung in the sky. He drove home and found Nicole sitting in shorts and T-shirt, barefoot, on the porch.

"Sky's still sleeping," she said.

"Put some shoes on," he told her.

She obeyed, returned, and together they walked out to the honey shed where he handed her a beekeeper's suit. Coveralls, veil, gloves. This was the outfit he had bought for Sue last year in the hope that she would share some interest in this life. She had worn it once. Nicole disappeared into the white stiffness. Paul zipped her veil. Her face was shadowed beyond the netting.

"You don't need one?" she asked.

"No."

"Never get bitten?"

"Stung."

"Never get stung?"

"Rarely." This was true. He often worked with no shirt on, just shorts. Hated the heaviness and heat of the suit. Bees danced around him, brushed against his skin, alighted occasionally, but didn't often sting.

"Sometimes I come across a nasty hive," he explained. "But I'm aware of those. I'll use a smoker then. I don't usually winter ill-tempered bees. Just let them die." They walked out beyond the honeysuckle hedge to the out yard where Paul removed the stacked supers on a hive to get a look at the hive body. "This is the brood box," Paul said, "or the main house, where the queen lives and the eggs hatch. There, that's the queen," and he indicated a bee slightly longer and wider than the workers. Nicole hovered behind him. Her covered arm touched his back.

"What's she doing?" she asked.

"Taking care of her family. Laying eggs. At her peak she lays two thousand eggs a day."

"And she's the boss?"

"Sort of. Though some people claim it's the workers who guide her. Still, she's the boss. Here, you hold it."

He handed her the frame. She took it carefully as if it were a freshly painted canvas. She was still, breathing slowly; bees circled her neck and shoulders.

"They look so harmless," she said.

Paul took the frame and slid it back in place. He restacked the supers. From the top super he pried free a frame. "Here," he said. "This is where the bees store the honey. Then they cap it with a thin layer of wax."

The frame glowed a deep yellow. Nicole bent to look, then straightened. They studied several more hives. Paul nodded at one where the bees were not producing. "May be a weak queen," he said. He marked it with a crayon. Dated it.

Later, walking back to the house, Nicole said, "And that's it? That's the bee's life?"

"What do you mean?"

"Flying out of the hive. Sitting on a flower. Coming back. Dropping honey. Covering it with wax. Flying out again. That's it?"

Paul looked at her, but didn't answer. In the shed, while Nicole changed, he thought how unimpressed she was and how ultimately that had to do with her age, her fascination with herself. Where he found creation, she saw futility. Her purpose, it would seem, was to satisfy her own needs, to fill herself up. And she wouldn't let this go, because as she handed him the beekeeper's suit, she asked, "How long do bees live?"

"The workers, six weeks in summer. Their wings wear out. The queen, three years, sometimes more, sometimes less. The drones, a summer."

"I'd like to be a queen."

"Sure you would."

"The queen gets to have sex, right?" She looked at him. Her eyes were bright.

"That's one way of putting it," he said. He turned. "Come."

She laughed. "You're such a prude."

"Am I?"

"Sure you are, Mr. Unger."

He felt a need to defend himself. Said, "Animals don't have sex like people, willy-nilly, as if it were their right to eat a special meal every day. Animals follow a cycle, and bees are no different. A queen mates once in her life but several times on that occasion."

"Oh." Nicole was disappointed. Then she said, "With?"

They were walking towards the house. Paul wondered if Sky was awake yet. He answered, "The drones." Pointed up in the air and his affection for facts took over. "Forty feet above the hive. Or higher. The strongest drones, those that fly the highest, are the lucky ones. The drone's penis goes into the queen's sting chamber, which closes around it, ripping it loose from the drone's body. The drone dies. The queen flies back to the hive with her back end weeping drone gut. It's all very much like the female praying mantis who actually turns and eats her partner while mating. Mating is all that drones are good for. In fall, those who are left are chased from the hive. If they come back, the workers tear off their wings."

"Kill them?"

"In a way. Drones are not terribly intelligent. They have big eyes and small brains and they hang out in gangs."

"I've heard that before," Nicole said, "about the praying mantis."

They entered the porch. Sky appeared in the kitchen doorway. He was naked, his stomach was tight and brown, his arms waved for his mother. She picked him up. Kissed his head. Said, "Sweetie. Mummy was looking at the bees. They gave me goose bumps. Crawling up and down my arms, buzzing around my face."

"Don't scare the boy," Paul said. He took out a pan. Put bread in the toaster.

"Oh, he doesn't scare," Nicole said. She lit a cigarette and balanced Sky on her knee. "Do you, love?"

Sky yawned. His eyes were oily.

"I was thinking," Paul said, "that you could clean pails. There are stacks in the honey shed. They all need to be readied."

"Sure," Nicole said, though she seemed displeased.

"Sky can help. He'd like that."

"Fine."

And so after breakfast Nicole changed into jean shorts and a loose shirt, runners. She took Sky and followed Paul out to the honey house where he pointed out five gallon pails. "Wash them with soap and water. Rinse well. Stack them over there." He motioned at the far wall, next to the gleam of the extractor. Then he left Nicole standing in the centre of the dim room, empty-handed, staring at the work that had been thrust at her.

Paul climbed into the half-ton and drove to town. He stopped at Lucky Foods, bought some more groceries, then drove over to Lise's house. Sue was home, suntanning by the pool, wearing a bathing suit with thin straps, not much on the hips. Her belly glistened with oil. She was reading, her arms extended; the book shaded her face.

"Hi, Daddy," she said. She sat up. Hugged her knees. A glass of water teetered beside the blanket. She picked it up, sipped, and put it back. She appeared stunned by the sun.

Paul picked a shady spot under the plum tree. He folded his legs. Sue squinted, shielded her eyes with one hand, and said, "So, how's the family?"

"Yeah," Paul said. "She said she'd seen you. Told you. I was kinda hoping I'd get to you first."

"Doesn't matter." Sue looked away. Dragged her fingers along the cement.

"You're right, it doesn't matter. They needed a place."

"They had a place."

"You're angry."

"No, I'm not." She flopped onto her back, put an arm across her eyes. The spiralled fineness of her ear. Neck just like her mother's. Her breasts flattened now. Paul was surprised by how naked she looked. He wondered if she always looked this vulnerable.

She looked at him again, peeked out from beneath her arm. Pupils, two rings of green. "Why?" she asked.

"Sue, Sue." Paul rose and went over to his daughter. Knelt and took her head and drew her upwards so that she was sitting. "What do you mean?" He touched her chin. Kissed her forehead. Sadness always made her beautiful. He held her head and said, "You're jealous."

"A little."

"For no reason. Sky is my grandson. How could I say no?"

"Oh, Daddy, you're so gullible."

He pulled away. Studied her and smiled. "Don't listen to your mother."

"Nicole's a slut."

"Is she?"

"Well, she gets whatever she wants."

Paul tried to hide his amusement. "And what does she want?"

"Your money." Then, looking away over at the driveway and Paul's half-ton, she said, "Daniel knows Nicole from way back. He says it's fishy, you and her in the same house." She turned, looked at him.

"Daniel said that?"

"Yes."

"And you agree?"

"No, I know you wouldn't do *that*. It's just I don't trust her. I guess I wish you'd asked *me* to live out there."

"You hate bees. The house is a mess and there's no TV and you'd have to cook your own meals."

"Nicole cooks?"

"Not really."

"See?"

"Well, come then. Join us. I'll build you and Daniel a bedroom."

Sue grinned now, pecked Paul's ear. She knelt, folded her blanket, took Paul's arm, and together they walked through the pool gate towards the house. Paul could taste the suntan lotion which had transferred from Sue's forehead to his mouth. Her hand was light on his elbow, petals brushing his skin. Inside, she ran up to her room, returned in jeans and sweatshirt. They shared coffee at the dining-room table. Sue talked about Daniel and how well he was doing. She said, "He'd probably make more money if you put him on commission."

"Would he?" Paul said. He was angry with Daniel. The boy had no right. How strange, to be talked about in that way. Perhaps others felt the same. Paul cleared his head, faced his daughter, and said, "So, you're happy then. You and Daniel?"

"Sure, we are. Daniel wants me to work in the fall. Not go to school."

"What do you want?"

"I'm thinking about it."

Paul nodded. "Does Daniel think you'll be happier working?"

"He's worried about money."

"Ridiculous," Paul said. "You're living with your mother, you have no expenses, what do you need money for?"

Sue shrugged. "Daniel thinks we should buy a house, and then he wants children, two, and we want new furniture, and Daniel just put a down payment on a new car."

Paul saw that his daughter was following the same path he had taken. This saddened him. He wanted to tell her this, but all he said was, "A new car?"

"Yes. One he's wanted since he was a boy."

"His money?"

"I don't know. We had some money from the wedding. We were gonna use it for my school but he wanted the car." Sue saw the darkness in her father's face. She added, "It's okay. I don't mind. Really. I've got a lot of years."

"I want you to be happy," Paul said.

"I am, Daddy. I am." Sue stood and kissed her father's forehead. Patted his crown. "You smell nice," she said.

"Know what I think?"

"No, what?"

"Marriage demands all this give and take, only one's usually giving and the other's taking."

"Like you and Mum, then?"

Paul shook his head.

"Grandma says you two are gonna get back together."

"She said that?"

"Did. Said little Harry Kehler will go back to Bunny, and you will go back to Mum."

"She said 'little'?"

"That's what she said. Then she said Daniel was young and he was still a boy and I should be good to him."

"And you're listening to her?"

"I'm doing my best."

"Of course you are."

"Sometimes I look up, you know, and I can see this window and I can't quite reach it to open it. That ever happen to you?"

"Lots."

"And then I imagine what's beyond the window." She shook her head. Said, "Oh, yeah, Mrs. Wish, the doctor's wife, came by the other day. She wanted your phone number. Something about buying honey. I gave it to her."

"Good," Paul said. "Can always use more customers." He had passed by the doctor and his wife on the road just yesterday in their white BMW, Dr. Wish in his dark suit, Emily staring out the windshield, bit of a pout, hair swept back. Funny about that little window of Sue's, but there were times when Paul imagined Mrs. Wish just on the other side, waiting.

The July days and nights that followed wrapped themselves, hot and then cool, around the house and its three occupants. Paul rose early, leaving Nicole and Sky asleep, and went to the honey house where he readied pails for the extraction of honey. He also scraped the brood combs and supers, peeling away the propolis of the previous year, shavings dropping fine and dark and sticky around his feet. The long warm days of summer were perfect for honeybees, who flew in the daylight and gathered nectar and pollen until dark. Whereas the bees, in spring, fed on the blossoms of hazel, poplar, willows, dandelions, chokecherries, saskatoons, and hawthorn, in summer they found clover, alfalfa, canola, sunflowers, and buckwheat, with clover producing the most popular honey. This, in any case, was what Paul Unger believed, though clover was becoming harder and harder to find, especially as canola took over the land. It was always surprising each July to discover yet more fields offering the brilliant yellow of that cash crop.

He had begun to school Nicole in the art of raising bees. Not just the simple elements of getting honey, but the philosophy of living with bees. He told her that bees were wise animals and it was not up to the beekeeper to dictate to the bees but to simply accompany. Bees had a definite plan for life, perfected through the ages. You could delay a bee's work or you could even hinder it, but no one had ever succeeded in changing the ways of a bee. The best beekeeper, then, was the one who followed.

There was a time, he explained one night, when beekeepers

would kill their bees every fall and then, in spring, order up new package bees from the States. No longer. It had become too expensive and there were too many diseases coming across the border. Now, he wintered his bees, right here, on the farm, in the winter shed. Four degrees Celsius. In fall, he made sure they had enough sugar syrup. In spring, he fed them antibiotics. Looked for healthy hives. A queen. Drones. Then he set them out in the fields near his yard, moving them later to their particular fields, hazel here, willows there, returning every few days to mark the hives and check their progress.

Nicole yawned and Paul saw that she was not very interested. Still, he talked on, of hives made from animal skins, coconut shells, cork, dung, fennel, and tuff. He told her about horizontal hives used in places like Mali and Menorca, hives hanging from trees, log hives standing on a hillside, or bee boles, which were holes carved into walls in which skeps, woven baskets, were placed upside down. He told her of Hippocrates, the like unto the like, crushed bee, the medicinal uses of honey. Etc. He had made it a habit of collecting books on bees and late one evening came across a tattered copy of Virgil. He read to a sleepy Nicole: *Bees themselves, unmated, gather their children in their mouths from leaves and fragrant herbs, and themselves supply their king and infant citizens and recreate their halls and waxen kingdoms.*

"Funny," Paul said, "how misinformed people were."

"And what will the future say about us?" Nicole asked. She had just put Sky to bed and was lying on the couch, one leg thrown up over the back. She was wearing shorts and her legs were dark in the dim light; they reminded Paul of Sky's legs, of babyfat and oil and the smoothness of the creek in the morning, just before the sun rose.

Nicole had a sliver in her foot, picked up from the rough wood of the front steps. She had mentioned it at supper, a Saturday night affair of fried potatoes, onions, corn, and bread, and now she kept drawing her foot towards her face to study the source.

"It hurts," she said. Paul got a sewing needle from his kit, trained the lamplight on Nicole and sat by her side. Her heel was soft and rimmed with the dust from the floors of his house. The sliver, long and thin, was near the back of her heel. He could hear Nicole breathing. He edged in the needle and her leg jumped.

"Don't," he said, "I'll slip." He worked at the flesh above the entry point and with tweezers extracted the culprit. "Here," he said, and handed it to her. He put her foot down and went back to the hard chair across the room. It seemed now that Nicole was too far away. He realized that he missed a regular sort of physical contact, though he had Sky and that had been a blessing. Still, Nicole roused in him a fierceness that was frightening and he wished she weren't over there, looking up at the ceiling, saying, "That's better now, really it is."

To stay this confusion he told her the process of forcefully immunizing a beekeeper. Sting and sting again.

"Really?" she said, interested now, sitting up and facing him, as if anything to do with the physical, of possible pain or pleasure, were truer than his earlier explanation of the beauty of a wafer of wax covering a hexagonal pool of honey.

"Yes," he said. "Though I don't practise the art myself. Immunization should come naturally, why magnify a painful process?"

"Tell me about it," she said. "How do you make a bee sting?"

"You pick it up and back it into your skin. Here," and he pushed lightly with his finger at his own forearm.

"And do I need that?" she asked, in anticipation.

"You could, but like I say, why?"

"So, I'll keep wearing a suit."

"Of course you will."

"You're weird."

"Yes, Sue tells me that as well. And Lise. My whole family."

Nicole looked up at him and he saw the colour of her eyes. That night he dreamed he was stinging Nicole. Rubbing ice across her forearm and backing the bee into her skin. Nicole smiled. Said she felt nothing.

When he woke, he rose and looked out beyond the screen to the yard. A hummingbird, barely bigger than his small finger, hung by a flower. Paul thought about who he was and what he knew. He believed that he was earth and he would return to it. He believed that the world favoured completion, that sexual desire was finite, and that possessions meant more to people than life itself. He believed that God could not be shocked, that pleasure was elusive, and that most people were selfish. He knew that goodness dwelt in him, in Sky, and in Nicole. He loved his daughter Sue but found her naive and simple. He had stopped loving Lise. He dreamed of Mrs. Wish, both sleeping and waking. He did nothing about those dreams. He remembered his father as a large presence, but he did not ache for him. When he said the world favoured completion, he meant that the answers had become more important than the questions. He believed that you either consented to wrongdoing or you refrained from it. In that sense, he believed in sin. He was no longer a possessive man. Since the death of his son, he cared little for ownership, though he liked to have enough to eat, and he enjoyed buying things for Sky. Sky, jabber, jabber, jabber, was Paul Unger's centre. The ball of the little boy's heel was the sun suspended. Sky. A blue bowl. Sinless.

That morning, driving into Furst to visit Stephen's grave, Paul went down Second Avenue and hit a dog that leaped out from behind a parked car. Paul was not going fast. He braked but still felt the bump and heard the yelp and then a white pellet skittered off the road and lay under the shade of a bush and whimpered, licking a rear leg. Paul stopped the half-ton, climbed out, and approached the dog. It was small, the shape of a poodle.

"Here, boy," Paul said. "You okay? Look at you. Who are you?" He bent closer and read the collar tag. Wish. "So, you're the doctor's, eh?" The dog growled, then it bit. Its teeth settled on the meaty part near the heel of his hand and broke the flesh and ripped a good portion loose so that when Paul pulled away and looked, part of his hand was flapping. He began to bleed and then the pain arrived. "You little SOB," he said. "Nasty dog."

"Look at that," he said, and looked. He went back to the truck and took a rag from behind the seat and made a compress of sorts. The dog yelped from the bush. "Yeah, yeah," Paul said. He drove to the house and parked in the driveway. The house was sleeping, the blinds drawn. Paul gathered up his hand and walked around to the back door. Rang. Waited. Rang again. When the door finally opened Mrs. Wish was there, her hair wet, wearing a housecoat, her feet bare. She looked at Paul, at his hand, and Paul said, "Emily?"

"Hi, Paul."

"I'm afraid I hit your dog, Emily. It's sitting under a shrub right now, back on Second Avenue. It bit me. Sorry."

"Andy bit you? That's not like him. Let's see." She took Paul's hand and unravelled the bloody rag. "Come," she said, and she sat him down in the gleaming kitchen. She left and Paul waited. The morning sun fell through the bay window onto his legs and chest.

Emily came back, holding a kit. She said, "Richard's at work. Otherwise I'd have him do this." She took out cotton swabs and alcohol and Band-Aids and tiny scissors. While she cleaned she said, "Poor Andy. Moaning under a shrub. This is the second time he's run under a car. Richard lets him out in the morning and he runs. He's a bit stupid." Emily's hands were cool and the smell of apple rose from her wet hair. She had changed from her housecoat into corduroys and a big black sweater. Her nail polish was green.

"You want to get him?"

"Right away. I'll finish this first."

"I'm surprised you remembered my name," Paul said.

"We danced, at your daughter's wedding. That was a wonderful wedding. If I were to get married again, I'd do it that way."

Paul took this to mean she would marry out-of-doors, though he wasn't sure.

She said, "How are Sue and Daniel?"

"Well, fine, I guess. They're young." Emily's hair was thick and wavy and now, as she bent over his hand, he saw that it was beginning to turn grey.

"Terribly young," she said. "But I liked that. So many people these days are cynical about love and marriage. Don't you think?"

Paul nodded, thought of his own marriage and said, "Perhaps with good reason."

"I was thinking more of the innocence at that age. The hope. When you get to be like us, we're jaded in some way. You know? As if we've run out of room."

Paul nodded again. Wondered how happy Mrs. Wish was. Her eyebrows matched her hair. Thick.

"There, see?" she said. "It's not that bad. Just a surface flap of skin. No need for stitches." She bandaged and taped. Told Paul to serve himself some coffee and then she drove over to pick up Andy. While she was gone Paul wandered into the living-room and looked around. It was a big house. Art on the walls. Expensive vases and artifacts everywhere. Books, too. The place was clean. Sterile. Paul was suddenly humbled, shamed by the perverse hope that he and Emily were equals. They weren't. He went back into the kitchen, poured coffee into a big white china cup, and sat down. When Emily returned, holding Andy, she said, "He's okay, I think, though I'll get him checked."

Paul stood and said, "I gotta go."

"Already?" Her free hand went up to her hair, and her sleeve slid to her elbow.

"Yes. Yes, I think so." He walked to the door, turned, and asked, "The dog doesn't have rabies, does he?"

"Andy? Well, I don't think so. He's had his shots."

"I had this picture," Paul said, "of me chained to a tree, foaming."

Emily smiled.

"Bye, then," Paul said.

"Yes, and thanks again," Emily said.

"What for? Hitting your dog?"

"No," she said. "For not killing him."

Paul walked back to his truck. He recalled the flash of forearm as her hand went up. Sweet notion. He found, behind the bench seat, a few jars of clover honey. "Unger Farms" written across the label. He took one, returned to the house, and left a jar by the back door for Emily to find later, perhaps when she stepped out to smell the air after a late afternoon rain, or opened the door to let the cat in. Paul wondered, as he left, if she even had a cat.

It was a nice thing, honey. A good gift. Most people liked it, even if only to spoon in their tea. His own mother liked hot water and a teaspoon of honey. Stephen had liked honey-baked chicken. Once, a customer sent Paul a recipe for fish and leeks and red-butter sauce which required two tablespoons of honey. Sky liked honey and peanut butter on Saltines. Paul's favourite was granola baked with honey. Lise was good at that. Nicole claimed honey was okay but she preferred jam and butter on her bread.

Paul drove to the Furst cemetery, parked, climbed out of his truck, and walked through the grass past the headstones to the grave of his son. He squatted, removed some dead flowers Lise must have left. Held them in his hand. Looked out across the cemetery to the highway which led to the city. A lone car passed, tires shushing. How silent. Paul imagined returning here, again and again, the years piling up. Coming to the grave like this was unremarkable, like driving out to the spot where Stephen's body had been found. Paul had done that a few months after his son's death. He had found a stubble field, the sky above, a bird singing. When he left that place he felt like he'd been shouting into an empty well and getting back his own voice.

Walking back to his truck now he passed the grave of his father and he paused and looked at the mound and the headstone. He took two quick breaths and then continued on to the edge of the ceme-tery where he found a stone that said Wish. Two brand-new roses in a vase. A living wreath. Emily, poor thing. Damp hair, a bare arm, money and culture, the doctor playing his violin in the evening as Emily sat and listened and held the rabid lapdog. Richard had played once at a community event. He offered classical when every-one wanted a fiddler. Still, the crowd had to admit he was good, those long surgeon fingers sliding across the strings. How did Emily stay there, in that house? That was why Paul ran, to scrape the smell away, all those reminders, the rip in the pool table, the basketball hoop, a bent spoon, chocolate sauce moulding away at the back of the fridge, a stray shoe appearing out of nowhere.

Restless now, Paul went to the store. He liked Sundays there, always did when he cared about the place, coming here to finish up extra work or simply to sit and admire the newness, the expansive floor, the TVs lined up like so many windows, the gleaming blankness of it all. Rich. He still liked the smell of the place. He entered and went to his old office and settled into what had become Lise's desk. Her things. A photo of Sue and Daniel at their wedding, Sue's face halved by the light, her mouth open in a glorious smile, Daniel slouched, his arm resting on Sue's shoulders. A photo of himself, taken not long ago, standing before his hives, holding a smoker, talking to Lise, who snapped the picture impulsively, catching him unawares so that he looked surprised. There was a folder on the desk and a paper, a memo to Jill Falk asking about payments and costs, with a happy face drawn at the bottom. Happy, happy. That was Lise. He opened a drawer. Sifted past a stapler, pens, erasers, Dictaphone, computer disks, and found a small picture of Harry Kehler, standing beside his cruiser. On the back he read, "For Lise, from Harry and his gun." Paul closed the drawer. Thought of Harry and his gun. He turned on the computer and played at a mindless game. He did not hear the front door open and close, and when he finally looked up, he saw Lise standing in the office doorway. She was wearing black tights and a red sweatshirt and a red bandanna. Her face was flushed.

"Hiya," she said.

"You've been running."

"I have." She approached, came around the desk, and stood behind Paul. "And you?"

"Playing," Paul said. He leaned back and looked up at the bottom of Lise's chin. Sweat dripped from her nose.

"I saw your truck," Lise said. "Are you okay?"

"Sure, why not?"

"You hate this place, so why would you come here?"

"I don't hate it. I was thinking earlier how smart I was to build out here, on the highway, what with the Pizza Hut a few doors down and the mall springing up over there. What foresight."

"All yours, then?"

"Well," Paul admitted, "you did help."

"Thank you." Lise took a chair and sat before Paul so that her knees almost touched his thigh. She wiped her face with a sleeve of her shirt. "Hot," she said.

"You a runner now? Getting in shape."

"I always was, you just never noticed."

"I hit Mrs. Wish's dog this morning. Andy. Then I went to see Stephen and came here."

"Sounds like a fun time."

"Yeah, that's me. Fun-loving Paul."

"Sue said Nicole and Sky are living with you."

"They are."

"Sue was upset, you know. Your daughter. I think she felt deceived in some way."

"I know she's my daughter," Paul said. "And I talked to her about it. Apologized for not telling her myself."

"I wonder sometimes what you're doing. What your motives are."

"What could my motives be?"

"Oh, stop it. Forget it, then. You get so put out, as if you were a child and innocent and everybody else was out to injure you."

"I don't think I ever intended to hurt Sue. But Sky is my grandson and Nicole is his mother and they needed a place and so I took them in."

"Sounds simple."

Paul looked at her. "'Bout as simple as Harry and his gun."

Lise pushed away from Paul and stood. "You have no right to go snooping. This is my desk."

"Is it?"

"Yes, it is. You walked away from here, from me, from your daughter. You just took off to your falling-down house and your bees and your hollow grief and now you can't come back here and make fun of us. I won't allow it."

Paul wondered if his grief was truly hollow. Watching Lise spit and rant like this had loosened a shard of memory in Paul, a winter's morning, Sunday as well, just before Stephen died, and he and Lise had come here to work, ending up on this office floor, making love. It had surprised him then and the thought still surprised him now. He said, "How can you call my grief hollow? What do you know about it?"

Lise laughed, quickly and bitterly. "Oh, yes, I forgot, your suffering is great. Greater than mine or Sue's or your mother's. You're so fucking worthy."

"Am I?" This saddened Paul. He shook his head. "Is that why he died?"

Lise closed her eyes. Came round now and loved him in his penitence, as if this were all she needed, to see him broken. She held his head to her chest and said, "Oh, my." Then she said again, "Oh, my."

They made coffee in the back room and come back and sat on soft leather chairs and Lise held Paul's hand. Her hands were like her body, small and sort of raw and he thought of how her knees would get all red and chapped in winter and she'd rub lotion on them before bed and after showers in the morning and she'd complain about Manitoba winters. Her ears were small, too, and spiralled so tightly that the skin over the cartilage shone like a finely polished stone, alabaster. He imagined Harry touching those ears and he said, "I think we should divorce. You know, move past this thing."

Lise didn't argue. She just nodded. Then said, "I love you terribly still, but it's the *terrible* part that makes me say yes."

"What about Harry?"

"Actually, Harry's decided to go back to Bunny. She was going crazy. Threatened to kill herself. Harry was all confused and he said this to me the other day, 'I'm a cop and cops are supposed to be honest and good and I can't go around deceiving Bunny because then how will the town see me?' Isn't that amazing? That he could say that?"

"Shouldn't he have thought of that a little sooner? Anyways, he's right," Paul said. "Bunny was all over me in the kitchen one night after baseball." Right away Paul regretted divulging this, as if this were Bunny's only shameful secret and he had given it away. "Don't tell Harry," he added. "Seeing as it doesn't matter anymore."

"I won't." She let go of him and wandered over to the long line of TVs. Ran a finger across the top of one. The black tights made her bum even smaller and there was no panty line and Paul imagined she was wearing nothing or perhaps one of those thongs, the thin lace tucking up inside the crack, all hidden and uncomfortable. It was odd, he thought, what women did for fashion. Stuffing their feet into little shoes, teetering around on heels, tight skirts, wired bras, all the wonderful accoutrements that made men crazy. It was suddenly obvious to Paul that someone like Lise dressed up for herself. It made her feel good, not him, or some stranger, or Harry. Just her. Such pleasure she took from her body and the way it moved. A pure self-consciousness: if she had had a mirror, she'd have used it, but instead she borrowed the dull reflection of the TV. Harry must have loved the hardness of her mind, her body, her heart.

"You love him, then?" Paul asked.

"I'm not sure." She turned and said, "But I like to have sex with him."

Paul was hurt by this sudden brutality. Confusion made him falter, his fingers shook. He swivelled in his chair and looked out across the floor to the large front window, and beyond, to the occasional car passing by on the highway. It was Sunday morning after all and most people in this town were either in church or in bed. He and Lise used to enjoy Sunday mornings together. He said, thinking both of this and back to that time just before Sue's wedding, "And you like to have sex with me."

"I shouldn't have done that, I was desperate."

"Thanks."

"No, I mean I shouldn't have planted that seed, the possibility, like it would be regular."

"I miss sex."

Lise didn't answer. She came back and stroked Paul's head. In the fluorescent light of the showroom he could see her face showing age, which was surprising, and he realized that all the exercise in the world couldn't stop the jowl from sagging. This made her more vulnerable, softer, and perhaps this was why Paul said, "We could have sex now, on one of those new hide-a-beds. It's worked before."

Lise shook her head. "I considered it. I don't think so."

This was pleasing to Paul, that she had thought about it, and the pleasure he felt made him, for a moment, generous and forgiving. He said, "That's all right," and he reached out for her, his palm caressing nylon and he saw that she was more distant than he had ever imagined. A creeping sadness.

They walked out to the front of the store together. At the door they hugged and Paul took Lise's jaw and gently turned it upwards and he kissed her. She let him, responded even, and then pulled away and said, "My, aren't we frisky for a man who just wanted a divorce."

"Did I?"

"Maybe you should get yourself someone."

"Too much trouble."

Paul watched her go. He went back inside the showroom, cleaned up the coffee cups, locked the doors, and climbed into his truck. He drove home slowly, taking a detour past his former house, imagining Lise at home now, in the shower, her black tights crumpled on the bathroom floor, and then he saw, in one brief glance, the taillight of Harry's cruiser which was hidden behind the house. Paul sucked in his breath. Stopped, backed up, and had a second look. Oh, Lise. How did the town see you now, Harry?

Dark thoughts. Lise bending over the bed, just the way she liked it, looking back over her shoulder, past Harry and into the mirror, finding there her own face, doubling back. She needed to verify her own existence. Still, it was all wrong. Mad. As if Paul Unger had died and Harry and Lise had every right to set loose on each other.

"Shit," Paul said. "Am I a fool?"

He drove home too quickly on the gravel road so that the truck swayed and he came close to losing control but didn't care. He found Nicole and Sky lounging in the porch, dirty dishes on the counter, clothes spread everywhere, and he barked at Sky and slammed around the kitchen until Nicole said, cigarette poised in the air, "I take it you had fun."

"Hit a dog," Paul said.

"Killed it?"

"Killed what?" Sky asked. "Conrad?" He looked around for the big black dog but couldn't find it. He began to cry. "Conrad is dead?" he said.

Paul went soft. He picked the boy up and kissed one cheek and then the other. The perfection there made him suddenly happy. "No, no," he said. "Grandpa hit a dog in town. With the truck. But the dog is fine. Andy. That was his name."

"His name was Andy," Sky said.

"Yes." Paul kissed him again and rubbed Sky's face with his own. Sky squealed and his voice rose with the ferocity of Paul's tickling. "Stop," he gasped and when Paul stopped he said, "Again." Paul rolled on the living-room floor with Sky, his face buried in the child's stomach. Coming up for air he saw Nicole's bare ankles and then he swung back to Sky and came back to the ankles and the toenails painted black and he recalled her clipping them the night before, the shards spinning off wildly and he had thought then that she would never retrieve them, it wasn't her nature, the path she left was slovenly. Sky sat on his neck. Said, "Say 'Uncle.'"

"No."

Sky stood and thumped down on his chest and Paul gasped, for real, and Sky laughed.

"Jesus, baby, don't hurt Grandpa," Nicole called from her perch. She had on her pouty face, her eyes were darker, a scheme in her head.

Paul tried to ignore her. He fried some potatoes and eggs. Cut a cucumber. Laid out some bread. A whole tomato. Sat down across from Nicole and began to eat. "What did you do this morning?"

"Slept. Ate. Sat around," she said. "You're the lucky one. Running off to town, seeing people, hitting dogs."

"You could go."

"Be more fun together. You could point out sights. You know."

"I know."

"You're embarrassed, aren't you? Don't want to be seen with us."

"That's not true."

"This place is so boring, sit around and watch bees make honey."

"Well, you chose to live here."

"I didn't have many options, did I? No money, no job. So I sit here and wait. I hate waiting. Don't even know what I'm waiting for."

"That's not so bad. Sometimes you learn from waiting."

Nicole stood now and walked over to the screen and looked out at the yard. "Here I am," she said. Perhaps it was the way the light came through the screen and fell on her face and her arms, but Paul noticed for the first time how long her forearms were, and her fingers, too. The light made her skin glow. Her toes were like her fingers, long and disproportionate and she curled them now and turned to Paul and announced, "Romel called."

"Oh."

"He wants me to come to Winnipeg. Talk."

"And."

"I said, 'Okay.'"

"How you gonna get there?"

"Your car?" Her nose lifted in anticipation. Her eyes narrowed. A long finger touched the screen. She waited.

"I don't think so. I don't want you seeing him."

"Who are *you*?"

"He'll hurt you."

"No, he won't. He promised."

"Oh, that's good."

Nicole slid several steps sideways across the floor and back again. Her bare toes whitened. Sky began to whine. He tripped over clothes and toys and found his mother's leg. Hung on, still wheedling. She ignored him. Said, "I want to see him. I can't stand another day in this shit hole, sun frying our brains, pretending I'm Winnie the Pooh, the mess. God, look at the mess."

Sky was still begging. Now he wanted up. He said, "Uppies." His little hands reached for Nicole's shirt and pulled. Nicole pushed him away. "I'll walk," she said. "You won't give me the car, I'll walk out to the highway and hitchhike and I'll be picked up by some pervert and he'll rape me and then you'll be sorry."

"It's either the pervert or Romel," Paul said, and again he was sorry, because this touched something in Nicole.

She swivelled and said, "You fucking prick."

Sky began to clamber up her leg again. "Don't," she said, and then she swung and her hand came down across Sky's cheek and jaw and his head snapped back, his hair flew out and fell back, and for several seconds there was silence save for Nicole's ragged rasps, and then Sky's eyes went wide, his mouth opened, and he began to howl.

"Oh, Jesus, I'm sorry, baby," Nicole said, and she bent to scoop up her child, but Paul got there first and he took Sky and held him, turned his back on Nicole and walked away, through the kitchen, into the living-room where he sat and cradled the boy. He heard Nicole sobbing and cursing, and then the screen door slammed, and the Camino started up and she was gone.

In the heat of the late afternoon, Paul blew up the wading pool and set it in the shade. Sky was tentative at first, testing a toe and then an ankle and looking back over his shoulder at Paul who sat on an Adirondack chair that his father had made years ago and which was now rotting. Sky's face, when he looked back, showed the imprint of Nicole's knuckles, but there was one place in particular where a purple welt had grown, the result of a wide silver ring Nicole wore on her index finger.

Sky had seemed to immediately forget what had happened and he began to ask where Nicole was and when she was coming home and why she had left. "She wasn't happy?" he asked at one point and Paul admitted, "No, she wasn't happy."

Sky began to hum a tune then and to walk around Paul's chair, touching Paul's back and his neck. It was not Nicole's fault, it was Paul's. He was willing to admit that. He had pushed her. Been resentful. Of Romel, strange thought.

When Sky had had enough of the pool he carried the boy into the porch and wrapped him in a large towel. Sky played then and Paul hovered and watched while Sky lay naked on his back and held a car up in the air. Vroomed slightly and then drew his knees to his chest and revealed his tight scrotum, an underwater animal. After a bit, Paul dressed Sky and decided on a wiener roast. In the fire pit he piled branches onto a mound of dry leaves and lit the whole bundle. It burned quickly and with such ferocity that Paul had to shoo Sky away. Together they wandered to the other side of the yard and whittled sticks. They fetched wieners from the fridge and again approached the fire which had become a few ashy branches glowing. "Perfect," Paul said, and he speared a hot dog for Sky and offered the stick. Sky promptly dragged the wiener through the mud. "That's okay," Paul said. "Bit of protein. Or we can give it to Conrad."

Sky thought this was a good idea and offered up six muddy wieners to the dog before he ate one himself. "Chew it," Paul exhorted, remembering a documentary he had seen years ago on wiener deaths in children. Got stuck in the throat and that was it. The perfect fit.

Sky chewed vigorously and walked around kicking at the earth. The sun had descended to just above the tops of the trees. The long days of July had become the foreshortened days of August and now, at night, there was a chill, autumn nipping at their heels, a warning to hunt and gather before the icy winds of winter. In the last while, wasps had descended on the farm and they were pesky and Paul knew his bees spent a lot of time chasing wasps from the vicinity of the hive, either sending them off or killing them. A few wasps circled Sky now and he poked at them with his wiener.

"Come," Paul said, and he gathered Sky and hauled him into the bathroom where he ran water into the tub he had installed the previous week. Blue, with claws for feet, so that Sky at first had thought he was bathing in the bowels of a large animal. Sky puddled about in the water while Paul sat on a stool and watched. Then he washed the boy's hair, tipped him back and scrubbed lightly, rinsed, and wiped gently at his face, around the bruise which was uglier now, the perfect outline of Nicole's long fingers, the ape in her tattooed on her son's face. He wondered where she was. On her back somewhere, he supposed, Romel flailing away at her, and allowing himself to imagine this he saw that she could no longer live here in this house, as if he were some benefactor to whom she could run whenever she was sick or lonely or grieved or needed money and food. He was not that, could never be. She would return, and when she did, he would give her a week to seek out some other place. And Sky? This was where he faltered, for he could not imagine life without Sky. There were moments when he believed that Nicole would gladly give up the child. Say, *Here, Paul, take him.* And he would take him, like a precious parcel that required years to unwrap, always fearing the return of Nicole who could sink back into their lives and ask for her son back.

Because the house had gathered up the heat of the day, he allowed Sky to sleep on the couch in the living-room where the breeze blew through from the porch and on out the big screens of the front window. Paul read him a book, offered him a glass of milk, and lay down beside him in the waning light. He sang several songs, his voice syrupy and the tunes with their half-remembered words forever slippery. Sky's leg jumped midway through the third song, a melody about a mockingbird and what mama's gonna buy. Recognizing that Sky was sleeping, Paul intended to get up and do some work around the house, but then he remembered a song his own mother sang to him as a child, a rhyme about crows, *One is for bad news, Two is for mirth,* and the rest he could not remember except that the song ended happily, with a wedding or a reunion of two lovers. He thought now that this was a strange song for so young a child.

He ran a finger along Sky's ear, down his neck to his naked shoulder. He would have Nicole's bone structure, the primate length which spoke both of awkwardness and deftness. That stretch of bone and sinew, a prowess, swinging from tree to tree, pink bare bum shining raw and rude, eating the lice from a brother's head, growing up to do battle, gaining a harem by conquering. Spend all your time fighting and no energy left for love. Not Nicole's problem. There were times when Paul caught her looking at him and he found at the edge of her mouth a sneer, or perhaps a subtle pitying smile, as if she were approaching him through the wrong end of a telescope and finding him diminished, unfortunate, a failure. There was that problem, of course. A child of twenty viewing any adult saw only the foibles, the lack of success, and the simple conclusion was, *I will be better; I will not go there.*

But she would go there. Everyone went there.

Against his will Paul slept then and when he woke, much later, he was disoriented. He touched Sky's hand, his hip, and began to focus. He sat up. It was dark. He sensed a third presence and looking across the room discovered Nicole sitting in the rocking chair, the outline of her a vague cut-out against the beige wall. He rubbed his eyes. Looked again. Sighed, and said, "I fell asleep."

"You looked so cozy, the two of you, I couldn't disturb you."

"You've been home long?"

"Half an hour."

Paul nodded. He had a crick in his neck, his mouth had a sour taste. "I wasn't going to sleep. I was planning to work." He squinted and tried to make out her face, her eyes, what she was thinking. "You want some coffee?"

"No."

"Okay."

"I was driving around. Never went to see Romel."

"You didn't?" This pleased Paul greatly. He believed suddenly that goodness and mercy would follow him the rest of his life. "You didn't?" he said again.

"No." Nicole stood and came over to look at Sky. "Does he hate me?"

"Of course not."

"He must. A mother who beats him." She began to cry and Paul reached up and patted her arm and looked over into the kitchen where the light from the stove gave off a yellow warmth. Was this the way it worked then? So quickly her scorn had turned to remorse.

"It was my fault," Paul said.

"*I* hit him."

"It was an exception."

"I've done it before." Nicole's chin pushed out in defiance as if daring him to hit *her*. She said, "It comes out of nowhere, his little face is there, in the way, and bang, I hit him. There, now you know. I'm awful."

Paul looked down at Sky. Nicole's hand rested on his shoulder. He stood, went into the kitchen, poured two glasses of rye, and came back, handing Nicole one glass. She took it and said, "The Camino ran out of gas. I had to walk to a farm and there was a woman who sold me a couple of gallons in a jerrycan. She was out in the yard with her husband. They were loading a horse into a trailer. The horse was fighting and the farmer was beating it. The woman said not to worry, the horse was going to market tomorrow morning. Isn't that awful? Killing horses? It was getting dark and I was frightened and I thought, I hate it out here. The city is better. At least there are lights and you can see the danger coming."

"There is no danger out here. That's the thing."

"The lady asked me about my soul. Was I going to hell or heaven. I laughed and said, 'Hell.'"

"She must have been pleased to hear that."

"She told me not to mock God."

"Well, that's good advice." The rye stippled Paul's throat, woke him up. Nicole had finished hers and was cuddling the empty glass.

"I'd like to be good, better," she said.

"You are good." As he said this, Paul wondered at his own motives. Why he would lie. He had never lied in this way for Stephen.

"But you don't know me."

"No, that's true. I don't." And he didn't. He knew only what he saw, and what he saw was fleeting, a girl who needed a centre. "You're young," he said. In the distance, through the front screens, lightning shifted across the sky.

"Oh," Nicole said. She hugged herself. Said, "It's going to rain. I could smell it while driving."

"Good," Paul said.

"Whenever it rains I dream of spiders."

"Spiders aren't bad."

"In my dreams they're big and ugly."

"So, that's where Sky gets it from. Running around killing them."

As if in response, Sky shuddered and turned. Nicole patted him. She said, "I wonder what children think. And see. Their world is knees and hairy calves and the bottoms of tables and always looking up and being pushed away. They must think they'll live forever."

"Children do. Think that." Paul found Nicole's soliloquy endearing, as if she had finally revealed, through the porch of her mouth, a glimpse into the sinuous working of her brain.

She added, "Stephen thought he would live forever."

A sudden ache, as great as any Paul had felt in the last while living here with Nicole and Sky. It was as if their presence had filled up his heart and now, with these few words, he had again been emptied, and that emptiness tore at him.

"I'm sorry," he said.

"Oh, don't be, Mr. Unger," Nicole said, and she placed a hand on his neck and leaned forward and with careful attention touched his cheek with one of those long fingers. An eye.

Paul was sitting at a right angle to Nicole and so her head was lying oddly on its side, in mid-air, as if she were a child studying something strange in the distance. She said, "There, that's better," and Paul could smell the rye huddling at the back of her tongue and he remembered when he was young and the stepping stones leading to the centre of the town pond where there stood a wishing well, and him leaping across those rocks to lean over and drop a penny into the well, waiting for the faraway clink of copper.

The day, now finished, he saw as a series of steps: Emily Wish's arm flashing and falling, Harry Kehler's taillight, Lise looking back over her shoulder, Sky dropping to lie on Nicole's belly, Nicole's simian hand falling across Sky's face, and the boy's hair flying out and falling back. Everything fell, or hesitated at the edge of the well and contemplated falling.

"There, there," Nicole said again and she patted his shoulder and he held her. She clung to him with a fierceness that surprised him, as if he had saved her from some danger, her chin pressing into the hollow where his neck and shoulder met. She smelled of cigarette smoke and the inside of the Camino. He was both relieved and slightly shamed. Regret and shame. He had lived with both long enough to recognize that what was tender and imprecise at that moment, the loose husk of Nicole there, the longing to enter some fleeting temporal space with her, all this would shift and later, perhaps the next day, or a month from then, seem flawed. What was perfect became imperfect. He loosened her grip and sat back, an arm's distance from her.

Nicole rose, properly confused and suddenly distant, and sifted through her bag for cigarettes. She found one, lit up, and went out into the porch. Paul could see her through the doorway, standing and looking out at the approaching storm. He joined her and they watched the storm arrive, first the wind and then a spitting, and finally a deluge, a wall of water that threatened to break through the screens of the porch. The lightning was brilliant and unforgiving and lit up the yard so that the Camino and half-ton and the honey shed and trees and swings appeared as if in daylight, and then they disappeared, only to reappear again.

The rain on the roof was loud, and for this Paul was grateful. He turned once to watch Nicole and, when the lightning arrived, her eyes were wide and untamed, and she was talking to herself, her mouth moving; in this primitive state she seemed to forget that Paul was there. Before the storm was spent Paul moved away and went to bed, leaving Nicole. He fell asleep and dreamed, and in his dream he was chasing butterflies down through the garden and out amongst the hives beyond the honeysuckle hedge.

Ellen and Jim Leclair, Paul's neighbours to the east, came over with their children one night for a barbecue. Their eldest daughter was sixteen and she took a liking to Sky; pushed him on the swing and followed him around the yard and talked to him. She was a tall big-boned girl with a broad face. She looked like her father who was sitting in a lawn chair by the fire pit. Paul had invited his mother as well and she was sitting next to Ellen, whose nose was a marvellous creation, long and slightly hooked.

Nicole, who had been inside, stepped through the screen door. She stood in the afternoon light and looked out over the yard. Sky with the sixteen-year-old on the lawn. The other five children kicking a ball. The adults by the fire pit. She hesitated, as if uncertain of her place, and then walked towards the adults. Paul stood and folded open a lawn chair, set it beside Ellen, and said, "This is Nicole, Sky's mum. Sky's almost three."

Nicole looked at Beth, Jim, then Ellen, and sat down. She was wearing black pants and a halter top that showed off, from the front, her belly button, and from the rear, the nubs of her lower spinal cord. She pushed at her bleached hair. Paul imagined the dire images spinning through his mother's brain. He said, "Nicole's helping me with the bees this summer. Which is good. Every year it gets busier."

Jim nodded and said, "I'm Jim."

"Hi, Jim."

"Ellen," Ellen said, and she pushed out her hand for Nicole to shake.

Released, Nicole turned to Beth and said, "You're Stephen's grandma. I met you a long time ago."

"Yes, I remember now. At Paul and Lise's. Yes, yes." She touched her mouth with a finger as if recalling something severe or unpleasant.

"Have you met Sky?" Nicole asked Beth. "He's your great-grandson."

"Sky's wonderful. It's the age of legs like sticks. I remember Paul, two twigs."

"Sammy's the same and he's three," Ellen joined in.

They spoke then of the tantrums of children and the daily fatigue and Ellen shared a beer with Jim, her mouth closing around the spout, her beak touching gently against the glass.

Later, Beth and Nicole walked into the house where Beth mixed the salad and when they returned they were laughing and Beth was holding Nicole's arm. Paul watched from a distance and thought how full of surprises people were. He cornered his mother near the barbecue and said, "You like her."

"Why shouldn't I? Though she's still so young. Naive in a way."

"What do you mean?"

But his mother wouldn't answer. She waltzed away and found Sky. Held him on her lap, fed him peppermints to keep him there. Touched the bruise on his cheek and whispered in his ear. He whispered back. She shook her head. Looked upwards and then over at Nicole, who was smoking and drawing with her foot across the grass. Sky finally squirmed away and ran over to the back lot where the older children were playing baseball. The sixteen-year-old, a thick shadow, dutifully followed him. Jim appeared to be on the verge of sleep over in his lawn chair. Ellen followed the children out to the field. She turned and called now for the other adults. Paul went, leaving Nicole and Beth chatting and Jim sleeping. When they returned, sweaty, thirsty, and hungry, Beth was leaning into Nicole and still talking, hands going up and down. Over supper, Nicole seemed stunned, had little appetite. She was short with Sky and then leaned over to kiss his head. "There," she said, as if that were proof enough.

The Leclair family went at dusk, a crying out of goodbyes and thank you's and the twins flanking the eldest daughter, who looked down to whisper at her baby brothers. Their departure left a hole in the evening and silence fell hard onto the smaller group. Sky's voice grated now, a whine that needed to be put to sleep. "Come," Nicole said, and took him into the house. Paul walked his mother to her car. She said, before getting in, "She hit the boy. The bruise on his cheek. I asked her and she said yes. Didn't even try to hide it."

"That's good, isn't it? Facing up to her sins?"

The mockery was too obvious. Beth pounced back, "Do you take no responsibility here? Just let her flail away at her child. The girl needs help."

Paul didn't answer.

Beth continued, "She loves him, I can tell, still, what about Sky?"

"Don't go phoning anyone," Paul said.

"You protecting her?"

Paul shook his head. Said, "It's not simple."

"I suppose it can't be easy, a child raising a child." She looked at Paul, considered, and said, "It's odd, you taking her in."

"I took *him* in," Paul said. "Sky. She came along."

"Oh."

"Is that how you see me?" Paul asked. "As hard and unbending?"

"No," his mother said, and she reached into her deep purse, looking for her keys, sighed heavily and said, "The child's beautiful."

No one is certain why bees swarm. Crowded conditions within a hive can induce a swarm, or perhaps a queen, as she ages, feels the need to move on. Sometimes a new queen, rather than killing another queen still in the cell, will fly out with a swarm. The bees, before swarming, gorge on honey; they will be without food for several days. Once out of the hive they land on any convenient spot, the eaves of a house, a stump, or a tree branch, while scout bees search for a new home. One time Paul found a swarm on the inside of a truck's wheel well. Another time the bees set up house on the screen door.

On Monday morning Paul got a call from the neighbour to the west, Sandra Leger, that a swarm had landed on a branch of an oak in their backyard. She was worried and Paul tried to calm her. He said, "The bees shouldn't be cross and they won't sting. Just leave them and I'll come over."

He took Sky and Nicole in the half-ton and they drove down past the mammoth pig barns and over to the Leger quarter section. Sandra was standing in the yard, her arms wrapped around her shoulders. She walked over to Paul and pointed over at the oak and said, "Up there. My son heard this sound, like a two-stroke motor-cycle, then it stopped in our yard. I've never seen anything like it. I've been keeping the children inside."

"You don't have to worry," Paul said. "I could pick up a handful of the swarm and not get stung. They have nothing to defend."

Mrs. Leger called her children and they arrived, three of them, and stood behind Paul, next to Nicole who was hipping Sky, who in turn was asking questions about the bees.

"A swarm?" he asked.

"Yes, that's what Grandpa said."

"And they're harmless?"

"Yes."

"What's 'harmless'?"

"Not dangerous."

"What's Grandpa doing?"

"Catching the swarm."

"Why though?"

"Just is."

Paul offloaded a hive body with ten frames of worker comb whose smell would attract the bees. He set the hive down and laid out a white sheet beneath the branch. He looked up. Normally the swarm would have been close to the ground and he'd shake the bees straight into the hive but this branch was too high. Paul found a ladder and a cardboard box and, taking a blanket along, climbed up to the swarm. He held the box with one hand and, with the other, shook the branch and the bees fell into the box. He covered the box with the blanket, descended the ladder, and shook the bees into the hive. There were bees on the grass, some still up in the tree, and many had crawled out of the hive entrance. The children cheered. Nicole did a little dance and Sky squealed. After twenty minutes things had settled down and Paul looked for the queen. He found it beside the hive, standing out larger and prettier than the workers. He called for Nicole to come see but she waved him away. Paul herded the queen into the hive and the rest of the bees eventually followed. He left the hive where it was, explaining to Mrs. Leger that he would return after dark, when the foragers and scouts had come back.

Driving home, Sky sat in the middle. He liked to hold Paul's and Nicole's hands and sing, imitating his mother. Not any particular tune but his own made-up songs that clattered up the octaves and descended. Sometimes he liked to sit on Nicole's lap and sing into the wind, his chin on the door, Nicole's bare arm wrapped around his tummy. Her shoulder was round and brown, a thin bicep, the sinew there. She leaned towards Paul now and said past the wind, "Do they like being trapped?"

"The bees, you mean?"

"Yes."

"They're not really trapped. They can come and go. I'm merely providing a home."

"But maybe they'd rather be in a tree, or an old tire."

"They don't really care," Paul said. At this, Nicole shook her head and answered, "You know, of course."

Since her return the other night Nicole had been elusive, as if she were planning something or preparing for flight. She paced the porch, walked outside to push Sky on the swing, filled the wading pool, and then sat in the shade, beer in one hand, and she stared off at the endless sky, her foot going up and down. Waiting. The beer and sun made her happy though and, like now, she seemed willing to wait, as if what she were sucking in was suddenly to her favour. She smelled her forearm and shouted, "I love the way my skin smells." She held up her arm for him to smell. He breathed in and nodded.

The week that followed was good. The sun rose and shone and set, the August winds blew, rain came and went, the fields of canola and rye and barley and flax ripened, and the bees made honey. Nature was heedless. Nature did not covet or seek revenge or hunt down the guilty or reward the pure. Nature simply was. Paul understood that. He remembered the day he learned of Stephen's death and how he had felt that the sun should stand still, or the sky should bleed, or at least a tree should fall in memoriam. But, nothing. Only the sun and the moon and the sun over and over until one night Paul stood on the back stoop and lifted his voice to the sky and cursed the silence, the constancy, the conspiracy of another sunrise.

But now, this month, August, the certainty of nature was a blessing and Paul and Nicole and Sky lived as if they had fallen back into the cycle and flow of the earth. Time was suspended, other people passed by unheeded, the beans overflowed the small garden plot in the rear of the house, the bees were feverish and absorbed. To Paul, the snapdragons, the ripped screen on the porch, the colour of the morning sky, these had all taken on a different smell and shape and colour. He sensed a release, a sinking away from self, as if Nicole, by striking Sky, and then leaving and returning, had altered his own view of the world.

He took to cooking large breakfasts for Nicole and Sky. Bacon, eggs, grapefruit, toast, sometimes biscuits and syrup, and for Sky he made waffles, retrieving the old waffle iron from the basement where it lay next to a tire pump and a deflated basketball. He picked raspberries one morning and threw them into a pancake batter. Sky didn't like those big red dots, so Paul cut them out and ate them. What Nicole liked best was strong coffee and a cigarette and though she accepted Paul's offerings she was quick to sit herself next to the screen and light up. When Paul handed her the mug and said, "Hot," she looked up at him and said, "Thank you."

One morning, a Thursday, she was wearing long baggy shorts and a loose sleeveless top and her face was sleepy. She yawned and her arms went up, revealing the beginning of hair under her arms where she had not shaved for several days. Her mouth gaped and the two silver fillings glinted, and then the darkness disappeared; the indifference at the edge of her smile and Paul thought, Do I bore her?

Nobody had come to visit. Even Herb, whom Paul was to meet Tuesday morning, had not phoned. The outside world didn't exist. Sometimes, in the stillness of the late afternoon, the tock of the neighbour's axe could be heard or a shout of a child, but other than those muffled reminders of lives being lived elsewhere, Nicole, Paul, and Sky were alone. And it was this aloneness that perhaps drove Nicole to announce that they should go to St. Malo, to the beach.

Paul demurred, thinking of the work he had to do, but Nicole insisted and so they went, the three of them, in the Camino, down the 59 through St. Pierre and beyond, to the man-made lake where they met, as if this were preordained, Sue and Daniel, who had laid themselves out on the sand, Daniel in tight trunks, Sue wearing that same bright green bikini. She was happy to see them. She got up and hugged Paul, her Vaselined lips sliding over his cheek, and he noted that her nose was cold, her hair damp. She nodded at Nicole and touched Sky's head.

"This is great," she said, "isn't it? It was Daniel's day off and I" — here she dipped towards Daniel— "convinced him to lie about in the sun and be lazy."

Daniel eyed Nicole. He said, "Nicole," and nodded at her. Her name in his mouth was more French and Paul heard it as "Knee-call," with the second syllable rounder and fuller and rising at the end. Hearing her name like that Paul suddenly saw another dimension: to his life, to Nicole's, to Daniel's.

"Daniel," she responded, and this too came out with a lilt.

They lolled about then and Sky dug a tunnel with Daniel. Daniel buried him up to his neck and Sky giggled until he panicked and began to cry. Daniel dug him free and ran him down to the water and washed him off. Together they walked the rim of the small lake, hand in hand. Nicole said to Sue, "Sky isn't usually this familiar."

"Oh, Daniel's great with kids," Sue said. "They like him." She was on her belly, hand holding her chin. Shoulder blades like wings.

Nicole had changed into a plaid one-piece and beside Sue she looked old-fashioned. She reached out now and touched Sue's hair and said, "I like that. Bleached, like mine."

Sue nodded and said, "Irma did it. My friend. I did hers, too, but it came out streaky and too yellow."

Nicole said, "Once, just after Sky was born, I shaved my head. I remember waking up one night, feeling my head, and wondering who I was." She laughed. Ploughed through her messy purse for cigarettes. "Here." She offered Sue one, who accepted. This surprised Paul.

"When did *you* start?" he asked.

Sue looked out at the lake and said, "Daniel likes it when I smoke. He says it makes me different. That's why I got my hair coloured." Here she put the cigarette in her mouth and shaped her empty hands as if holding a ball. "He claims that when he holds my head, it's exciting. New. So I do it." She shrugged, tugged at her bikini top, and rolled over onto her back. She made a visor with her hand and looked up at Paul. Nicole.

Nicole was wearing a baseball hat. It shaded her nose and eyes. She said, "Guys are weird."

Paul was suddenly uncomfortable, aware of all that flesh, the bottoms of Sue's feet staring at him, Nicole's round shoulder there, her stretching now to lather on lotion, his own naked legs, their whiteness, and the confessions just now of these girls, as if he had been plunked down to listen to the intimate disclosures of his own daughter.

They talked some more and then Sue buried her spent cigarette, stood, brushed off her belly, and said, "Come, Daddy." She took his hand and they walked down to the water and swam out. Beyond the buoys, as Paul remembered now, the floor of the lake fell away quickly and the water was cold and dark. He floated on his back and watched the sky. Sue paddled beside him. She said breathlessly, "*She's* weird."

"Is she? I think she was trying to identify with you."

"Oh, I don't think so, Daddy. Did you see the way she was eyeing Daniel? And that bathing suit. Was it her mother's?"

All that initial joy on the beach had disappeared. Paul righted himself so two bodiless heads bobbed around in the puddle. Sue's eyes were black buttons. He said, "Sue, sweet darling. You're jealous. Why?"

Sue's shoulders appeared and disappeared as she shrugged.

"Is it Daniel? Or me?"

"A bit of both."

"You needn't worry, I love you dearly," Paul said, and saying this he thought that she had every right to worry, to infer betrayal and deception. The heart marched far ahead of the mind. Sue had turned away. The smallness of her head, the complexity, the fineness there.

"Has Daniel hurt you?" he asked.

"Oh, no, Daddy, not like that. I just don't think he's happy sometimes."

"What, he's got everything."

"That's it. It's too easy."

Paul took her hand and pulled her back towards shore. They rose out of the water to meet Sky and Daniel returning. In the distance, on the beach, Nicole appeared to sleep. Paul touched Sky's nose. "Would you like to see the dam? The one Grandpa slid down as a boy?" Daniel's toes appeared, long, hairy. Paul looked up at him. His son-in-law was elongated, big head blocking the sun. Paul looked back to Sky. "Come." And he took the child's hand and called out to Sue and the three of them walked the edge of the lake to the dam with its algae and slime, only to discover that access was denied; a chain had been drawn across the top of the dam.

The dam appeared smaller, just as earlier the lake seemed smaller and the trees surrounding it bigger. Memory was tricky. Paul recalled years ago standing in this exact spot with Lise, his new wife, and she was holding Stephen, and they had looked out over the lake and Lise claimed joy and Paul echoed that, and the baby purled. Now, holding Sky's hand, he pulled Sue close and kissed her sunny hair. They retraced their steps to find Nicole and Daniel swimming far out beyond the buoys, Nicole emitting little screams and Daniel diving and staying hidden underwater, surfacing finally to frighten Nicole. Sue watched this for a while and then walked to the water's edge and waved at Daniel. He waved back. Dove. Came up and waved again. Sue beckoned him in. He came, dragging Nicole by the elbow, both of them speaking French. She halted, in knee-deep water, and splashed her face. Paul watched Daniel pass by Sue, who turned to say something. Daniel ignored her and kept coming, grinning at Paul, who looked away. Daniel gave off an odour of possession and conquest; he was a looter at heart.

Sue came back to her towel. Lay down, lifted a bottle of lotion Paul's way, and said, "Could you, Daddy?"

He complied, rubbing the lotion around and above and on her winged shoulder blades. He passed his hand up to her neck, and then back down to the small of her back, the thinness of her waist always a bit of a shock. Paul, lost in the reverie of essence and need, heard finally Sky's small voice claiming he had to pee, and so he fell away from Sue, who feigned sleep, and gathered up Sky and walked him up to the lip of the trees where Sky aimed onto a bed of dried pine boughs. When they returned, Nicole, Sue, and Daniel were laughing at some shared joke.

Driving home later, the sun on the verge of setting, the day salvaged by a hearty barbecue served by Daniel, who had become suddenly the good husband and doted over Sue, kissing her shoulders and calling her "love," Paul asked Nicole if it was possible that she may have hurt Sue by flirting with Daniel. "I don't think so," Nicole said. "I wasn't flirting. It didn't mean anything. He could have been anybody. A dog. Another girl. You." And with this Nicole smiled and looked down at a sleeping Sky, tracing his forehead with her long finger, singing a song to herself, too softly for Paul to hear the words or catch the tune.

The two weeks which followed were full of long days. The nectar flow was almost over, the honey was ready, and the bees were slowing down. To get at the honey the bees needed to be drawn away from the frames and out of the supers. Paul used a chemical called Bee Go. Mrs. Ernst, over in Kleefeld, used a bee escape, an attachment to each of the hives that allowed the bee to exit but not get back in. This method was clumsy and slow, but then Mrs. Ernst claimed she would never infect honey with chemicals. Paul, who was modern and impatient, fumed the bees out of the supers. First the top super, load it on the truck, then the next, load, next, load. Paul could do ten stacks of supers in an hour.

Paul brought the load back to the farm where he taught Nicole how to pry loose the frames and draw them out. Then they removed the top layer of wax on the honeycombs with a hot knife in a decapping machine. From there the frames were placed in the honey extractor which was like a large metal salad spinner. The force of the spinner threw the honey against the metal sides and the honey slid through a funnel into forty-five gallon drums. From the drum, the honey was filtered through Paul's notion of a sieve, a nylon stocking, in order to get rid of the final particles of wax, and then it was poured into smaller containers.

Nicole's job, because it was lighter work, was to decap the frames and fill the smaller containers with honey. She managed to work sometimes for a three-hour stretch and have Sky putter at her side. She resented Paul correcting her and, when he did, she tended to pout or stop working altogether, pretending that Sky needed her help. And so Paul had learned to ignore her sloppiness, preferring to follow behind and correct her mistakes. She was not used to working and one time Paul entered the honey house to find her and Sky sitting on the floor, shaping honeycomb in their fingers, Nicole smoking, the extractor spinning wildly, the decapper still sawing away at empty air. Paul shut down all the machines and said, "Are you done, then?"

Nicole looked up. "Yup. I'm done."

A stack of frames awaited her. Paul looked at them and back at her. Sky said, "Grandpa." Paul ignored him. He said, "I've just brought another truckload. It's outside."

"Goodie," Nicole said. "More honey." Her finger looped the air.

Paul waved her away and turned towards the work she had abandoned. He heard her stand. A prissy yawn.

He said, without turning, "Maybe you could find the energy to make a meal."

"Oh, yes, that's good. Come, Sky, let's make food for our sugar daddy."

He came to the house late that night, past dusk, and found the table set for him, a napkin laid out, glass of water sweating, the food on the stove, cold now in pans, and Sky and Nicole sleeping, fully clothed in their bed, as if they had eaten and immediately dropped onto the mattress. Exhaustion came early to them both. Work was for others; Nicole had neither the constitution nor the desire for work. Fine, Paul thought as he spooned at his watery chili and chewed wearily. Fine. He had experienced, earlier in the honey house, the exhilaration of nearing completion. Another good week, he thought, and then the honey would all be taken, and then he could finish bottling, begin preparing for fall, and make his sales. And yet, with the fall came the certainty of Nicole's departure. She had mentioned, a whispered aside which meant much more than any direct comment, that money was to be had for a woman like her, single, child and all, to go back to school.

"Where?" Paul asked.

"In Winnipeg."

"That would be good," Paul said, and he believed this, though he could no longer imagine his house emptied of Sky's voice, the rub of his bare feet, Nicole's empty coffee cups scattered about, the smell of her burning cigarette. "That would be good," he said again.

Now, sitting over his cold coffee and raw carrots and empty chili bowl, the prospect of another sleepless night—he had not been sleeping well—frightened him. He worried. About the winter, Sky, Nicole, Stephen. He stood. Rinsed his dishes and wrote a note thanking Nicole for the wonderful supper, pinning it to the fridge.

Mrs. Wish came by on a Sunday afternoon with her camera and her notepad and the empty honey jar. She found Paul at home. Sky was sleeping, Nicole had gone to Winnipeg to shop. As she left she had said, *"Je m'en vais,"* and then she blew up her cheeks at him, did a pirouette, and left. She was prone to doing that more and more lately, speaking French to a man who understood none. Still Paul found it endearing and always responded with a "Wee, wee."

Mrs. Wish arrived in her dark blue BMW. She was wearing a black dress that was simple but Paul figured must have been expensive. The hem came just above her knee. When Mrs. Wish sat and crossed her legs, her calves shone. Paul served her coffee and asked, "Did you like the honey?"

"I did. Richard prefers honey that is hard and crystallized. I like it smooth."

"So Richard didn't eat any."

She laughed. Her throat moved and her laugh came from somewhere deeper.

He said, "Tell Richard that he prefers honey that is not heated. Honey straight from the comb. Most people like smooth honey so beekeepers heat it enough to break down the crystals before it is sold."

"I'll tell him. He's fascinated by trivia."

"It's not trivia."

"Of course not, I'm sorry." She did not seem at all repentant.

She looked around the house. Paul was embarrassed. "I've got Nicole and Sky living here as well," he said. His arm flew out and back, as if this would make the mess disappear. They were sitting in the kitchen and through the window they could see the honeysuckle hedge and the garden that Paul had been working at. Paul said, "My tomatoes are big this year. My carrots are small."

"Richard is our gardener. He likes cherry tomatoes and beans. We've been overrun by beans."

Paul acknowledged that it had indeed been a good year for beans. Emily turned and said, "I've convinced my editor that a bee and honey story would be necessary and interesting." She was wearing shoes that had white piping and low heels.

"Interesting, perhaps, but certainly not necessary."

Sky woke and niggled through the kitchen and onto Paul's lap. "Hi, little guy," he said, and kissed the boy's head. Smell of straw. "Say hi to Emily." Sky pushed his head lower into Paul's lap. Emily watched. Then she said, "Sarah would have been one already." She leaned forward and touched Sky's bare foot.

Paul looked at the top of her head. He remembered her thickness when they danced and how it seemed a consequence of grief. He said now, "It never goes away."

"No, it doesn't." She was still rubbing Sky's foot. When she finally pulled away she brought her hand to her nose. She breathed. "What can you do?" she said.

Paul didn't respond. Emily looked up and said, "Richard doesn't want another child. He says it would just bring more sadness. And he's right. And he's wrong. Richard fixes sadness, you see. He's a doctor."

"Yes, he is," Paul said. Sky slid to the floor and lay on his belly beside Conrad.

"He believes suffering is wrong." Emily dug around in her purse and pulled out a caramel. "Here, Sky," she said. He sat up, offered a palm. Emily scooped him up and sat him on her knee. Helped him with the wrapper, his pudgy fingers scampering through the air. As he ate, Emily stroked his head and touched his ears.

"Where's Nicole?" she asked.

"Shopping. In Winnipeg."

"Is it odd, to have her living here?"

"Odd?"

"I mean, she was Stephen's girlfriend and then she was gone and then she came back with your three-year-old grandson. That strikes me as impetuous."

Paul liked this inquisitive quality which bordered on impertinence. The roving reporter. Why, he wondered, was she not asking about bees and honey and hives. He said, "Nicole is twenty. You don't get much from a twenty-year-old. A bit of work, some conversation. She's even cooked a few meals. She was lonely, I was lonely. Sky is lovely."

"Yes." Emily smelled the child. Said, "Everybody's lonely. I talked to Lise the other day. She seemed lost."

"She admitted that?"

"No, I thought she *seemed* lonely. Do you like my shoes?" Impetuous herself now, she lifted a nyloned leg for Paul. Waggled her foot. "Richard bought them. In New York. He was at a conference. Nine hundred dollars."

"Well."

"Of course Richard made a point of letting me know that. He likes his things." She bent forward and slid off a shoe. She had a tiny hole in her stocking, near the heel. She gave the shoe to Sky who promptly dribbled caramel over the fine leather.

"That's okay," Emily said, and watched as Sky licked the shoe. "Yum," she said, and continued, "I don't love Richard anymore. I think maybe I did once, but now I don't."

Paul nodded and thought he should say something. He watched Emily's foot, the tiny hole, the shape of her toenails through the stocking. She kissed Sky's head again and then carried him over to the sink to wash him. She held him with one arm and ran the water. From Paul's vantage point she appeared off balance, standing there half-shod, Sky pressed between the sink and her stomach.

He said, "I remember with Lise, one day I woke up and thought, I can't continue this. *This* was everything. Living in that house, running the business, golfing, curling, listening for Stephen to come home. Lise put up no fight. She let me go."

"Richard wouldn't let me go."

"He wouldn't?"

"No. I am too precious." She was drying Sky's hands. He wriggled free and ran off outside into the yard, down to the swings. Emily watched him go and then turned and said, "Do I scare you?"

"No, no," Paul said, but of course she did. This intimacy of words was foreign. With Nicole and Sky it was the physical knocking up against each other, but with Emily it was language, the words, *I am too precious*, dropped into the lap of his brain. She was still standing by the sink. She turned, pulled in a hard breath and said, "The world is made of ice."

Paul stood and went to her. Held her. His hand could feel the line where her bra pushed into her back. She fisted his shirt and then said, "There."

Sky called, from the doorway, "Are you sad, Grandpa?"

Paul could see Sky past the tangle of Emily's hair. He said, "No, not sad."

"Is the woman sad?"

"Emily."

"Is Emily sad?"

"Are you sad?" Paul asked Emily. He had pulled away. The afternoon sun had found the window and the new light in the room flattened the objects so that Emily seemed smaller now. Paul saw that she had a little nose.

"No, I'm happy," she said. She squatted and Paul watched the backs of her arms, the bones of her elbows, the movement of her dress against her back as she gathered in the boy, held him.

Sky said, "I have to poop."

Paul took him down the hall. Watched as his bottom disappeared into the bowl. Chin almost on his knees. "Go away," he said.

Paul went and rejoined Emily. Paul said, "Do you know anything about bees?"

"Nothing. I saw this documentary once on bees talking to each other. It had a religious tone, as if to say, If the bee is this wonderful, there must be a God."

"It could be true," Paul said.

Emily ignored this. She continued, "And I came across this really old book called *The Hive and the Honeybee* by a man called Langstroth."

"He was very strange," Paul said. "Suffered from melancholy. He was going to be a preacher, but delivering his first sermon he was struck dumb."

Emily laughed and said, "That all churches should be so lucky."

Paul said, "His madness came and went. He took up beekeeping for his health. He invented the modern hive. When he was mad he couldn't bear the hives nor even look at the letter *B*."

"Really?"

"You should write this down."

"The local reader wouldn't care."

"But it is up to you to make them care."

Sky teetered in. Wanted his pants buttoned. "Did you wipe?" Paul asked. Sky nodded.

"Can I come back? Here?" Emily asked.

"Yes." Paul fished in the cupboard and produced a jar of honey. Handed it to her.

"Another?" she asked, but took it.

She got some photos of him in the out yard, holding a smoker, bending to inspect a hive. She said, "When I come back we'll talk some more." She played with the word "talk." Pronounced the *l*, an odd lilt.

"Yes," he said. He held Sky. They walked out to the car. As the door slipped shut he sensed a sudden distance, as if the creak and scent of leather, the way the seat held her, were pulling her away. Then, without warning, she took Paul's hand and held it to her nose.

"You have a certain smell," she said. "Not bad. Just different." Then she left Paul standing in the wake of her dust, holding his hand to his nose, wondering what he smelled like.

With the arrival of September and the chance of night frost, the bees were storing up their winter honey, flying out to the patches of late-blooming goldenrod or seeking out asters, an ethereal white-and-golden flower. It was still too early to move the hives. In October or early November Paul would haul the bees in from the fields and feed them in preparation to store them in the winter shed, next to the honey house. Manitoba winters required that the hives be given some shelter. One year Paul had wrapped a few hives in insulation and black plastic and left them outside for the winter, but with the coming of spring, only a few bees had survived and the hives were devastated.

One morning Paul asked Nicole if she would help. She hesitated and then said, "Fine," but promptly wandered off into the porch for a cigarette. She had taken to reading fat novels about other worlds, fantasy she called it, and this habit had made her inaccessible. One day Paul had said, "Why not read something edifying?" She looked up and said, "Edifying is boring."

"Needn't be."

"You're always right, aren't you?" she said, and left the room.

He had been sorry. He didn't want to be right and, today, he sensed a storm as well. Nicole was short with Sky, snapped at him when he refused his oatmeal, told Paul that she had no money.

"Here," he said, unfolding a twenty and placing it on the breakfast table. She ignored it, but later it was gone, slipped into her jeans pocket, he supposed. He had, on occasion, punched some bills into her pockets at night, entering her room and fumbling in the dark for her jeans. One night she called out, disoriented, and he left her room, feeling oddly like a thief.

She had taken to leaving in the evening, after Sky was sleeping. She preened in the bathroom and dressed up; short skirts and brief insubstantial tops which revealed the thin straps of her bra and the circle of her belly button. Daylight turned to dusk coming earlier now, making her darker, a collection of shadows, the narrow knees, leg and calves, the clap of her shoes' fat heels on the wooden stairs. She didn't tell him where she went. She didn't ask if she could go. He assumed the care of Sky and slept poorly, waiting for her return, which was often towards morning, the knock of the Camino a warning, then the dieseling and sigh of a needy engine, and then her entry. Softly she came, removing her shoes, and sometimes Paul was sitting on the veranda, unable to sleep, and as she passed and stopped briefly to offer a few words, he could smell her and, doing so, his heart ached for the loss of the unfathomable, the unspoken, the space in his own heart that lay fallow and untended. And as the sun came up she slept a pure and rich sleep and he posed, a weary sentry, looking at a reddening sky, deeply aware of the callow nature of the heart.

On a Sunday, planning a sales trip to Winnipeg, he sensed danger and didn't want to leave Sky with Nicole, so suggested bringing him along. Nicole was pleased by this and said, "Lucky Sky," and kissed the boy and then Paul, on the cheek, and he saw she loved the notion of being left.

He loaded the half-ton with pails of honey, gathered Sky, and they left mid-morning, driving away from Nicole who stood in the yard, waving diligently, her hand passing back and forth as if she were not saying goodbye but, in fact, denying something. No.

They travelled through Furst and up past Tourond and on to the 311 where they turned east towards the river. They passed through Niverville and Sky pointed at a forklift in a parking lot and a dog wandered across the quiet main street. Paul had to drive around him. They passed fields left fallow and fields with thick swaths of wheat and oats that sat there, waiting. Through St. Adolphe then and past fancy houses on river property and on to Saint Norbert where Paul set up a stall at the farmer's market. The stall next to Paul's sold pinwheel fans and Paul bought one and Sky wandered about blowing into the centre of the wheel, his mouth puckered into the shape of a purse string. Paul had a hand-painted sign hanging above his booth: Unger Apiaries. His sales today were poor. As sometimes happened, he was assailed by people who believed honey was a cure-all and assumed that he, because he was a beekeeper, believed the same. Today he was assaulted by a young woman in a red kerchief who claimed that venom from a bee could cure syphilis.

"So can antibiotics, if I'm not mistaken," Paul said.

The woman, who had large hands and no chin, said she was allergic to chemicals.

"I see," Paul intoned.

"It is a fact, isn't it," the woman said, "that bee venom can cure arthritis as well?"

"I've heard that," Paul said. He was watching for Sky, who

tended to wander. His head appeared and disappeared beyond a stall which sold patchwork potholders.

"My mother suffers horribly from arthritis," the chinless woman said.

"I'm sorry," Paul said, though he wasn't. Then, before more could be said, he added, "Would you like a pail of honey?"

"Is it pure?"

"Straight from the hive," Paul said.

"Chemicals?"

"None."

"From the plants, I mean. Did the bees work canola that was genetically altered, or sunflowers that were sprayed?"

"This is clover honey. Perfect in every way."

The woman nodded. Stared off into the distance. Then she left without buying any honey and Paul had to tend with the next customer, a deaf man holding a knobbed cane who threatened to fall over with each breath.

The afternoon passed. Sky slept at his feet. They returned home before supper and arrived to find Daniel's car parked in the driveway. Paul said, "Look, Sky, your aunt Sue is visiting."

"Soo?"

"Yes."

Paul was glad. He'd missed talking to his daughter, though he wondered why she would be visiting Nicole. They unpacked the truck and stacked the unsold jars of honey. Sky wandered off to the swing and Paul went onto the porch, through the door, and made to call out for Sue and Nicole but hesitated as Nicole's voice bled together with another voice, lower. A glottal gasp. Nicole cried out then as one could only cry out believing the world was an empty place, that no one else existed, certainly not the father of the daughter whose husband was holding you.

Paul couldn't breathe. A bright and vital memory of himself standing at the window and looking down on the pool and Nicole's knee pointing at the sky, her face lifting to seek him out. He turned and exited the house, saw Sky's curls, the motion of the swing, the squeak. He squatted beside the boy, who asked, "Where's Nicole?"

"She's coming. She's sleeping."

"Sky will go." He bumped off the swing and began to run towards the house. Paul grabbed him and threw him to the ground. Tickled him. His squeals lifted and carried.

"Don't, Grandpa," Sky gasped.

Paul released him and they lay side by side and looked up. Sky pointed and said, "Moon."

"Yes, it is," Paul answered.

Sky sighed hugely. Tucked his head against Paul's shoulder and said, "Grandpa."

The screen door slammed, someone descended the stairs, and Paul, eyes closed, waited.

"Hello."

"Hello, Daniel." Paul kept his eyes closed. He did not want to see the boy.

"You been here long?"

"Long enough."

"Oh."

"Tell you what," Paul said. "You get in your car and leave now. And don't come back."

"Okay. Okay." He walked away, stopped, and turned back. "It didn't mean anything."

"You son of a bitch," Paul said. Sky put his finger in his mouth and said, "Bite."

Paul kissed his knuckle.

"Sonuffaditch," Sky repeated.

Daniel left. The car offered its expensive rumble, the whine of reverse, then the ping of rocks in the wheel wells and the diminishing thrum of the engine. Paul and Sky stood up to go inside. Nicole was sitting in her chair, smoking.

"Sweetie," she said, and gathered up Sky. "How was your time. Sell any honey?"

"Uh-huh. Grandpa bought me a toy. A girlywig."

"Whirligig," Paul corrected. He was standing looking at Nicole. Waiting.

She ignored him. He stepped forward. Nicole's left eye closed. She looked up. Looked away.

"Why?" Paul asked.

Nicole shrugged. A slight and meagre lift of one shoulder.

Sky wanted toast. "I want toast," he said. "And milk."

"Didn't you think?" Paul asked.

"You jealous?" Nicole said. Her voice was soft but cold.

"Ahh," Paul said, and then, as if to match her, he said, "You little bitch."

She stood and swung at him, swept sideways with her left arm so that the palm of her hand caught his right cheek. The blow was hard and unexpected. A fingernail flayed his cheekbone and left a quickly rising welt.

"Oh, Christ," Nicole said. Her hand went out and back again. Paul stood and looked at her for several seconds before kneeling and picking up Sky. Nicole was nervous now. She tried to dab at his cheek with a finger. Inspected the finger and said, "You're bleeding." Paul was still holding Sky who squirmed away and said, "Grandpa hurt?"

"Not bad."

"Mummy, too?"

"I don't know, is Mummy hurt?" Paul could not resist the opportunity to mock. This sudden attack had both surprised and fortified him. He said to Nicole, "You have no shame."

Nicole laughed. Sullen again. "Shame?" she asked. "Who are you? You seem to be doing just fine with the doctor's wife."

"What do you mean?"

Nicole laughed again, a brief and unhappy gurgle. Paul had followed her to the bathroom now, where she eyed herself in the mirror as if she could discover something there. She said, "Men think sex is so simple."

"I never slept with Emily Wish," Paul said, and even as he spoke he was amazed to be confessing this to Nicole who obviously didn't believe him.

"Sky saw you holding her and children don't lie. You do that to all your customers?"

"She was sad."

"Well, so am I." She pushed past him and walked down the hall to her bedroom. She began pulling clothes from drawers and tossing them into boxes and the one suitcase she owned.

Paul had followed her. He stood in the centre of the room and asked, "What are you doing?"

"Leaving."

"Where?"

"Don't know. Somewhere. Daniel wants to go down to Las Vegas."

"Sky's staying with me," Paul said. He was still holding the boy, who had begun to whimper.

Nicole came over, stroked Sky's cheek, and whispered in Paul's ear, "No, he's not, and don't scare him."

She stepped back. Porcelain neck, subtle veins there, her loping fury as she stuffed clothes in boxes. Paul looked around the room. Imagined it empty. Nosed Sky's head and thought that if the child left, he'd never see him again.

"Going?" Sky said. "In the Camino?"

Paul latched onto this. He said, "How will you go?"

Nicole had figured this out. She said, "I'll call Daniel. He'll come get us."

"Don't. Don't do that to Sue."

"But he likes me. Sue bores him. She doesn't like sex, that's what he said. See, it's a sex thing."

Paul had no space left for rage. He went weakly back down the hall. Sky muttered in his ear, shook himself loose, and ran back to his mother. Paul could hear them chattering and packing, Nicole talking about the sun, the desert, and big mountains. "Should we go?" she asked.

"Okay," Sky answered, and then there was a pause and he asked, "Grandpa, too?"

"No, sweetie, he'll stay here and guard the bees."

Sky seemed to accept this. Paul, listening from the kitchen

where he sat at the table looking at the far wall, heard Sky playing, talking to a toy. Paul considered taking Sky and driving away. He could have, but he didn't want to frighten him. Or he could just refuse to let Nicole have him. It would be best for Sky. What kind of life could she give him?

Nicole was on the phone now, her voice rising and falling, a whispering, pleading, sudden anger, and then a cajoling. She hung up and re-entered the bedroom. Sky, hungry, began to cry. Nicole appeared, wary, and poured Sky a bowl of Cheerios. Sat at the table and fed him. Milk dribbled across the grey-topped chrome suite and onto Sky's bare chest. His little fist rubbed it away. Sensing defeat in her, Paul felt suddenly generous. Giddy with relief.

"What will you do for money?" he asked. This was not meant as a taunt.

"Daniel said he had money. But now he's afraid. Doesn't want to go. Says we should wait."

Paul experienced both pity and glee. He didn't speak, just watched Sky's mouth open, the spoon go in and the cereal disappear. Nicole seemed tired now. Paul's cheek hurt. He rubbed it and said, "I'm going out to work."

Nicole ignored him. Paul bent to Sky and kissed him on the head. "Night, night."

Sky looked up. Said, "Kiss."

Paul kissed him. Tasted Cheerios. He looked at Nicole and said, "Don't go."

She looked back at him and asked, with a softness that surprised him, "What do you want?"

"I'm afraid," Paul said. "Afraid that you will leave and I will never see Sky again."

"That's ridiculous."

"You running off with him. *That's* ridiculous."

"I can't stay here. I'll end up like you."

"I don't see that as a possibility."

"I couldn't stand it. Knocking around with bees and hives and honey. Stuck out here. It's lonely. Boring. Haven't you figured that out?"

"Perfectly," Paul said. "But I'm afraid for Sky. You're a selfish girl, and he'll get lost."

"Am I selfish?" She seemed surprised, almost pleased.

"Of course," he said, and then he went out to the honey house, entering the smell of that small space, the coolness, the silence.

Later, he returned to the house and went to bed, but he did not sleep well. He drifted off and then woke quickly, confused, tortured by the chance that Nicole would leave during the night. At one point Paul went to Sky and Nicole's room and found them, limbs entangled, Sky in his pyjamas, Nicole in panties and a T-shirt. How normal everything seemed at that moment. Paul returned to his bed wondering if he did believe, as Nicole said, that sex was simple.

Towards morning, just before the light appeared, he woke from a dream in which he was looking for a lost shoe. In the dream he had been filled with unreasonable panic and now, awake, aware of the silence of this room, this house, the panic remained.

She was gone.

He knew this.

He left his bed and walked to her room and discovered there the snarled blankets, the suitcase and boxes gone, and, stepping to the front window to look out at the yard, the absence of the Camino. The dawn was cold and grey. Rain beat against the front window. The trees let go of their leaves. Paul walked back to the kitchen. Put on water for coffee. Then he sat down and put his face into his hands.

Because it was raining Paul worked in the honey house through the morning. At noon the phone rang. It was Lise. She sounded breathless and agitated. "Paul," she said, "Daniel's run off with Nicole."

"Yes, I thought so."

"And you did nothing?" Lise asked. "You knew?"

"I didn't *know*. I assumed. They'd been seeing each other."

"Oh, my. How long?"

"I don't know. I just found out yesterday."

"You sound like Sue. *Oh, well. Too bad.* Like her heart isn't broken. She must be suffering."

"Maybe she's glad to have him gone."

"That's cruel, Paul. I called Daniel's mother and she was defensive, but then her boy can do no wrong."

"No, he's perfect."

"It's all so messy," Lise continued. "I hate it."

"You hate it. That surprises me. Weren't you quite happy about this wedding?"

"So were you. Don't get moral. I told Sue to go see you. She left the house but I don't know where she is."

"Poor girl," Paul said.

"How about Sky?" Lise asked.

"She took him. They left during the night."

Silence, and then Lise asked, "You okay?"

"Not great, but okay. I feel worst for Sky. You think Daniel cares about him? All he thinks about is money and fame. They're going to Las Vegas, I'm sure of it. Daniel wants to be a stand-up comic, Nicole said something about being a Rockette."

"Jesus," Lise said. She laughed. "Have they no brains? Daniel wasn't even funny."

"Some drunk on their honeymoon laughed at a few jokes and now he's convinced he's a genius."

"Well, at least Nicole has long legs," Lise said, and then added, her voice going up slightly, "Sue said just the other day, 'Why is Daddy living with Nicole?' I couldn't answer her. You know?"

"No, I don't know."

"Well, it seemed odd, you and her, out there. It wasn't natural. I think Sue felt the same way. Everybody did."

Paul waited.

Lise rushed on, "She can't be trusted. She's a siren."

"Funny," Paul said, "just yesterday Nicole accused me of sleeping with Emily Wish. And now you have me in bed with Nicole."

"I didn't say you were in bed with Nicole. Don't be perverse."

"Oh, so now it's perverted."

"Well, of course it's perverted," Lise cried out. "She's the mother of your grandson."

"Oh, so you admit that?"

Lise avoided this question and said, "That girl has brought us only grief."

"Yes, she has," Paul agreed.

Lise became wary. "What about Emily Wish?"

"She's doing an article on beekeepers and I'm the beekeeper."

Lise was thinking, but Paul interrupted the silence. "Conrad's barking," he said. "It's probably Sue."

"Take care of her."

"I will," Paul said, and he hung up and walked out into the yard to find Sue bending over Conrad, rubbing his ears. He went up to her, hugged her, and said, "You hungry?"

She wasn't sure. Her eyes were dark. She was too thin. She smelled of defeat. "I'm so embarrassed," she said.

"Oh, no, you shouldn't, you shouldn't."

"Three months. Everyone's going to say, 'Look, Sue Unger wasn't even married for three months.'" She was crying. Paul wiped her tears. Kissed her head. He held in his heart a hard hatred for Nicole, for her health, her vigour, her energy, her sexual treachery.

"It wasn't you," he told Sue. "It was Daniel and Nicole."

"I hate her," she said.

"And you should." He pulled her up the stairs and settled her in the kitchen and poured her coffee. She lit a cigarette and when he looked back over his shoulder and saw his daughter sitting at the table, a raggedness around her edges, the smallness of her head and shoulders, Paul thought Nicole had returned.

"Daniel left in the morning. I heard him getting dressed and asked, 'Where are you going?' and he said, 'Las Vegas, with Nicole Forêt.' He didn't even bother lying. I thought he was joking. I was watching from the window. Nicole pulled up with Sky and they all got into Daniel's car and drove off. Like they were married or something." She stopped. Started again. "It was like I had known

Daniel all my life, the games we played, his love for insects, I knew him, and then we got married and I didn't know him." Conrad clicked across the floor and laid his muzzle across Sue's leg. She put a hand on his head. His tail swept. "He wasn't happy." She stubbed her cigarette. "Maybe Nicole can make him happy."

"Maybe."

"Hélène thinks it's my fault. She said to Mum, 'He'll come back. They always come back.'"

"Maybe he will."

"I don't want him back."

"That's fine. You don't have to."

"You liked her, Daddy?"

Paul looked at Sue. "I guess. In a way. I'm angry with her now."

"I wish you hadn't ever invited her."

"She asked." Paul found himself building a defence. "She was lost. No money. No home."

"You loved her?"

"No, no," Paul answered, too quickly. But he saw that love had filtered in like the sun and filigreed his heart. And the hatred he felt now was because of love. Nicole had a claim on him which passed through Stephen and Sky and if asked to separate those three shapes, Paul could not have, would not have. He said, attempting to save Sue from more pain, "She won't come back. Ever."

"Good." Then she added, as if this were the natural progression of things, "Is that the way it always is? You look forward to something and then, after, or even during, it just isn't as good as you imagined?"

"Sometimes, though that doesn't mean you should lose faith." And yet, why not? He himself had lost faith, he had become alien, far-off. The brief contacts he had with others were like passing pinpoints of light in the night sky. Which was why Nicole and Sky, with their constant presence, were like tunnels of radiance shining back onto him. And with their departure he was blind. He thought of Sue, having to sleep with a boy who had no notion of sanctity or mystery. Paul wished he were a violent man. Sue lit another cigarette. Her knuckles were delicate. He traced the bump on her left wrist, wrapped his index finger and thumb around her like a bracelet. Told her she was the most beautiful girl in the world.

Emily Wish wrote an article on beekeepers. She began:

> Beekeepers smell of homemade candles, propolis, alfalfa, clover, Bee Go, Aristaeus, blackberries, royal jelly, nectar, leatherwood, bee venom, Virgil, hunger, prairie grass, plum trees, and beeswax. They wear white uniforms with masks like fencers and carry smokers to overcome the bees. Some beekeepers wear only shorts and shoes and walk barefoot among the hives like a landowner among the serfs.

Emily went on to describe the process of collecting and extracting honey. She quoted Paul Unger, a beekeeper near La Broquerie, who said that beekeeping was a form of meditation. Then, in an about-face near the end of the article, she likened the hive to a prison, with its cells and honeycomb and its warden, the keeper, and the little white box and the bees who seemed not to understand that they *could* leave.

Paul read the article and phoned Emily the following day and said, "The nature of an animal is to follow its design. A bee's only purpose is to make honey."

"Did I say otherwise?" Emily asked.

"You implied that the bee was an ignorant animal. Trapped."

"Well, it is, isn't it? I didn't say that was bad."

"I felt accused somehow," Paul said. Holding the phone, he imagined her mouth close to her own receiver, her breath leaving an invisible mist. "Why is it," he asked, "that humans assume superiority, as if they stood outside of nature?"

"We're afraid?" Emily asked.

"Nicole left," Paul said. "Took Sky."

Emily expressed surprise, though she must have known.

"Yes," Paul said. "And she took Sue's husband, Daniel."

"Oh." There was a pause and then Emily said, "I can never quite understand how some people do that, devour life around them. It's odd, but I get slightly jealous."

"Jealous?" Paul imagined her leaning forward now, on the edge of confession, the physical distance between them allowing intimacy.

"Yes, I think that's the right emotion. Like I could only imagine, in the darkest corner of my head, doing something like that, running off with someone else's husband. I'm talking hypothetically now. It could just as easily be climbing a mountain. Or skydiving."

"I know," Paul said. "Only, it's not really freedom."

Emily doubted this. It was her pause. She asked, "How's Sue?"

"I can't tell. She hates Daniel and Nicole, and possibly even me."

"Not you."

"I miss Sky."

"Yes, I guess so."

"Anyways, I thought the article was great."

"Thank you."

After he'd hung up Paul stood and looked out the far window onto the garden and he thought that he had just passed Emily by, that where there was the notion of something, even just a friendship, he had cut it loose, like most things.

Over the next two months Paul wintered the remainder of his hives and painted the house inside and out. He redid the bathroom and put a new rug and windows in Nicole's bedroom. He sanded down the hardwood floor in the kitchen and fixed the screens on the front porch. The outside stairs were rotten and sagging, so one warm Saturday in October he tore out the old stairs and built new ones. The stringers were tricky and he wasted a couple of good pieces of planking before he figured out the rise and run and came away satisfied enough to sit on them in the afternoon sun and drink a beer. Conrad lay at his feet in the brown grass, nose across his paws.

"It's an even keel," Paul told his dog.

One night he found himself in Sky and Nicole's bed. The pillowcases held Sky's spoor, and he imagined himself a child again, folding into his mother's belly, the smell of sleep on her breath. The presence of the departed pair hung about the house. Nicole's musty perfume rising from the medicine cabinet, cigarette smoke on the porch curtains, Sky's breath in the fall air, Conrad's whimpers, like Sky's, lifting out of some feral dream. These memories congregated in his head like precious idols.

Paul had seen Lise twice in the last month. She was no longer with Harry. It was all over, she said, this was certain. Today, she would be coming for supper and the thought of having her sit across from him made him happy. It would be nice to see her naked, rub chests with her, draw his tongue along the hard muscle of her thigh. It was not something he'd propose, though. She was still too far away; the circuitry of her mind looped elsewhere, concerned itself with more important things than bedding her former husband. Still, he dreamed, and the sun on his nape made him sleepy, and Conrad shuddered at his feet, and when Lise arrived, directly from work, dressed in a dark skirt and sweater, Paul had to look twice before he saw the Lise he used to know, found her finally in the shape of her head seen in profile. He said, "How perfect you are."

"Yes, and that's what you ran from."

They went into the kitchen. Lise said, "You've cleaned up." Her nylons were red. They were reflected in the hardwood.

Paul showed her the new bathroom, Nicole and Sky's room, and Lise was blunt, "She won't come back."

Paul shrugged, looked around the room. It was on the shaded side of the house and so the light was dim, the corners disappeared into shadow. The fresh paint had scrubbed away the scent of Sky and Nicole, and standing beside Lise, Paul smelled her; it was a familiar odour, nice, a mixture of perfume and ink, the hint of leather, soap perhaps.

Walking back to the kitchen, Lise said, "Hélène called and Daniel's in Las Vegas. He was alone. He said Nicole and Sky were in North Dakota or Wyoming. One of those states."

"What do you mean, '*one* of those states'? He didn't know?"

"He didn't say."

"What about Sky? What about Daniel and Nicole? All that love?" Paul felt panicky, impatient with Lise's nonchalance.

Lise sighed. "Hélène said Daniel had a job interview. Stand-up comic. Sometimes, Hélène surprises me."

Paul thought about Sky out there somewhere on the Great Plains. A speck. He took two beer, pushed one at Lise. She said, "I'll have tea."

He put water on. Said, "Remember that goldenrod you pressed and kept in the attic?"

"That was my flower stage. We were just married and you were teaching me about wild plants."

"You loved goldenrod for its name, not for its looks."

"I don't remember."

"Do you remember anything about me, about us?"

"Of course, Paul, lots of things. You made the best fried eggs."

"I saw Harry and Bunny yesterday. Driving out of town together. Bunny'd slid right over next to Harry, like they were teenagers."

"Yes?" Lise said. This information hurt.

"Must be odd, eh? You *did* like him."

"I guess I did." She got up to make her own tea. Stood by the stove and said, "Sue is happy. She's pretending she was never married."

"Well, that's good," Paul said. He waited, pondered the tabletop, and continued, "If I knew where they were, I'd go get them."

"Maybe Nicole doesn't want getting."

"Do you ever suffer?" he asked.

Her cheeks reddened. She turned away, looked out the window. Said, "You need your grief. If it were a meal, you'd devour it."

Paul wondered if this was true.

Lise continued, "Sky is not your boy. He's Nicole's. If she wants to take him and go to Wyoming, then she can go. Sky will survive. He will grow up and he will be fine."

Paul waved a hand, dismissed her. And sensing that she somehow merited his disdain, Lise talked on and on, attempting to recover what she had lost.

Later they ate chicken, carrots, rice, a salad, and a gingerbread cake that Paul baked. Lise ate two pieces of cake and then complained that her skirt was too tight. She said, "Your mother thinks it's wonderful that I'm here for supper and about time that we got back together."

"Is that what we're doing?" Paul asked. The meal had made him sleepy. His face was flushed from the beer and overeating. Lise slouched slightly, her neck bent, and this for some reason reminded Paul of Nicole and he suffered a brief sharpness, a dip and a rise, guilt at having forgotten. But thankfully the guilt did not last and he let Sky and Nicole slip away, two helium-filled images floating upwards and disappearing.

Lise doodled across the table with a spoon. "I'm not a rabbit, always needing someone in my bed."

"Rabbits are okay."

"Awfully quick though, you know, getting it off."

"Harry tell you that?"

"Huh. Well, he did run back to his Bunny, didn't he?" And here she laughed, briefly, and then her face went distant and Paul thought that what appeared to be happiness wasn't always the case. The thought that Lise was unhappy produced his own surge of joy; it was easier to forgive the disconsolate. They drank scotch and talked. Lise petted Conrad. Later, she went to the bathroom and Paul said to Conrad, "Would you like to stay?" His voice got quieter and he tried, "How about sex?" A sip of scotch. Another. He leaned forward. "I was thinking, since you're here, and the hour is late, why don't you stay the night? Sleep in Sky's room." Conrad looked forlorn. His tail cleaned the floor, left a wiper patch in the dust near the couch. This was the one room Paul still had to clean. The toilet flushed. Paul said, "Wanna fuck?"

Conrad's tail thumped expectantly, his eyes brightened. "Okay," Paul said, "subtle, then."

Lise returned. She stood in the doorway and said, "So, you want me to stay?"

"You want to?" Paul asked.

"I guess."

"You're not sure?"

"I'm sure."

"Okay."

Conrad's tail swept.

Paul woke in the night to find that Lise had thrown a leg over his stomach. In the darkness he made out her hip, her shoulder, her hair, and the profile of her nose and chin. He smelled her head. He slid out from under her and stood looking down at the bed. She was as grasping in sleep as she was in sex. They had first made love on the couch, Paul looking up into Lise's small breasts as she skidded across him, her breath sharp, rising and falling, rising again. Paul filling his mouth. Lise ducking her nose into his neck. The edge of the couch in his back. The smell of her on his fingers even now as he left her, sleeping. His unfurling of the condom, a rubbery vote of non-confidence, which had soured the event slightly and made her tilt her head briefly as if reconsidering, but then she charged on without protest.

They did it again on the bed, after a few more drinks, and this time it was less desperate, more aware, and Paul felt as if he were standing outside the action of his own body, looking down onto the scene: Lise slow, Lise kneeling, Lise's mouth an *O*, her eyes flicking upwards past his belly to his studied gaze, "Okay," and finally, on her knees and him gazing down at the twiggish movement of her vertebrae an arm's length away as he entered her. The thought that he could so easily break her neck. And then, after, the pity. That was the strangest, the pity.

He remembered sex with Lise, as if what were important to Paul

Unger over the last twenty years was the act of calling out, of numbering, of setting down a record of love. The first time in the heat of the midday in St. Malo, the nylon tent a thin skin beyond which life continued, mundane, oblivious to the marvel of Lise and Paul, naked and fumbling and breathless. And in that first year of marriage, after Stephen's birth, on the floor close to his crib, Lise clutching the bars of the crib as Stephen watched, ohing and cooing, on his side, black eyes wide, breast milk still rolling from his puckered mouth, and Paul, in his haste, picking up the leftovers from Lise's large nipples. And he remembered when Stephen and Sue were adolescents and they couldn't find the space or time to have sex and finally driving out one summer evening to the gravel pits where Lise threw off her clothes and lay down on the gravel and said, "Come, fuck me."

For Paul, riches and fame were less important than sex. It was like falling and knowing you would be caught. Yet, before tonight, never had he felt pity, except for himself perhaps during those times when lust had won out over consideration, and so pity had been a new notion, leaving a residue of shame and loss.

He was restless, wide awake now. He walked out, naked, into the living-room, where he retrieved his shorts, his jeans, and his shirt and put them on. He recalled the clatter of change and keys as he had shed his clothes earlier and so he bent now to look under the couch. Eased the table lamp down onto the floor. Found his keys, a few coins. A toy of Sky's: a blue metal truck with the paint scratched off. Paul drove it across the hardwood, into his other hand, smelled it and set it up on the couch. He saw, further back, more objects, so he swept with his arm under the couch and gleaned dustballs, a comb of Nicole's, and, cluttered like little glass shards, her toenail clippings, a fair number, and he recalled the night she had sat in this room and snipped her nails and how the cuttings spun like spears through the air. And here they were. There was a trace of black from the nail polish. Paul blew away the dust for a better view. He picked one up. Rolled it between his fingers and then put it in his mouth. Tasted like dust. He took it out and put in his palm. He gathered up the clippings that remained and stored them in a blue glass bowl in the kitchen. Lise slept on. Paul made himself toast and honey. It was three a.m. He sat at the table in the kitchen and listened to a hard rain beat against the roof. He had put the bowl on a top shelf where only he could reach. He looked up at the bowl now. The bowl looked back. In the bedroom Lise slept the sleep of the forgiven.

Paul had given up any hope of Nicole returning or calling. Or writing. And so, when a postcard arrived, Paul experienced the headiness of salvation, even though the words offered were cryptic and spare. She told of a place, Great Falls, Montana; a parting, Daniel gone; and another man named Wyatt, who had a house, a job, a dog, and two trucks. "Just like you," she concluded, and Paul imagined a wistful tone there, regret perhaps. He put the card in his pocket. Took it out to read throughout the day so that, by evening, the paper was worn and dirty, the ink smudged.

The following morning he had breakfast with Herb. He took Conrad along. Fed him a chocolate bar and drove with one hand, too fast, his rear end swaying in the loose gravel. Paul showed Herb the postcard. Herb read it and nodded.

Paul said, "It's a mystery. Why there?"

"There are bigger mysteries," Herb said. He did not speak meanly and Paul did not take it that way.

Paul said, "Imagine doubt as a large pink eraser, the size of a heart." He indicated the tip of a finger. "I've got this much faith left."

Herb was not surprised. He spooned sugar into his coffee and said, "Faith is not reasonable. It is difficult."

"And rare," Paul said.

"Not true. It isn't rare. It's for everyone."

"There's the preacher in you," Paul said. He tapped the card. "It's Sky I worry about. Not her."

"Yes."

ul said, "Lise would like me to live with her again."

"Good, that's good. Isn't it?"

"I guess it is. Her eavestroughs need cleaning."

Herb ignored this.

Paul said, "I like living alone."

"It is a selfish thing."

"We're all selfish."

Herb shook his head. Impatience made his eyes widen. "Acch, that's ridiculous. Like saying we are all equally guilty. The new order. Utmost tolerance for deviance and sin. *It's just different.* You have been very selfish, Paul. I don't begrudge you that. But then I'm not your wife or daughter. Sue, of course, has suffered the most. Do you see that?"

Paul nodded. Admitted failure. Said, "For some reason Nicole slithered in." Here his hand waggled across the table.

"Sue called her a wayward whore."

"That's quite a strong statement."

"I thought it was charitable. The wayward. Sue was doubly deceived."

Paul held up his hands, "Fine, crucify me."

"Not at all. Have you talked to Sue?"

Paul shook his head. "Lise says she's doing great. Quite happy to have escaped."

Herb was not satisfied.

Paul said, "Okay, I'll call her. I'll take her out for dinner."

But this would not happen, because that afternoon, as Paul was moving the remainder of his hives into the winter shed, Nicole called. The phone hung on the post in the middle of the shed and Paul answered it on the third ring.

"Hi," Nicole said, as if she had returned from a day's outing.

Paul stood there, slightly out of breath. The sky was falling.

"It's me," she said.

"I know. Where are you?"

"Montana. Didn't you get my cards?"

"One. I got one."

"Did I only send one? I wrote more, you know. Several. They must still be sitting on the fridge. It's where I put my notes and letters. On top of the fridge." Her voice slipped away.

"Are you all right?"

"Yes. I am."

"And Sky?"

"He's fine. Talking even more now. Can you imagine?"

"What happened? Why Montana?"

"Oh, you'd like it here. It's flat and tough and ugly and hard. You'd like it."

"You don't?"

"That's why I'm calling. I want you to come and get Sky."

"Really?" Paul could see an elongated reflection of himself in the honey extractor. He was being stretched. Nicole's voice was banging around inside him, leaving him shaky.

"I've decided it would be best."

"And so I get there and you've changed your mind?"

"I won't. And, well, if I did, you'd get a chance to see Sky. And me." The *and me* trailed the rest of the sentence, as if she were suddenly ashamed of her aimless ways. Then, she sucked a quick breath and chirped, "Come soon," and she gave him vague directions, an address, described the house as small and run-down. "Wyatt's house," she said, as if Wyatt were an intimate and close friend. "Gotta go," she whispered abruptly, and then she was truly gone, had disappeared.

Paul kept holding the phone. He imagined himself a bird, a small hawk, and the route to Montana laid out beneath him like a map, the thin black lines of road, the small twisting rivers, the Great Plains, the ragged land.

MONTANA

JUST EAST OF GLASGOW, MONTANA, ON HIGHWAY Number 2, he picked up a woman, her husband, and their two children. They were coming back from the Red Lake Indian reserve in North Dakota. The family had spent the night sleeping in their broken-down car. Paul, as he approached, saw the children peeing in the ditch and the woman flagging him. He slowed down, wary now, aware of the isolation. Perhaps these people would rob him. Still, he stopped, rolled down the passenger window, and the woman stepped back towards the ditch. A man crawled out of the parked car and walked over and said, "We're going down to Roundup. Can we borrow the back of your pick-up?"

Paul nodded and asked, "Where's Roundup?"

"Lavina, Harlowton, along the Musselshell River. Highway 87. Where you headed?"

"Great Falls."

"That's good. We can go there. Chicky's got a half-sister lives in Helena." He turned and motioned to his family. Lifted the children into the box, hoisted Chicky, who was a large woman, in beside the kids, settled them, and climbed into the cab beside Paul and Conrad.

"Are they cold?" Paul asked. He reached behind the seat and pulled out his sleeping bag. Climbed out and offered it to the mother and children. They accepted and the children crawled right inside. Paul handed the mother a loaf of bread and a jar of honey. She took it, opened the honey, and pulled out a fingerful. Conrad scrambled into the ditch to do his business, then came sniffing around the front of the truck, and leaped back in.

Later, when they were on the road, the man said, "My name's Nicodemus. She's Chicky and those are our kids."

"I'm Paul." They shook hands and then Paul said, "Nicodemus and Chicky." He lifted an eyebrow. Nicodemus nodded.

They drove on in silence. Nicodemus slept as the sun rose behind them and spread its light across the plains, little bits of shade here and there, from an abandoned house or a billboard. That was all. The light seemed meagre. The sky was too big. The world was empty save for the occasional clump of cattle out on the pasture land. They passed through Hinsdale and Sara. Prickly-pear cactus grew in the ditches. Paul saw a man on a horse. A fox. When Nicodemus woke, Paul said, "What about your car?"

"Wasn't mine," Nicodemus said, and he didn't offer any more.

They stopped for gas in Dodson. A single-bay garage and one pump and a tiny restaurant that boasted a breakfast special. The kids remained sleeping, deep in the bag, and Paul wondered if they'd suffocated. Chicky hauled herself over to the bathroom and Nicodemus bought coffee in a Styrofoam cup and stood in the sun at the edge of the highway and smoked. His legs were bowed, he was wearing cowboy boots and his shirt was stained in the back. He came back and said, "I had a brother lived here once."

Paul was washing the windows. Nicodemus stood beside him and said, "You got kids?"

"Two," Paul said. "Only one's dead."

Nicodemus nodded as if this made perfect sense. He tipped his head. Scratched his belly.

"Hungry?" Paul asked.

Nicodemus nodded.

When Chicky came back they woke the children and went into the restaurant and Paul bought everybody breakfast. Pancakes and bacon and coffee and milk and juice. There were three tables and one large waitress named Emma. She huffed and puffed and tweaked the children's cheeks. Chicky smoked and said, "Emma, I'd like a Coke."

"Okay, dear," Emma said, and when she returned she looked at Paul and he saw her round face and the pale eyes buried in fat and he said, "Thank you," for Chicky.

Paul asked the youngest child, Frank, how old he was. He held up three fingers and said, "Four."

"I've got a grandson who's close to three."

"I'm four," Frank said.

Chicky ordered another breakfast. Frank spilled his milk. Nicodemus mopped it up with paper napkins and said, "That's a good glass of milk."

Paul was anxious to leave. Chicky kept eating. Nicodemus smoked and said, "When I was a kid I went to a white school where the teachers pulled my ears. See?" He pushed his ears out. Paul looked. Nodded. The ears looked normal. Before they left Paul gathered up the scraps, put them in a bag, and carried them out to Conrad, who bolted everything beside the truck. Then he licked the syrup off Frank's face. Frank laughed and put his fist in the dog's mouth. Paul let Conrad drink from the squeegee water.

Back on the road Nicodemus slept and Paul studied the map as he drove. Nicole's thin voice was in his ear, Come get Sky. Distant and dream-like, perhaps imagined. All this space out here, forsaken, unused, made the idea of Nicole's and Sky's existence elusive, as if they had run out onto this flat earth and fallen away. She had said, "I'm living in a house at the edge of Great Falls. I have no money and Sky wants you." He distrusted her. Imagined Sky as quite happy. Children that age had short memories. Still, he had come and in the pocket of his jacket was a sheaf of forty one-hundred-dollar bills, American, that he would give her and for that she would give him Sky. Vulgar, but easy.

Three hours later Nicodemus was awake and they drove through Havre. It was just after lunch and the town was sleepy and slow. Nicodemus took the map and pointed out the Blackfoot

Indian reserve. He said, "With a small detour you could take us here. We'll feed you supper."

Paul considered. He could sense Sky and Nicole out there, waiting. Still, he thought of the children in the back, the cold wind, the possibility of another night on the road, and he shrugged and said, "Okay."

He drove on. Hills in the distance, the shape of mountains, the flat land disappearing. Crosses on the side of the road marked fatalities. The sun beside them now, extending the shadow of the half-ton, the backs of the rolling hills darkening, the sky and land turning purple, the Lewis Range ahead, the Big Belt Mountains to the south, and black clouds roiling in between. Nicodemus stretched and yawned, pointed at the clouds, and said, "Maybe snow." The two boys in the back woke and peed into an empty Pepsi bottle. Chicky tossed the bottle over the side.

An hour into the reserve Paul stopped at a small shack with one gas pump. He served himself while Nicodemus and his family disembarked. They shook hands, said goodbye. No mention was made of a meal. The family disappeared. Four teenage boys huddled by the shack and threw rocks at a cat. Inside, when Paul paid, he saw more children playing video games. Paul, back on the road, was lonely. He smoked a cigarette from the pack Nicodemus had left on the dash. His fingers tingled, he got light-headed. The sun fell through his windshield now and warmed his chest. He looked for his sunglasses, patted about through the mess on the dash and came up with a pea-sized piece of gum hard as a pebble from that first day when Paul walked out onto the driveway in St. Pierre to meet his grandson. Sky's gum. Paul rolled it between his fingers, smelled it. Lemon flavoured. Put it in his mouth and sucked on it. It softened and he began to chew. He chewed until the gum was flat tasting and then tossed it.

An hour and a half before Great Falls the I-15 skirted around a place called Conrad. Paul said, "Look at that. Conrad." The dog lifted an ear.

He arrived in Great Falls around suppertime. He had the

address where Nicole was staying. He drove around looking for the street but couldn't find it. Grit-eyed and dirty, he decided to take a room at a motel, a cheap one with a bed, a shower, no restaurant. He dropped his bag in the middle of the room and went to the window. Looked out at the parking lot and beyond to a mesh fence and the highway. Trucks passed, running lights on. He took Conrad out for a quick run.

Later, Paul showered and lay in his underwear on the bed. He slept deeply and dreamed that Stephen was a toddler and Sue a baby in Lise's arms and the four of them had travelled down through North Dakota and west to Montana, into this vast and empty space where the howl of a wolf floated down from a far mountain and they lived, the family, in a small house at the edge of a stream from which they drew water and bathed. And in the dream, what began as an idyll slid into horror as he could never see Stephen's face and Paul spent one long and never-ending day following the child around the yard, thinking that evening would bring reprieve but evening never came and the sun hung forever in an unforgiving sky and Lise turned old and Sue grew up and walked naked with the carriage of a monkey through the grass, crying that she was tired and would the day never end, and when it did finally end Paul lay down beside his now-grown daughter and smelled her breasts and looked up into the face of Nicole and he cried out and his cry woke him from this troubled dream.

He lay in the stale silence of the motel room and heard the TV from the next suite and he wondered if his own voice had woken him. It was not yet midnight. He thought about his dream and then decided that it was futile. *Nicole.* Vowel following consonant following vowel. And *Sky*, soft and wild child, the fragility of him an answer to a prayer of sorts, as if Paul had asked specifically for a pale and malnourished child to enter his core.

The dream had left a residue of fatigue and slow desire. Near Minot that first night he had stopped to eat and the waitress who served him was called Sally. Sally wore a short brown uniform and her calves were long and her voice found a spot in Paul's head.

Unable now to picture anyone else, Paul retrieved Sally and imagined pinning her against a wall and pulling up the hem of her short skirt. He came quickly and then lay with his eyes closed and thought that nothing could be more sorry than this place, this time, this century coming to a close.

Later, just after midnight, Paul dressed, took Conrad, and went out to drive around town. He stopped for onion rings. Drank coffee. Great Falls was sleeping. The occasional car floated down the street. A state trooper went by. Finally, Paul tried to find the house again. The dark made it more difficult but he eventually came across the street, a lane really, which was a dead end. The house was a bungalow, no basement, tiny, with a front porch that was really a slab of wood laid out on the grass. There was a truck parked in the gravel driveway. Two motorcycles, one torn apart. A small window offered an orange light through a curtain. No sign of movement. Paul imagined Sky inside: he slept on his side, naked, curled up, ribs and spinal column like a small prehistoric animal, his hand curled like a spur. Nicole, on the phone, had said, "Wyatt's a nice man. He really likes Sky."

Where did she find these men? How easily she moved from one bed to the next. Paul turned off the engine and sat and watched. He had parked down the lane slightly, behind a four-wheel drive with monster wheels. His engine ticked. A few late geese passed by overhead, telling the world that winter was coming. "Cold, cold, cold," they called.

The door opened and a man stepped out onto the porch. The light fell onto his back. His face was shadowed. He was a big man, thick arms, large head and neck. And tall.

"Hello, Wyatt," Paul whispered. Conrad whined.

Wyatt lit a cigarette. Paul waited for Nicole to appear but she didn't. Wyatt smoked and stared out at the night. At one point he looked over at Paul's half-ton. Tipped his head. Concentrated. Then he looked up at another *V* of geese. His neck was wide. He spun his cigarette out onto the driveway. Sparks sprayed up. Wyatt turned, entered the house, and closed the door. The orange light went out ten minutes later.

Paul sat for another hour and he watched and thought. He thought that forgiveness was elusive and slippery for a man like him. More than three years ago he had let his son fall away. Since then he had looked for release but had not found it. Not in the isolation of his farm or the sheltering of Sky and Nicole. Perhaps, briefly, he had experienced the notion of grace, the passing of it as he had held Sky or slept beside him after a dream, or sung him to sleep. Still, forgiveness did not exist. Forgetting was possible but that too was tricky: consciousness could not be separated from memory. Nicole, impatient with Paul, had said, "Let him go. Do something for him. Set up a memorial fund. Buy a horse and call it Stephen." In her flippancy, she was wise. She hated to wallow, which was why she was here now, living with Wyatt, the man who felled trees.

Paul started up the truck and patted Conrad, who was jumping in his sleep. "Come," he said. "Let's go to bed."

In the morning he ate breakfast at a restaurant close to the house. He ate a bran muffin and drank coffee. The woman sitting at the table next to him was eating waffles and bacon. She picked up the bacon with her fingers and then wiped her fingers on a white napkin. She looked over at Paul and smiled. Lipstick had found its way onto her teeth. Paul nodded and looked away. After, he drove over to the small lane by Wyatt's house and parked by the curb. The truck was gone. Paul climbed from the half-ton and approached the house. Conrad barked from the box, scratched the metal. Paul stood on the useless deck and knocked on the screen door. The big door was open and he could see inside. A child sang from a distance. Paul's heart fluttered. Then Nicole was there, standing on the other side of the door.

"Hi," Paul said.

"Hi," Nicole answered. Her hand went up to her cheek. And down again. He looked at her and found there the same girl who had run away. Her hair was longer now, it covered one eye. Dirty hair, as if she didn't have time for hygiene. "You came." Nicole stepped back. She was barefoot. Black nails, chipped, too long. The beautiful blue veins flowing like many rivers from her heart. A relief map. Her hands went up, out to him and back at the room; she was drawing him forward on a rope. She motioned at the table, a chair. Said, "Wow, you came."

"You called, remember?"

"I know, it's just weird. Seeing you here."

"How's Sky?"

"Oh," she brightened. "He's fine. We took him up to Glacier Park last week. He loved it. The mountains. The deer."

"We?"

"Wyatt and me. And Wyatt's friend, Gary. Wyatt's great with Sky. And Sky likes Wyatt." She paused, looked at her hands and said, "You want something? Coffee?"

"Just had coffee. Thanks." Sitting here, watching Nicole, he was uncertain. On the phone she had begged him to come, now she was surprised to see him. He said, "So, Daniel?"

"Oh, yeah. Well, we stopped here in Great Falls, see. And Daniel was getting tired of Sky. I could tell and so we had a fight and he left."

"Just left you here? No money? Nothing?"

"Yeah." Nicole poured herself a cup of coffee. Lit a cigarette. Exhaled back over her shoulder. "Matter of fact, it was a blessing. I met Wyatt. He's a lumberjack. Was married once and has two kids. They live with the mother in Helena."

"How'd you meet him?"

"Hitchhiking. But just in town."

"Uh-huh," Paul said.

"It was funny, he picked Sky and me up and the first thing he said was, 'Are you nuts?' He says I can't hitchhike any more. It's too dangerous."

"And you listen to him?"

"I like him. He's got size-fourteen shoes. Here." She got up and went out. Came back holding a pair of dress shoes that resembled skis. "Sky flops about in them. Aren't they huge?"

The mention of Sky made Paul look up. He could hear him out back somewhere. He said, "Can I see Sky?"

"Come. He'd love to see you. I didn't tell him you were coming 'cause I didn't really expect it, you know?"

Paul didn't know. Still, he nodded and followed Nicole, who had slid into Wyatt's shoes, out to the backyard where Sky was kneeling by a pile of leaves and burying an orange cat.

"Sweetie, look who's here," Nicole said.

Sky looked up. "Grandpa," he said and knocked his way through the leaves to Paul, who scooped him up. Sky smelled of the outside, things falling, the air. He allowed Paul a kiss and then squirmed earthward and ran back to the cat. How quickly the boy had forgotten, just slipped away like a cloud going elsewhere.

There was a man raking leaves in the yard. He was watching Paul and working. Nicole motioned at him and said, "That's Gary." She went up on tiptoes. "Gary, say hi to Paul, Sky's grandpa."

Gary waved. Paul waved back.

Nicole confessed, "He's Wyatt's friend. Stoned most of the time, but Sky likes him."

She talked then, about Montana, Great Falls, the Missouri River, about going fishing with Wyatt. Paul wondered if she would ever admit to running away, to stealing Daniel from Sue. He thought not, guilt and remorse were foreign to her. Nicole looked at him. He could see the thin blue lines that ran through her nose. Her lips were chapped. For all her animation she looked rheumy and run-down, as if she were addicted to something.

She paused now, tipped her head, and said, "You wouldn't have let me go."

"I would have. Yes," Paul confirmed, "I would have." Then he added, "But Sue, she was shaken."

"That's between her and Daniel." Nicole blew on her hands to warm them. "He didn't give a fuck. You see? About me, neither."

"Sue's happier," Paul said. "That's a fact."

"Well, there," Nicole said, as if she'd accomplished some good in her life.

"And why'd you call me?" Paul asked. "You look perfectly content."

"I panicked one night. Felt this place closing in like every place eventually does. Life's always better somewhere else. Don't you think?"

"I used to. Now I don't."

Nicole carried on. "Wyatt says we can drive down to Las Vegas together. When he's finished logging. He says he can be my manager or get a job as a bouncer. He's done it before. He's got this neat trick where he grabs your arms and pulls them back through the legs. Easier to throw you through the door. Maybe he'll show you. Wanna stay for lunch?" She was talking too fast. When she walked back into the house and kicked off Wyatt's shoes, her hands were shaking.

"I could take you out," Paul said.

"That's good," she said. "Sky'd like that."

The afternoon folded around Paul and he didn't want to let it go. After lunch they drove around Great Falls, Sky stuck between him and Nicole, Conrad at his feet. The day offered a pocket of warmth and they found a park down by the river. Paul pushed Sky on the swing and hoisted him up the slide. When the wind blew off the water Sky's nose began to run. Later, they sat in the half-ton to warm up, looking out over the river, and Nicole said, "You're lucky. That you don't need to run. Look at this. It should make me happy, but it's not enough."

"You're spoiled," Paul said.

"Not really," she answered. "I just live differently."

"And by living differently you hurt people."

"I hurt you?"

Paul looked out at the river. A small fishing boat passed. He shook his head. Patted Sky's leg. Said, "I'd like to know what you want."

"Not now," Nicole said, nodding at Sky.

"How about Wyatt?"

"Oh, he's got his opinions."

"Even about your child?"

Nicole laughed. Said, "Wyatt adores him."

Paul floundered. "So do I."

"Of course you do, you're his grandpa." She smiled at him. He had forgotten her long and ropy forearms. He liked seeing them again, comfort there. She was vital, even in her waywardness. She said, "Let's go home. I want to make Wyatt a nice supper. He's always so hungry after work. You wanna stay?"

"Sure," Paul said. "I'll drop you off and then go back to the motel and then be there for supper."

"You should just stay at the house. We've got room."

Funny, how she had just settled in and claimed Wyatt and the house. *We*. Paul didn't want to stay at the house. He said, "I'm going to move actually. To the Best Western on Fourteenth. It's got an indoor pool so Sky can come swim during the day."

"Would you like that Sky, go swimming?" Nicole asked. Sky nodded. He was sleepy. Paul took his head and pushed it gently down onto his own lap. During the drive back Sky napped and Paul asked Nicole again, "What do you want?"

"I don't know. I called you because I want to leave and I don't think Sky'd do well down there. He's been having nightmares lately, crawling all over the bed, gasping and wide-eyed."

Paul stepped carefully. He said, "If I took him, it would only be until you're settled. Or could see your way."

"Wyatt figures we can see our way already. He says if I give Sky up, I'll never see him again."

"You believe that?"

"No." She was thinking. Her tongue touched an eye tooth. Slid out, then disappeared. Paul saw that he had lost Nicole. He saw it in the wildness of her eyes, the fervour with which she threw out Wyatt's name, the hesitance now to trust Paul.

He said, "I brought you money."

"You did?" A quick stutter of her chin, the realignment, a calculation. "How much?"

"Four thousand."

Nicole was suddenly wary, "Why?"

"You'll need it."

"And Sky?"

"I'll take him back with me."

They'd reached the house. The sun was falling away. Dark clouds were approaching in the west. Paul stopped the half-ton. He said, "You fooling around with stuff?"

Nicole shook her head. "No," she said. "Why?"

"Your eyes. Nose."

"I've got a cold." She sniffed for emphasis. Tried to smile at him.

"I'd hate to give you money and see it wasted."

She gathered Sky and climbed out. Leaned back and said, "Come for supper, okay?" Then she shut the door and went inside.

Paul drove back to the motel, packed his bags, checked out, and moved over to the Best Western. He went up to his room, turned on the TV, and looked out the window to the parking lot below. A woman tottered on high heels towards her car. She had red hair, a fur coat. Earlier, even an hour ago, the sky had been open and infinite, but now the clouds were pushing Paul earthwards. Snow hit the window and melted. He closed the curtains and lay down and slept. When he woke the TV newswoman told him that a man in Missoula had killed his wife and four children. The man was shown being herded into the courthouse; he seemed stunned, vacant. He was wearing glasses.

Sky, seeing Paul enter Wyatt's kitchen, said, "Grandpa," and came to him. Wyatt was drinking beer and watching TV in the living-room. He rose, stooped through the doorway, and said loudly, "Paul."

"Wyatt."

"Hunger, right?"

Paul, confused for a second, caught the joke and laughed. Weakly. "Unger," he said. "And you?"

"Earp." Wyatt chuckled and shook his head. "Wainright," he said. "Double-u, double-u. Ain't that great?" He studied Paul. He said, "So, Sky's grandpa."

Paul nodded. Accepted a beer and followed Wyatt past Nicole, who was mashing potatoes at the stove. Wyatt stopped to pat Nicole's bum and kiss her neck. She went up and down and said, "They're lumpy."

"Lumpy's fine, isn't it, Paul?"

Paul nodded again. He was suddenly a stupid puppet. Holding Sky and a beer and following a meaty man who molested Nicole in broad daylight.

Wyatt sat and said, "You must have travelled through the night. When'd she call, day before yesterday?"

Paul said, "Yes, in the morning."

Wyatt agreed with his head. Held out a hand, "Come, Sky."

Sky refused. Burrowed deeper into Paul's lap. Wyatt tipped his head as if the scene before him had suddenly changed and he had to get a new look. He finished his beer. Deep draughts. His throat shone, thick neck. His teeth clinked the bottle.

Purl of hazard in Paul's ear.

Sky went up to his ear and whispered, "Where's Conrad?"

"In the truck," Paul whispered back.

"Get him."

Paul asked Wyatt, "I have a dog, can he come in?"

"Sure," Wyatt bellowed, "as long as he isn't belligerent. I like dogs. What kind is he?"

"A Lab."

"Good, get him. We have a mastiff but she's in heat and so we have her kennelled out back."

Paul went out to the truck with Sky. Brought Conrad back on a leash. Made him sit by his feet where Sky pulled his ears. Wyatt watched.

Paul said, "You're a logger."

"I am. What people don't know about logging is the danger. When you fell a big tree there's always a chance it'll kick back and kill you. Had a friend last year whose head was crushed."

"He died?"

"Absolutely. Do you smoke?"

Paul shook his head.

"I do." Wyatt lit up and leaned forward. Said to Sky again, "I've got something in my pocket for you." He patted his hip.

Sky wiggled. Lifted his chin. "Go see," Paul urged, aware of Wyatt begging. "Go see what Wyatt has." He gave him a little push. The boy walked over. Wyatt tucked him up and tickled him. Sky gasped and giggled. Looked at Paul, eyes wild. Paul leaned forward. Waited. Wyatt put Sky beside him and reached into his pocket. Pulled out a ball of fur. Shook it out and said, "Here." It was a squirrel's tail.

"Found it today," Wyatt said. "Just lying in the bush. Some squirrel is running around out there right now without a tail. Want it?" He waved it at Sky who pulled away. Wyatt laughed and hugged Sky.

"A squirrel?" Sky asked.

"Yeah," Wyatt said.

"It's dead?"

"Oh, I don't think so. Just doesn't have a tail."

Nicole called everyone for supper then. Paul found himself sitting across from Wyatt, who opened two more bottles of beer and gave Paul one. "You want a beer, hon?" he asked Nicole.

Nicole nodded and laid out the bowl of potatoes and a salad and a plate of pork chops. She smiled at Paul and patted Sky's head as she passed. The scene appeared to please her.

Wyatt fetched another beer. Everybody sat. Nicole pushed her hair behind her ear and said, "Well, here's to Grandpa." They all drank and then Wyatt ate. Sky lifted his chin and said he wanted Shreddies.

Nicole blew up her cheeks and said, "Jesus, Sky, you're gonna just disappear."

"Ah, let him have his Shreddies," Wyatt said, and he looked at Paul and said, "Sky's got tunnel vision." He waved his fork. "Help yourself."

Paul did. Nicole came back from the kitchen with cereal in a bowl. Sky said, "Feed me."

"Ask Grandpa," Nicole said.

Paul reached over and spooned up some cereal. Milk dribbled down Sky's chin. He began to cry.

"What's wrong with you?" Nicole asked.

"He's tired," Paul said.

"You're a beekeeper, I hear," Wyatt said.

"Uh-huh."

"Ever get bit?"

"Stung," Paul corrected.

"Hey?"

"Bees sting. Dogs bite."

"He gave me the same lesson," Nicole told Wyatt. She leaned over to wipe away Sky's tears.

"*Woof*," Wyatt went. He said, "Ever get stung, then?"

"Many times."

"We lived the whole summer on the farm and never got stung," Nicole said. "Did we, Sky?"

"Why?" Sky said.

"Funny," Wyatt said, "but I'd never thought of it as a bee *farm*."

"Well, it is in a way," Paul said. "Bees cull and gather. I'm lucky, they do all the work."

Wyatt nodded. Thought a bit. Pushed his plate away and lit a cigarette. "Kinda like soft work, isn't it? Beekeeping."

Nicole looked up. Said, "Not everybody can be a logger."

Wyatt waved her away. "It just seems soft."

"It isn't," Paul said. "A super full of honey can weigh over a hundred pounds."

"Wow," Wyatt said. "You hear that, baby? A hundred pounds. I had an uncle who was a beekeeper. He was small and pale." He closed his eyes, opened them, and asked, "You like history?"

Paul waffled. Opened his mouth to speak but Wyatt jumped in ahead. "Here's some bee history. Seems around 1889 there was a pair of Cincinnati brothers, both wonderful shotgunners."

"What's a shotgunner?" Nicole wanted to know this.

"A man who shoots a shotgun at flying animals."

Nicole nodded. Tried to say more but Wyatt pursued his story. "So, the flying animals they mastered were blue-rock pigeons, blackbirds, and sparrows. All kinds of birds, but birds were too big and easy, so they had a go at bats. Then they discovered bees." Wyatt laughed and leaned towards Paul. "Bees," he said again. "Bang."

"Bang," went Sky.

"That's not history," Nicole said.

Wyatt looked at her. "Sure it is."

Her hands paused in front of her chest. She smiled.

Paul watched Nicole, who kept looking over at Wyatt as if expecting something. Sky drank the milk out of his bowl and left the Shreddies. He climbed down off his chair, took Conrad, and pattered to the living-room. Turned on the TV.

Wyatt was suddenly sated. Sleepy. "That was great," he said, and he leaned forward to take Nicole's hand. Paul could see that his hands were tanned and big. They buried Nicole's fingers. Wyatt tripped up Nicole's forearm. Down again. He had a tattoo of a wolf or a dog on his forearm.

"The thing about Sky," he said, as if this were a natural sequence to the conversation, "is Nicole doesn't know what's best for him. She thinks handing him off to his grandpa is the answer. She doesn't understand that a boy needs his mother."

"Hey," Nicole waved, "I'm over here."

Wyatt looked at her. Looked away.

Paul said, "Why are you so interested in Sky's welfare? I think it's great, no problem, I'm just curious."

"You think I'm stupid, don't you?" Wyatt said.

"Wyatt, no, no." Nicole patted his hand. Played with the hair on his arms. Paul aped Nicole, "No, no," and had a sudden and perfect image of Nicole and Wyatt having sex. Nicole yanking at the hair on his head, her long legs twining his hairy rear, Wyatt with his eyes closed, big vacant head.

Wyatt said, "You probably brought money. Pay for the kid."

Paul shook his head. Nicole got up to clear the table. "Don't be ridiculous," she said.

When she was gone Wyatt said, "She'd take the money. I love her, but she's simple. How much?"

Paul experienced a nudge of fear now, as if he had stepped into an unfamiliar place; everything had moved sideways. He shrugged, said, "The money wasn't to get Sky back. It was for Nicole."

"Of course it was. How much?"

Nicole reappeared. She'd baked gingersnaps and she passed them around. Paul declined. He could hear Sky singing along to an ad.

Wyatt said, "He'll pay three thousand for Sky." He lifted his eyebrows at Paul.

Nicole laughed and said, "Wyatt thinks he's a kidnapper." She stumbled and leaned forward to kiss Wyatt. Put her tongue in his mouth and moved it around. When she resurfaced she rubbed her forehead and said, "Sorry."

She was stoned again. It was obvious now. Paul wondered how she managed to look out for Sky, make supper, and shoot up, snort, or whatever it was she did. And when? While she was making supper?

Wyatt said, "I'd say the boy's worth at least forty thousand."

Nicole stared at her beer. Looked up at Paul finally and lifted her nose and smiled bleakly. Paul said, "I'll go now."

"Oh, don't," Wyatt cried. "We could watch some football, play cards." His voice was too high, all wrong for his bulk.

"Yes, don't go," Nicole said. "Wyatt was joking, weren't you, Wyatt?"

Wyatt said, "I have two children. They live in Helena with their mother. I hardly ever see them. Their mother tries to keep me away. As far as I'm concerned, children aren't objects that can be bought and sold or used as a form of bribery or punishment. My wife likes to punish me, you see."

"I'm not stealing Sky," Paul said.

"We're happy here," Wyatt said. "Aren't we, hon?"

Nicole inclined her head. She was fascinated by the shape of her little finger. She looked at Wyatt finally and said, "Of course."

"Listen," Wyatt said. "On Saturday we want to drive out and do some fishing. Before the river ices up. You wanna join us?"

"I don't think so," Paul said. "I want to drive back to Canada and I want to take Sky."

"Oh, my. Sweetie, did you hear that?" Wyatt asked.

Nicole nibbled at a cookie and wagged her head. Sky scampered in and sat on her lap. She smoothed his head. Her long fingers pulled at the little obstinate knot of hair near his crown. She sang, "There was an old lady, who swallowed a fly." Then she paused and said, "I want to go to Las Vegas and be famous. I'm not gonna get famous here in Great Falls, Wyatt. And if I go to Las Vegas, the best place for my little one is with his grandpa. And when I'm famous, I'll get him back."

"You'll never be famous, Nicole," Wyatt said. "Don't you get it? Long legs and a lovely pussy don't mean much. You gotta be smart."

"I'm smart."

"Oh, Christ," Wyatt said. He spun an empty beer bottle on the table. It stopped, pointing at Nicole.

"Gimme a kiss," he said, nodding at the bottle.

Nicole sang, "I don't know why she swallowed a fly, perhaps she'll die." She stopped.

Paul held his breath as if waiting for the next line but there was no more. Nicole had suddenly huddled into herself. Worried now about who would care for Sky, Paul stayed on into the evening and helped bathe him. Later, when Nicole was more focused and was putting her boy to bed, Wyatt brooded and lost the edge he showed at supper. He took Paul into a small back room of the house and showed him his gun and knife collection. Paul, who didn't know anything about guns, was nevertheless impressed by the size of the collection. Wyatt let him hold an ancient Remington.

"It's from the 1870s, 'bout the time of Crazy Horse. My

mother's grandfather was the half-brother to Nellie Larrabee, Crazy Horse's second wife. So, I've got some Indian blood in me. I'd show you a picture of Crazy Horse but the amazing thing is no one has a sketch, painting, or photograph of the man. Just word of mouth." Wyatt shook his head. This room had had an effect on him. It was like a shrine. He said, "When I die, I want to lie out on the earth like Crazy Horse did. Nobody owned the man. You understand?"

Paul handed him back the gun. The smell of oil and metal. Wyatt cradled it back into its nest. Picked up a thin-bladed knife with a steel handle. "A fleam," he said. "Used to bleed horses. You like horses?" Then, not waiting for an answer, he confided, "I'm not a bad man. Nicole and Sky dropped into my life one day. I was lucky. Take them away and I'd be lost. I bet *you're* lost without them."

Paul looked away.

Wyatt said, "It's a good thing, to be loved."

"She'll leave you," Paul said. "She leaves everybody."

Wyatt shrugged. Said, "Maybe. Maybe not. She leaves, I'll follow her."

"Think of Sky, running around this country. He'd be better on the farm. With me."

Wyatt shook his head. "We're a package. Take away Sky and we'll fall apart." He motioned at the door and they stepped out into the hallway and walked back into the living-room where Nicole sat, watching TV. The three of them played cards then around the coffee table. Wyatt drank whisky, Paul had coffee, Nicole wine. Wyatt said at one point, not really addressing anyone, "Why is it that everybody wants to be famous? Especially the young?"

"Look around you," Nicole said, her hands launching, gathering in the room and its occupants. Her eyes were slow, pupils too big. She was still stoned.

"She doesn't want to be like you and me," Wyatt said to Paul, and with this he fell into a silence that lasted until Paul left, Nicole walking him out to the truck, moving her hands through her hair, saying,

"Oh, my," and then holding Paul's hand. There was an icy wind blowing off the river and Nicole leaned close to the truck while Paul started it. He said through the open window, "Wyatt's scary."

"That's just the drinking. He's really a puppy."

"He won't let Sky go."

"He will, it's just he's lost his own two." She bent through the window and kissed his cheek. "You're sweet."

"Think so?" Paul felt a pull near his stomach, shook it away.

Nicole's head was back outside. She nodded and pushed her chin down onto her chest.

"He's mad," Paul said. "He's got this shrine of guns and knives."

"And he thinks he's Crazy Horse," Nicole added.

"Right, see, he's mad."

"Actually, I find it quite precious," Nicole said. She clutched herself. "He gets jealous. When you're not around he's terribly nice."

"Why don't you just leave? Go on your own? Fly out of here?"

Nicole looked back over her shoulder. Faced Paul again and whispered, "He'd go crazy. He needs me."

"You love him?"

Nicole laughed and tossed her head in a loop. Said, "He asks me the same thing every day. What is it with you guys?" She ruffled Paul's head. Enjoyed his embarrassment. Kissed him again and said, "I'll call you tomorrow after he's gone to work." She backed off and ran, light-footed, to the house. Paul watched her, and thought of Wyatt sitting there waiting for her, his big thighs, his rough palms, the heavy whiskers making her lips raw. He started the truck and rolled away, turning on the lights when he reached the main road.

He phoned Lise that night. Her voice fell into him as if she were lying beside him and whispering in his ear.

"Were you sleeping?" he asked.

"I don't think so, though I was watching TV and I don't remember the news ending. What time is it?"

"Ten-thirty here. You're an hour ahead."

"Did you find Sky?" she asked.

"Yes, and Nicole."

"So?"

"Well, it won't be easy. Wyatt's an obstacle."

"Wyatt?"

"Nicole's new man. Bit of a thug, though she says he's sweet."

"She doesn't waste any time."

"He's a logger. He could crush me."

"What, you having a duel?" Lise laughed. A bubble burst in Paul's chest. He thought that everything was fine. No worries.

He joked, "Wyatt fancies himself an outlaw. Frontier mentality. He keeps telling me he's not stupid."

"I thought Nicole asked you to come get Sky."

"She did. Now she's torn 'cause Wyatt wants Sky."

"What a mess."

"How's Sue?" Paul asked.

"Good. I just talked to her. She's liking school."

"Good for her," Paul said. He enjoyed the idea of his daughter grasping at knowledge he himself abandoned so long ago for televisions, stereos, and sectional couches.

"I dreamed about you last night," Lise said. "We were birds."

"What kind of birds?"

"Small ones. Common sparrows, something like that."

"I dreamed about us, too," Paul said. "We lived, the four of us, by a river. We were settlers."

"Stephen, too?"

"Yes, only as usual, I couldn't see his face."

"That was nice," Lise said, "the other night, you making me supper, feeding me."

"I'd do it again," Paul said, though that final sense of pity still sat inside him. He gathered she never noticed, or was just happy to have someone after losing Harry.

She said, "I cleaned your house yesterday. I figured you could use the help."

"You did?" Paul suffered a touch of panic. Stifled it and asked, "The whole house?"

"Everything. The kitchen, especially, needed work."

Paul could see the eye, staring down at him. Brief panic. He asked, "That blue bowl, up high?"

"Oh, yes," she said. "Little bits of plastic, like a rat had been making a nest. I threw that out. It wasn't important, was it?"

"No," he lied. He could taste his own desperation.

She said, "I was thinking about us. I was thinking that we still have habits. We know how to live together."

"Do we?"

"It's hard to erase twenty years."

"You don't want to live with me again."

"Maybe," Lise said. She didn't want to beg, he could tell, and his awareness of this made him falter.

"All I want," he said, "is to forget." He was conscious, as he said this, of how innocently she was helping him forget, scrubbing his house, tossing out the contents of the bowl. "In any case," he added, "I plan to return with Sky."

"And then she shows up and takes him back. And you chase after him. And around you go. The poor boy."

The familiar churlishness. Paul welcomed it. A safety there.

She asked, "Are you running?"

"I don't know," Paul said. "This is a great place to run to."

"You're serious?"

"It is. There's all this room and most people are happy here. Except for Wyatt."

"You know what I liked best the other night?"

"What?"

"Doing it on the couch."

This sounded so juvenile, coming from Lise, that Paul had to smile. To keep her happy, he agreed, and later, hanging up, he thought of being sandwiched between Lise and Nicole, one alive and whole, the other mere remnants, tailings of memories.

He slept poorly and woke before dawn and went to the hotel

restaurant for coffee. He sat and watched a man in a suit talk to a woman in a blue dress. By eight he was restless and went up to his room and phoned Nicole. Wyatt answered. Paul hung up. He looked out his window a bit and then walked down to his half-ton and drove over to Wyatt's house. It was quiet, though Wyatt's car and both motorcycles were in the driveway.

Paul waited, then started up the truck, and drove to a payphone. This time he got Nicole. She said, "Paul?" and then she disappeared and was replaced by Wyatt. He was drunk. He said, "Hiya, Paul, how are you?"

Paul didn't answer. He could hear Nicole talking behind Wyatt's head. Paul asked, "Is Nicole okay?"

"Of course, she's okay, Paul. Why wouldn't she be okay? I'm looking at her right now. She's got two arms, a head, legs. She's talking, can you hear her talking?" His voice disappeared.

Nicole said, "Stop it."

"Wyatt? Wyatt?" Paul called.

He came back. "Yes, Paul."

"Where's Sky? Is he okay?"

"He's quite happy," Wyatt said. "Very happy. Ate breakfast. Brushed his teeth. Such beautiful teeth. Perfectly white. I helped him brush. Up and down."

"Wyatt," Paul said, "I'm not going to take him. If you and Nicole want him, you can keep him. I want Sky to be happy."

"He is happy. Very happy. Where are you now, Paul?"

"At a restaurant."

"That's not true. I can hear the traffic."

"I'm phoning from outside the restaurant."

"Uh-huh. You know what I'm scared of? I'm scared you'll come and take Sky. That's why I didn't go to work. And tomorrow, I'll take Sky to a friend's house. Keep him safe."

"What do you want?" Paul asked.

Wyatt smothered the phone, said something to Nicole, came back.

"Don't hurt him, okay, Wyatt?"

Wyatt's voice went sad. "I wouldn't hurt him, Paul."

"Good. Do you want something? Money?"

"You're a real rich fuck, aren't you, Mr. Unger? Think money'll save you. Christ, it didn't save your son, did it?"

There was a pain at the top of Paul's head. He whispered, "What do you know about my son?"

"Nicole told me. He died. He was drunk and he died."

Paul groaned, began to hang up and then came back to the phone. He opened his mouth, closed it, and finally laid down the receiver. His hands were cold. His knees and feet were cold. A wind blew up under the spaces in the phone booth. Paul sat in his truck. He wondered if he should buy a gun. He had seen a gun shop at the north end of town. He pondered this and then thought the best thing to do was wait. He drove to a tourist information centre and talked to a woman in a red suit who gave him maps and brochures and told him about the parks and about Custer County and while she talked Paul wondered if she had children. She was wearing a ring so she could have been married and Paul figured that meant she might have children. He wondered how many and, as he wondered, he said, "How many children do you have?"

The woman in red looked up, tipped her head, and said, "Three."

Paul agreed. He said, "I have one child and one grandson. The grandson's living in Great Falls."

"That's nice. So, you're here on holidays." The woman asked, "How old is your grandson?"

"Three next month."

"Well, you should take him to the fish hatchery. He'd like that."

"I might," Paul said.

He left the tourist information and went to the C. M. Russell Museum where he looked at watercolours, sculptures, and oil paintings. He stood in front of one painting which depicted cowboys and Indians at battle. The effect was peaceful, serene. A sense of distance. The violence seemed safe. Standing before another painting of a warrior on horseback looking out over the plains, Paul's hands began to shake. He found the washroom and washed his face, drank from the tap. His hands calmed down but there was a fear now that wouldn't go away. He dried himself, looked in the mirror, and said, "What are you doing?" He wandered around the museum and then stepped outside into the wind. Snow blew across the sidewalk.

He ate Chinese food at a buffet. Two State Troopers sat next to him. He formulated possible questions, and at one point almost leaned over to speak, but the troopers stood up, brushed off their uniforms, put on their hats, and left. Weak tea and a fortune cookie completed the meal. His cookie had no fortune. The sugar pastry melted in his mouth. He was still afraid.

Around dusk Paul drove towards Wyatt's house, parked at a distance, and watched the lights through the wet windshield. He turned on the wipers once in a while to clear his vision. Orange glowed from the kitchen, a shadow passed back and forth. It looked like Nicole. Paul sat until the lights went out, then he sat some more. The cold from the outside entered the truck, his legs ached, his wrists were cold. He returned, emptied of hope, to the hotel. He went to bed, slept surprisingly well, and woke to a world buried by snow, icicles hanging from the eaves of nearby houses and the TV calling for more snow by noon. He showered and dressed.

After breakfast he left Conrad at the hotel and drove out to the gun shop. It was located off the highway in a white bungalow. The owner was a small man with glasses and a ponytail and a belt with a big rodeo buckle. He seemed too young to own all these rifles and pistols and ammunition. There were duck decoys hanging from strings and the head of a deer was installed over the doorway. Paul was the lone customer. The owner said, "How do you like the snow?"

"I like it," Paul said.

He was standing by the counter looking down through the glass onto an array of pistols and what he assumed were miniature machine guns. Black metal and dark stocks.

Paul said, "I'd like a gun."

"Okay, this is the place."

"A small gun, nothing too big."

"A handgun?"

"Yes, I guess."

The owner opened the glass case and pulled out three pistols of varying size. He handed Paul the smallest one. "Half a pound of butter," the man said. "Here." He tipped up the barrel. "Single action, eight shot."

"That's fine," Paul said. "I'll take it."

"I'll need your identification, you'll get checked out, and then in a few days you can pick it up."

Paul shook his head. "I need it today."

The man tilted his head. "Can't do that." He studied Paul's chin, ran down his chest, then back up to his eyes. "There's a three-day space. I call it the suicide wait. So you don't walk out of here and kill yourself. Or someone else. Gives you time to think about it."

"If I wanted to kill myself, I'd find another way," Paul said. "And as far as that goes, do I look like a killer?"

The owner lifted his eyebrows. He had blue-brown eyes. Like stones at the bottom of a mountain river. "No, you don't."

"So?"

Shake of the head. He leaned forward. Confided, "I've got a friend who's got something just like this. Private. Only it'll cost."

Paul looked around, the sense of espionage deepening. Fool, he thought. Then he nodded and said, "Okay."

He drove to the address given and discovered a woman, about his age, who had him wait in her living-room where a cat slept on a rose-coloured cushion. She returned and said, "Walter called ahead." She was holding a replica of the gun Paul wanted at the shop. She handed it to him and said, "Beretta." She sat and patted the cat. Said, "This is Charlie. He killed a rat today. Didn't you, puss?" She stood and offered the same demonstration Walter gave. Then she sold him a box of ammunition, took his money, and saw him to the door.

The gun sat in Paul's jacket pocket. He could feel its weight, the presence of something important. He drove out of town and detoured onto a gravel road which led to a dirt lane where he stopped, got out, and walked through a ditch out onto a field. He was wearing runners and the new snow stuck to his socks and began to melt around his ankles. He shivered, took out the gun, released the safety, aimed at a lump of dirt the size of Conrad's head, and fired. A heartbeat in his hand, a whine through the air. He had no idea where the bullet went. "Huh," he said. He aimed and fired again. This time he saw the earth move near the lump. Again. He hit the lump. It fell apart. "Okay," he said. He looked around. Wondered if anyone had heard the shots. There was nothing, no buildings, no cars, no animals. Just the earth and the sky and Paul Unger and his little gun. He reloaded, thumbed the safety catch, put the gun in his jacket pocket, and walked back to the truck.

He started the engine and drove back to the hotel. He asked for messages. There were none. He took the elevator to his room, where he shed his jacket and sat in a chair. He wondered how his gun compared to Harry's. What Lise would think. He'd had a thought during the night, something about hypocrisy and Harry, but it was unimportant now. He picked up the phone and dialled Wyatt's number. Nicole answered.

"Where've you been?" she asked. She sounded worried, breathless. This pleased Paul.

"Out," he said. Then, thinking there was some advantage to her knowing, he added, "I bought a gun."

"Shit, Paul, what for? Wyatt's not dangerous."

"He isn't? The Wyatt I met is."

"He *collects* guns, he doesn't use them."

"Uh-huh."

"I've been talking to him, making sense, and he's leaning my way. And now you want to walk in here with a gun like this was a movie or something. What's happened to you?"

Paul considered this question. He said, "Sky still there?"

"Yes, right here? You want to talk to him?"

"Okay."

The boy came on. Breathed into the phone. Paul imagined him staring past the receiver as if looking down a well for his grandpa.

"Sky?" he said. "This is your grandpa."

"Hi, Grandpa." His voice was thin and far away.

"What are you doing?"

"Baking cookies."

"That's good. What kind?"

"Peanut butter."

"I like peanut butter."

"Me, too."

"Good. Are you having fun?"

"Will you come visit, Grandpa?"

"Sure. Sure, I will." Paul wondered if it was better to shoot someone in the heart or the head. The head would be messy.

The phone was fumbled and Nicole came back on. "Throw that thing away," she said. "You won't need it."

"I hope not," Paul said. "Where's Wyatt?"

"He's walking the dog. I promised you wouldn't take Sky."

Paul's mouth was dry. He swallowed, shook his head. "Why?"

"He's reasonable. I'll convince him yet."

"Can I come over?"

"No, don't. If he finds you here, he'll think we're planning something."

"I won't lose him."

There was a sudden coldness in Nicole's voice. "Sky's not yours to lose."

Paul said, "You shouldn't have told him about Stephen."

"You're right. But, I did."

"And then he throws it back at me."

"He was upset."

"And so am I."

"I know you are. I know." These words were an ointment. Nicole was softer now, he could tell. She was holding Sky, who was jabbering about the cookies. Paul saw them, twinned, their backs to the window, crouching now to gape at the burnt cookies. He could hear the creak of the stove door.

"Don't be like Wyatt," she said. "I don't think I could stand it."

Paul nodded at the phone and said, "Were you smoking some-thing the other day?"

Nicole sighed. Said, "I was sucking on the tiniest bit of acid. Gary gave it to me. Wyatt hates that shit, but it was a lousy day, and there it was, a pick-me-up."

Paul remembered the lumpy potatoes, Nicole singing about spiders and horses, Crazy Horse, the smell of Sky's head, and the winding down of the evening into cards and a despondent Wyatt eventually retiring verbally, and Nicole singing on, pretty butter-flies in her head, he supposed now.

"What does it feel like?" he asked.

She laughed. "You wanna try. I'll get you some. We could do it together 'cause it's quite nice. Everything stops, like walking on one of those exercise machines, except more fun, less work. No worries. Sometimes the top of your head opens up."

"Neat," he said, mimicking a voice she offered him long ago: a mockery. Only he was partly serious.

"Better than a gun," she said.

"So, Wyatt hates it?"

"He's like you that way. Kinda moral."

"I'm moral?"

"Sure, you are. That's good. I like that."

Sky squawked. Nicole said, "I'll call you. I will." She disappeared and Paul sat in his chair, looking out the glass doors at the dull sky.

He went anyway. Believed that not acting was the worst sin. He stashed his gun in his jacket pocket and drove over to Wyatt's house. With Conrad on a short leash he approached the front door. Before he could knock, Wyatt's mastiff came around the corner, headed straight for Conrad, knocked him over, and grabbed his throat. Conrad howled and scrabbled at the deck floor, seeking footing. Paul was pulled forward and snapped over against the doorway. The screen ripped. Wyatt came around the corner of the house, at a run, large stick in hand, and brought it down on his dog's head. "Suzy.

Bitch," he yelled. Suzy was unfazed. She had a death-hold on Conrad and wouldn't abandon it. Paul fumbled in his pocket for the half-pound of butter. He had it, then it squirted away. His arm hurt where he hit the door. Wyatt bellowed and planted one of his big boots under Suzy's jaw. A crack and she let go. Wyatt grabbed her collar, noosed her skywards, and hauled her off back around the house, her rear legs pumping. Paul knelt beside Conrad, who tried to stand but fell over.

"Okay," Paul said. Conrad whimpered. Paul picked him up and carried him to the truck, laid him in the box. He could hear Nicole calling. She was standing by the house, holding Sky. Paul walked back to them.

"What are you *doing* here?" Nicole asked.

Sky was rubbing his eyes and yawning. He'd just woken up. Wyatt came back around the house, his big boots sliding in the mud. He said, "Where is he?"

Paul nodded back at the truck. Followed Wyatt and they stood by the box and looked down at Conrad, who lifted his head and licked himself.

"His leg's broken," Wyatt said. "You'll have to take him to the vet. Here." He pulled out a card and handed it to Paul. Paul released the gun in his pocket and took the card. Looked up into Wyatt's face, the flat forehead. Right there.

"Suzy hates other dogs," Wyatt said. He touched Conrad's head. Conrad growled and wagged his tail. His breathing was sloppy, loose and ragged, the wind was coming out the hole in his throat.

Paul went then, drove over to the veterinarian whose office was attached to a flat-roofed bungalow in a residential area. The vet came out to the truck and inspected Conrad. He said, "You should put him to sleep. Best thing." Paul shook his head. Then he watched while the vet carried him inside and sewed up Conrad's throat and reset his leg. Put on a splint. He talked to Conrad while he worked, let him know what he was doing.

"He should be dead," the vet said. He was an older man who breathed through his mouth as he worked. He said that Conrad couldn't be moved, the wound to the throat was deep, went right into the windpipe.

Paul said, "I have to take him. I'm going back to Canada."

Paul was given tiny white pills that the vet said should be crushed and added to Conrad's water. Then he injected Conrad with painkiller and said, "Make him drink. He'll refuse because swallowing will hurt. If we kept him here we'd put him on an IV."

Paul paid and carried Conrad back to the truck, putting him on the seat in the cab. They drove back to the motel where he placed Conrad in the corner of his room, covering him with a blanket. It was dusk, the evening news was on TV. Paul watched, ordered room service, and talked to Conrad. Patted his head and touched his nose. It was hot and dry. He tried to get him to drink from a cup but Conrad turned away. Paul pried his mouth open and poured water in. Conrad choked and tried to bite. "Okay," Paul said. He crushed one of the pills and attempted to lay it on Conrad's tongue. "Here," he said. Conrad refused, turned his head away.

Later, Paul phoned Nicole. No answer. He went to bed early. The rattle of Conrad's breathing made him uneasy. Just before dawn he woke and he could hear Conrad sucking for air. He got up, turned on the light, and found Conrad lying as he had been the night before. His throat bubbled as he breathed. Blood had seeped from the wound onto the rug. Paul poured water into the slit of the mouth. It missed and mixed with the blood. Conrad's eyes were shut.

"Not good, eh?" Paul said.

He sat and watched Conrad breathe, then went back to sleep. He woke up to the phone ringing. It was late in the morning and the boy at the front desk announced that a Nicole Forêt was coming up. Paul dressed, opened the door, and waited. Looked down the hall towards the elevator. When Nicole appeared she had Sky in tow and was carrying a small duffel bag. The three of them entered the room and sat on the beds.

Nicole was out of breath. Her cheeks were red from the wind.

She looked around and said, "Nice." Noticed Conrad in the corner. Said, "How is he?"

"Not good."

"Suzy's a mean dog," she said.

Sky sat on Paul's lap, said, "Mean dog," and then got up to jump from one bed to the next.

"Don't," Paul said. "You'll fall."

Sky kept jumping.

Nicole said, "Sky's going with you."

"Why?" Paul asked. He thought he would remember, forever, the pink dots of her cheeks, and the brightness of her eyes, and her chapped lips as she leaned forward to give him this news. She seemed unaware of his question. He said, "What about Wyatt?"

"I figured he loved me more than Sky. And I was right."

"And you'll stay?"

"Yes," she said, so easily that Paul had to look away, at his hands, at Sky still jumping on the bed.

"Stop it," he said.

"Hey." Nicole took his hand. "You okay?"

Paul nodded.

"You got what you wanted." She hugged him then and Paul registered three things: her hair was dirty, she smelled of a nutty oil, and she was too thin. He let her go. She went to Sky. "Come," she said. They hugged. She whispered in his ear. Kissed his forehead. At the door Paul handed her the four thousand dollars. Took it out of his back pocket, felt his own body's warmth on the envelope, and put it in her hand. She went up and pecked his jaw, just below his ear. "Thanks."

Her head dipped and she almost smiled. Then she was gone, forgoing the elevator for the stairway. The clank of the metal door, her steps descending, the room silent now save the whish whish of Sky still jumping.

"See?" the child cried, behind Paul's back, and Paul turned and found Sky in mid-air, mouth open, and, yes, he saw.

They drove south and east along the 87 and then directly into the sun along the Number 3 to Billings where they stopped for a late lunch. Sky ate oatmeal and toast. Paul ordered coffee and a sandwich. French fries. Sky drank his milk and said, "Where's Nicole?"

"With Wyatt, back in Great Falls."

"Great Falls?"

"That's right."

"Why though?"

Paul leaned over and kissed the boy's head. They'd talked about this all the way down, like a circle to walk around, Paul explaining that Nicole was going to look for work and would come and get him soon, but for now he'd live with his grandpa. Sky was not frightened by the idea of this, but he kept turning his head to look behind him.

"Why?" he repeated.

Paul stroked the boy's neck. He giggled.

"Tickle me," he said.

Paul did. Sky's mouth dropped open. He whooped.

"Shhh," Paul said.

"Again."

"Don't spill your milk."

"I want ice cream."

"Finish your toast."

Sky refused. Paul ordered ice cream. Mixed it into a creamy froth for Sky. The child ate slowly, his tongue went in and out. He said, "Conrad likes ice cream."

"Yes, but Conrad's sick."

Sky was disturbed by the lump of Conrad on the floor of the truck. His rattle filled the cab, flooded upwards, and unsettled the boy. Still, Paul believed Conrad would be fine. The bleeding had stopped, he had swallowed some water and crushed pill, and just an hour ago he had recognized Paul and licked his hand.

After lunch, against all common sense, Paul took the I-90 south to the Little Bighorn Battlefield. Sky went willingly. Slept sitting up, fell over and hit his head on the door, woke up and cried, then fell asleep again. Paul woke him when they arrived. Paul got a brochure and talked to a ranger who said that the fight between Custer and the Indians lasted only an hour. "Isn't that amazing?" the ranger said.

Paul studied the brochure and the map. Then he and Sky drove out to the spot where Custer and two hundred and sixty-five of his men were killed. Sky wanted to stay in the truck. Paul got out and stood by the stone memorial. He walked out and studied the white markers that honoured Custer and his men. Nothing for the Indians. From here, looking out, he could imagine them swooping down, the earth moving, the sun above all those heads. Up on the bare ridge a thin layer of snow covered the ground. He was alone. The sun was weak. History came and went. Paul felt something but he wasn't sure what it was or where it was coming from. He looked back at the truck. Sky was leaning into the dash, his forehead pushed against the windshield and for a moment Paul thought he was Nicole, dark hollowed eyes.

He walked back to the truck and said to Sky, "Time is a tricky thing."

"Tricky?"

"Yeah. Goes like that," and he opened his hand and closed it.

Sky imitated him. Said, "We'll go now?"

"Sure," Paul said.

"Nicole?"

"Soon. Soon."

He drove back to the information centre, regained the highway, went north to the I-94, and they fled, the three of them, east, into the dusk towards Miles City. Paul kept checking his rearview mirror, imagining the snout of Wyatt's Explorer suddenly appearing out of the mist. A senseless fear, really, because if Wyatt did give chase, it would be north through Fort Benton.

The road was a dark strip against the newly fallen snow. Tractor-trailers passed and with each gale Sky mewed and went, "One truck, two truck, three truck, four," and Paul was lulled by the warmth of the truck and the rhythm of Sky's chant. The horn of a tractor-trailer woke Paul as the half-ton's wheel slipped off the edge of the shoulder and the running lights of a black rig slid by, heading east like them.

Paul slowed down. Opened the window. Fear and adrenalin and the wind made him shiver. Afraid of his own fatigue he watched the afternoon slide into dusk, the light disappearing like water being sucked out of a cup.

Someday, a hundred years from then, the light would disappear in that same way. And then the next day it would come back and fill up the sky, and the wind would blow from the north and cover the plains with a fine dust that was in turn blown from the west, and a boy or a man or a woman, or all three, would cross that place and fall away into the earth.

Nicole had said she would write and Paul imagined her sending postcards from points across the United States, little towns like Great Falls that she and Wyatt travelled through, never quite making it to Las Vegas, afraid of actually arriving, finding it easier to pick up odd jobs here and there, looking ahead to that time when she would be a Rockette and he would be her manager, or a bouncer, or a drunk sitting by the poolside waiting for her to come home.

Paul stopped in a place called Terry and they ate supper in a restaurant attached to a service station. Sky had oatmeal again. Was sad about Nicole. Paul talked to him and had soup and coffee. They took a motel room at the edge of town. Conrad was laid out on the floor and Paul slept in the same bed as Sky, both fully clothed, as if they were on the run.

Towards morning, Paul woke, shivering from fear. Conrad was doing badly. His eyes were full of fever, his breathing was quicker and lighter, at times inaudible. He refused water. Paul understood now that Conrad could not last another day. He stood by the window and looked out onto the shiny asphalt parking lot. What had been puddles were now ice as a north wind had brought frost, the final settling in of winter. Paul expected to see Wyatt's Explorer in the lot. It wasn't. Still, Paul picked up Sky, laid him down on the front seat of the half-ton, placed Conrad on the floor, and drove over to the motel entrance. He woke up the owner who cursed and grumbled but in the end thanked him for not running off. Paul climbed back in the truck and picked up the Interstate towards Glendive. Conrad laboured. Sky slept.

At the edge of Montana, as the light began to fold back the night, he exited the highway and found a back road that led beside stubble fields. He stopped the half-ton, got out, retrieved a spade from the box, gathered up Conrad, and dipped through the ditch and out into the field where he laid Conrad down and dug into the clay and mud. He went down three feet, deeper than any harrow, plough, or disker.

He took out the gun from his pocket. He touched Conrad's nose. His eyes. Conrad looked up at him. "Poor boy," Paul said. He slid back the bolt, held the snout to Conrad's head, and pulled the trigger. The sound of the shot fell upwards and sideways. Conrad bled from a small opening just behind his ear. Paul picked up the body and put it in the hole. Then he laid the gun and ammunition in beside the dog, shovelled the mud back into place, went back to the truck, scraped off his shoes, put the spade back in the box, and climbed back into the half-ton.

Sky was awake. He was crying, his head buried into Paul's jacket. His face came up wet. Went down again.

"Here I am," Paul said. "Come on." And he held Sky, who shuddered and sucked for air.

"There, there."

"You were gone," the child said.

"I'm sorry."

"Why?"

"I had to go out in the field."

"Why?"

Paul veered away. "You were sleeping."

Sky stopped crying. Said, "It's morning time?"

"It is."

"I'm hungry."

Paul handed him a package of crackers. His little fingers worked the cellophane. Paul regained the I-94, stuck to the slow lane. He opened his window slightly. The air was warm. He was light-hearted. He touched Sky's head. His hot little nape. Sky looked up, cracker crumbs on his lips. He had still not registered Conrad's absence. High in the sky, beyond the windshield of the truck, they saw, simultaneously, a bird circling. A hawk, perhaps.

Sky's head was like his mother's, the same shape, only more deli-cate, a thinner skull, but the truth lay in the crown, the falling back in towards the neck, the last bit of down and the first precious vertebrae. Skull of a rat, a horse, a dog. Washed up on the plains. He hoped that Nicole would be safe. That she would flee Wyatt. Sky rested his chin on the dash and sang a nonsense tune. His ears were red. There was much to consider: things dead, prayers said long ago, the durability of love, the perfection of Sky's wrists there, the bumps, bone of his bone.

All that day Paul sensed that he was being followed. It wasn't possible, but he thought it was. A black dot appeared in his rearview mirror, then it disappeared and reappeared fifteen minutes later. He slowed down, even pulled over to wait for the dot to get bigger, but it never did. Other vehicles passed but not the black dot. In Bismarck, Paul bought some bread and ham and apples and juice at a convenience store. The half-ton idled outside; Sky was curled up in his seat. When Paul had told him that Conrad died during the night, Sky cried for an hour, calling out, "Grandpa, Grandpa," over and over until he fell asleep. He was still stunned. Paul paid and watched the traffic pass by on the road. He'd expected to be closer to the Canadian border by now. It was mid-afternoon and a good five hours to go. Back on the road, still unsettled, he decided to leave the I-94 and head cross-country towards the Number 2 which would take him into Grand Forks and up to Emerson.

Paul was tired. His head kept dropping sideways and hitting the window and he was startled once to find the half-ton on the wrong side of the road. He finally pulled onto a smaller road, drove a little and stopped on the shoulder. Darkness was coming. Sky slept. The truck idled. It was snowing. Paul fell asleep.

He woke as his door was pulled open and he fell out of the cab onto the pavement. He banged the back of his head and his left elbow. Wyatt stood over him.

"Hiya," Wyatt said. He looked into the cab and then shut the door. "Let the boy sleep."

Paul got up on his knees. Put his hand in his jacket pocket and rued the buried gun.

"Where's Conrad?" Wyatt asked.

"Dead."

"That's too bad. I like dogs."

Paul stood, leaned against the truck, touched the back of his head. He was bleeding. "What do you want?" he asked.

"Sky."

"You can't have him. Nicole brought him to me. It's what she wanted."

"Nicole doesn't know what she wants. Right after you left she sent me after you. Changed her mind." Wyatt snapped his long fingers. "Like that." A single car passed, illuminating the side of Wyatt's face, and then moved on, its taillights eventually disappearing. Wyatt's Explorer idled behind Paul's half-ton.

Paul imagined Nicole prancing into Wyatt's kitchen, the four grand folded into her pocket and pressed up against her little bum, calling out like a bird for Wyatt to run after him. His heart was empty. "What are you going to do?" he asked.

"With you? I'm considering that. I'm not mad. You think I'm crazed or something. I'm not."

"I know you're not. Take Sky. I won't follow you. I won't come back to Great Falls."

Wyatt surveyed the road, looked over the fields, down at his feet, and back at Paul. "I've gotta make sure. You're a nuisance." Then he said, "He's not your blood, you know. She was fleecing you all along."

"You're a liar."

Wyatt shrugged. Said, "You drive, I'll ride along."

"I don't think so," Paul said. He was scared. Thought it best not to get in the truck.

Wyatt pulled out a knife. It was that thin fleam which he had held up two days ago in his gun room. "I could walk you out into that field and cut your Achilles tendon so you'd flop around like a fish and bleed to death, or we could do it different. Here's the plan. We'll drive out to some field, drop you off, and you can walk back to your pick-up. That way you'll have time to think and I'll have a leisurely drive back home."

"You won't hurt me? I don't want Sky to witness that."

Wyatt applauded. Said, "My, you're thoughtful." Then he told Paul to pick up Sky and join him in the Explorer. He circled the front of Paul's half-ton, opened the far door, shifted the sleeping Sky, and waved at Paul. "Carry him over. You'll drive."

Sky woke, sat up, looked at Wyatt, and began to cry. Paul pulled him in close and went, "Shhh, shhh."

"Hey, Sky," Wyatt said. "It's me, Uncle Wyatt."

Sky cried on as he was moved. He ended up with his head on Paul's lap, dragging air through his nose, his feet falling down into the space between the bucket seats of Wyatt's truck. It began to snow, flurries that dipped past the headlights. Paul imagined himself as weightless. His head ached. He did as Wyatt said and drove north. They passed the light of a farmhouse, a distant beacon. Several miles further on Wyatt waved at a small side road and Paul turned off. The Explorer's wheels followed the ruts. The mud was slick.

"I'll get stuck," Paul said.

Sky lifted his head as if that were something to consider and then fell back into Paul's lap. He whimpered. Wyatt grunted. Paul could see the blade of the lancet pressing against Wyatt's wrist. What scared him was not the knife but the prospect of being left out in the field, of dying out there and not being found till spring. He drove slowly, kept track of the odometer. Wyatt's truck smelled new. The leather upholstery reminded Paul of Lise and, oddly, he thought of her now, sliding into her low-slung car, a sleek foot into a red shoe.

Or Mrs. Wish riding beside her husband in their white BMW. Paul remembered holding Mrs. Wish in his kitchen, the outline of her bra strap beneath his fingers, like the relief map he would trace as a child, a river leading him down the mountains to some safe harbour.

Wyatt said, "The thing is about a girl like Nicole, you have to believe in her."

Paul looked over at Wyatt. "What do you mean?"

Wyatt didn't listen to the question. He said, "She's great in bed. Greedy." He looked across Sky's head at Paul. "You jealous?"

"No, why?"

"Thought you might."

"She's the mother of my grandson."

"You ever fuck her?"

"Jesus, Wyatt, the boy's listening."

"Did you?"

Paul didn't answer. Watched the narrow trail and fought the ruts. Listened to Wyatt breathe through his mouth.

"I could tell that first night, when you came for supper," Wyatt said. "You were jealous."

"Was I?" Paul wondered how Wyatt knew this. What gesture or words of Paul's had given that message. He himself had been unaware, or at least thought others were unaware. Nicole was complex and puzzling; if there was jealousy, it had to do with men like Wyatt and Daniel and Romel not deserving her. He said now, "She should have better."

"We pick and choose," Wyatt said. "Get what we deserve."

"Not always."

"No?" Wyatt seemed surprised. "When's that then?"

"Not everything's earned. For instance, you dropping me off in the middle of nowhere."

"Meddling. That's not earned?"

"She called me. Said, 'Come get him.'"

"She's fickle." Wyatt sighed. Asked, "How much money did you give her?"

"I couldn't say."

"She claimed it was two thousand. That's a paltry sum for some-one you love."

"Well, no matter. It's hers."

"Actually she said four." Wyatt laughed. "Or was it six. Do you think she's lying?" Then, not waiting for an answer, he said, "Here, stop here."

Paul stopped. Looked out his window at the snow. The dark. The headlights made a tunnel.

"Explain to him," Wyatt said, nodding at Sky. "Make him believe."

Paul touched Sky's temple. Said, "Hey." Sky's eyes were open. He was staring past Paul's knees at the dark space under the dash.

"You know what?" Paul said. "You're gonna go back and see Nicole. She sent Wyatt to come get you. Grandpa's gonna go in his own truck. He'll see you at Wyatt's house later. Okay?"

Sky was thinking. Knew something was wrong. He blinked. Said, "Nicole?"

"Yes, Wyatt will take you."

"No, you, Grandpa."

"Wyatt's truck is warm and big. Safe. Here, I've got a chocolate bar for you." Paul rummaged through a jacket pocket and came up with an old bar from the trip out to Montana. Handed it to Sky, who took and held it. Wyatt climbed out. Passed in front of the head-lights. A ghost. Paul put Sky in the passenger seat, drew the seat belt around him. "There. You be good." Kissed the top of his head.

Sky nodded. He ripped at the bar wrapper and smelled the chocolate. Took a lick. A bite. Filled his mouth. "Bye," Paul said. Sky nodded. Looked at him and then back at the chocolate bar.

Paul opened his door and climbed out into the wind and snow. Wyatt, who was standing beside him now, said, "Here," and handed him a hat and gloves. "I'd give you boots but mine are too big."

Paul looked down at his own feet. Thin runners, thin socks. He pulled on the hat and gloves. Said, "Thanks," as if this were a great kindness.

Wyatt leaned forward and shouted into the wind, "Come back

to the Falls and I'd probably lose it, kill you or something. Okay?" He waved at the fields, the sky, and said, "Don't chase your tail!"

Wyatt climbed into the Explorer and closed the door. Rolled down the window and said, "I'll let Nicole know." Paul wanted to step forward and ask what, let her know what? but Wyatt rolled up the window. He put the Explorer in gear and drove forwards, then backwards, then forwards again until the truck was facing the direction it came in. Then he went.

Paul followed the taillights of the Explorer till they disappeared, then he put his head down and looked at the ruts and tracks as he walked. The snow was thicker now. He was thankful for the mitts and hat. Still, his feet were already wet and numb, and he knew he had a long walk. He wouldn't die out here. He was familiar with snow and ice and wind and the cold. The point was to keep your direction. Walking would keep him warm. He could walk for miles; it was like Christmas back home, the hush, the snow on his face, the emptiness, only back home there were groves of alder and thin spruce to offer protection. Shelter of sorts. The wind was cold, that was something to consider. Wyatt, that son of a bitch. Nothing Paul could have done. Wyatt was bigger and stronger and there was Sky to consider; best to keep the child at peace. Others might have looked at this situation and wondered, but Paul understood heroism. It belonged to fools and depended on luck.

Paul looked up at the sky, for a hole in the heavens, but there were only clouds and flurries and the wind. The Explorer's tracks were eventually covered and he had to guide himself by sliding his runners along the ruts. Snow pushed up inside his jeans and around his ankles, made his skin ache. At one point he found himself in the field and he stopped, looked around, and wondered how he got there. His quick breaths were a form of fright, the onset of something bigger. Perhaps he was lost. Not impossible. The highway should have been reached already. He turned back and stumbled up onto higher ground. Briefly, a light flickered, which he took to be the farmyard passed earlier, or maybe the highway. Elation. He beat his hands together as if applauding his own success and dipped back down onto the field, running in the direction of the light, now gone. He ran, head up, directly into the wind. The sleet drove against his forehead and up his nostrils. He watched for the light, another brief flash, but saw nothing. Still he ran, frantic now, breathing with great gulps, his feet splashing through what could have been a lake. He tripped and fell into the lake, which turned out to be a vast puddle in a field. He fell face first and soaked his jacket, his face, his mitts and jeans. He sucked up water and mud, sputtered as he surfaced. He threw his head back and howled, "Wyatt, you fucker."

"You fucker," he said again and the wind took his words.

He stood. Sobered, he decided to walk with the wind. Backtrack. He stripped off the wet mitts and threw them away. Put his hands into the soaked jacket pockets. Thought that his fingers maybe weren't there and removed one hand to verify. His fingers curled like claws. He put them back in his pocket. Moaned. He remembered a story of a man and a horse in a blizzard and how the man saved himself by killing the horse, slitting his belly, pulling out the entrails, and climbing into the hot belly. Paul had no horse. A dog would be enough to warm up the hands but Conrad was already dead. The past had become a litany of failures.

Walking with the wind was easier, almost an ease to being pushed along, though the trail seemed aimless and void. The front of his jacket and jeans had turned to ice; he could no longer feel his thighs. He was light-headed and believed he might be either hungry or freezing to death. Still, he walked, purposeful, with great intent, and when he arrived at a raised road he talked to himself and said, "This is the track I left earlier. See, here are the ruts." He calculated directions and turned to the right, followed again this same trail, intent now on seeing it through. The wind blew against his right side and he ducked his chin lower, turned his face south.

He knew when he arrived at the highway by the feel of the

smoother road. Though his feet were lumps of ice he sensed the change and stopped suddenly, his nose in the air, as if he were a buck scenting the territory, waiting to be shot. He turned left and counted the miles he had yet to walk. Five, six perhaps. A vehicle might appear out of the sleet and rain. Pick him up. Or hit him, toss him into the ditch, and keep driving. These were the possibilities. It was more difficult to follow the paved road. It was too smooth, blended too easily with the ditch. Paul found it easiest to walk the gravelled shoulder, to hear the occasional click of stones under his feet. At one point he fell, and because his hands were in the pockets of his coat and he was tired, he did not catch himself and so landed heavily, on the side of his face. He lay, cheek against the gravel, and found this to be a safe place, warm, out of the wind. He thought of Lise, of the shape of her and how he liked to lie just like this, cheek on her belly, tracing her mound with his finger as she lifted towards him, a rasping in her throat. What one got was never enough. Were he to have laid his life out against some greater pattern, he would have come up short. But doesn't everyone? Wouldn't Harry and Lise? Mrs. Wish? If he would have the chance again, he would invite Emily into his bed, touch his finger to the hole in her stocking, lift her dress over her head, say, Lie with me. And Nicole. He had been negligent. Wyatt was right, four thousand was a paltry sum for someone you loved. And it was fine now to admit this. He should have told her, in Montana, about her toenails. They were just there, a fine little pile. She would not have found this dire. It was an act of love. He saw that now. She would have seen that. Giggled and touched her nose and said, Well, Mr. Unger. She was not a child anymore, she had put away childish things. He remembered Sky as he had last seen him, huddled inside Wyatt's truck, his face glowing from the dash lights, his hands, immobile, folded around that bit of chocolate as if he were praying for something.

A car passed. A flash and then the pink of the lights and then gone. Paul lifted his head. Called out, on his hands and knees. He stood and began to run. Waved his arms, ran till exhausted. Bent over to regain his breath. Then, just as quickly, he continued to walk, full of hope now. He walked on for perhaps another hour, stopping often to check his watch, and then taking aim once again at the road, counting his steps out loud, up to a hundred and then beginning again. He thought he would walk another hundred and sit down and rest. He was at sixty-seven when he ran up against something hard and fell over. It was his half-ton. He tried the driver's door. It was not locked but ice had gathered on the door handle and his thumbs couldn't depress the button. Like useless clubs. He looked in the box for a hammer, something to smash the ice or the window. Found the spade, aimed it at the door, and swung. The metal banged and bounced back. Some ice had shaken loose but not enough. He walked around to the passenger's door and tried that. No success. He kicked with his feet at the door handle. Ice broke off the door and fell to the ground. He used both thumbs, stacked, to push at the handle. A grinding, like two steel bearings moaning past each other, and he pulled the door open and fell into the cab. The wind shut the door. Paul lay on the bench seat, knees up to his chest. The keys were in the ignition. He reached out, and using the heels of his hands, turned the key. The engine caught. Ran. Kept running and then Paul began to shake, convulsions that began at his head and followed through to his feet and then started again. Later, he realized this was good, because the shaking kept him awake long enough to fall onto the floor, curling up by the vent where the heat began to blow, slowly at first, then warm and thick as he pushed his fingers up the opening and moaned, safe in the walls of this, his own shell.

MANITOBA

THE FOLLOWING SPRING, ON A WARM DAY IN LATE APRIL, Paul moved his hives from the winter shed to the out yard. He removed the covers on the hives, used a little smoke to calm the bees, and assessed each hive for queen problems, diseases, food stores, and strength. The strong hives had eight to fourteen pounds of bees and at least five frames of brood. Brood frames held eggs, larvae, and pupae. A few colonies had died over the winter and Paul cleaned out these hives and set them away from the apiary. He found one colony that was failing and decided to unite it with another colony. He located the weak queen, crushed it with his hive tool, and searched for other queen cells. They resembled a peanut shell, were an inch or more in length and hung vertically from the comb. Paul found five of these and destroyed them. He opened the hive top on a strong colony and placed a sheet of newspaper over the upper brood chamber. He cut slits in the paper and placed the weaker colony on top, knowing that the bees would gradually chew through the newspaper and join the other colony.

He worked through the day, grateful for the sun, the warmth, glad to be rid of a winter that had been long and dark. He ate a cucumber sandwich at noon, sitting on the porch steps, facing south towards the fallow garden and the honey house. The bees were foraging already, seeking out willow and early maple. A few bees were working the early-blooming wild spikenard at the edge of the lawn. Paul had placed pails of sugar syrup mixed with antibiotics around the apiary to supplement the feeding. Earlier, he had found one colony robbing the store of honey from another colony. The attacking workers were furtive, setting up decoys, parrying and diving, eventually entering the weaker hive to rip off the wax seal from the comb and steal the honey. The robber bees were single-minded and careless; they left debris and moved in and out in a hurry. In order to save the weak hive Paul had moved it to another area and placed a sugar pail beside the stronger hive.

By mid-afternoon he was tired and went into the house and lay on the couch and watched the light move across the ceiling. He napped and woke to the phone ringing. It was Sue. She said, "Two things. I'm worried about you and how about coming with me and Chris to Jill Falk's wedding social?"

Paul said, "That's sweet of you to worry, and no, I won't."

"You're a hermit, Daddy. I've seen you two, three times this winter."

"I'm here. I'm not going anywhere."

"Mum said you *want* to disappear."

"She did, eh?"

"Do you?" Sue asked.

"I don't think so. But maybe she knows best."

"I'm thinking we should see each other more. It's a bit of a distance from La Broquerie to Winnipeg, but you can't just push everything away. You're my father."

"I am," Paul said, and he pictured her now, face too serious, the lines on her brow like her mother's when she was considering something important.

"I love you," Sue said.

"You do," Paul answered. This sounded more like a question than a statement, and so, to correct it, Paul added, "I know." And he did. He was surprised by that admission, as if love were meant for others.

"So, come with me then," Sue said. "You can sit in a corner and drink. I'll sit with you."

The light in the room was changing. The sun had dropped beyond the bare branches of the maple hedgerow. A dimness now.

"Okay," Paul said and even as he spoke he saw that he would regret the decision, this descent back into the world.

The wedding social was held at a hall on the outskirts of Furst. Paul drove out together with Sue and her friend, Chris, a boy slightly younger than herself whom she had met at a winter bush party. From the back seat Paul asked Chris about his family. His father was dead. There was his mother, himself, and a three-year-old sister. His mother was a chicken farmer out near Île des Chênes. Layers. Two barns. Chris said he hated eggs but helped his mother when he was home.

"Is she remarried?" Paul asked.

"No. She almost did. Might still." Chris lifted his eyebrows. A hint of something darker there, as if his past were not all rosy.

"Chris wants to be a firefighter," Sue said. "Isn't that neat?" She was driving, and as she spoke she wrapped a free arm around Chris's neck and pulled him close. His head was shaved and Paul could see the imperfections of his skull.

"Yeah, neat," Paul said.

"Mum was wondering if you were coming to this social," Sue said. She was still hanging on to Chris, who was listing to his left, his head on her shoulder.

"She was? I wonder why?"

Chris slid out from under Sue's arm and lit a cigarette. Sue held out two fingers. Chris handed her the cigarette and she drew and blew at the windshield. Handed it back. "I dunno," she said and then talked about what everyone was thinking, about Jeffrey, this young boy, twenty-three, who Lise was seeing. A baby-faced travelling computer salesman who had come into the store one day, midwinter, and wooed Lise.

Sue said, "You met him, Dad?"

"No, I haven't. Lise told me about him, though."

"That's so rude," Sue said. "Don't you think that's rude?" she asked Chris.

Chris nodded agreement, opened his window, and blew out the smoke. Sue said, "Mum's lost it. Jeffrey's okay, he's a nice boy, but he's a boy. You don't sleep with a boy who could be your son. He's pretty much the age Stephen would be. That's gross."

Paul thought about Stephen being that age. Thought that there was nothing more painful than a lost child. Left a hole in your chest that couldn't be filled. He'd given Jeffrey and Lise some thought throughout the winter and he couldn't say he blamed Lise. There were moments when he envied her.

He remembered when she had first told him about Jeffrey. "I'm awful," she whispered, "Aren't I?" She had arrived on a cold day and was still dressed in a coat and toque and boots and was standing in the middle of his kitchen. The winter sun was bright and came in through the south windows, and if you sat in the direct light, it warmed your knees and hands and made summer seem less distant. Paul looked at Lise, looked at the curls protruding from under her toque, the faint age lines around her eyes, and he found he could easily picture the shape of her beneath all that clothing and he wondered what it was like to lie beside a boy whose skin was taut and unblemished, a boy who would inevitably break her heart.

He had told her to sit and she did. They talked about Stephen and Sue and Sky and Nicole. Paul confessed that he had failed in Montana. He had been selfish and vain. A coward, too. He told her about Wyatt and being left out in the storm. "There is nothing more frightening," he said. "I wanted to lie down out there."

"Oh, Paul," Lise said. "That man should be arrested."

"No. No. He didn't mean to kill me. In some strange way he allowed me to see differently."

"I think Jeffrey helps me see differently," Lise said. Her small hands moved her mitts around on the table. He kissed her at the door. On the cheek. Saw that she was unsettled and lost and this saddened him more than he would have thought.

The next morning a buck had been stranded in the drifts formed along the windward side of the tree break. The buck was buried up to his neck; a tremendous amount of struggling had only sent him deeper into the heavy drifts. Paul had to dig him out with a shovel, working slowly around the animal, who, wild with fear, sucked in great quantities of air and made a noise which resembled a pallet of bricks being dragged across gravel. The buck smelled of wet fur, piss, skunk, and sap. He foamed at the mouth. The whites of his eyes were moon-like and red-veined. Paul stood, waist-deep in the snow, just aft of the buck's head, and thought how easy it would be to slit the animal's throat. Stock the freezer. But Paul knew nothing about bleeding a dead animal, about gutting and quartering. His business, that morning, was to free the buck. After digging out one side Paul shifted to the other. The buck heaved and blew. To no avail. He looked around at Paul as if to question his intention. Paul leaned his shoulder against the buck's shoulder and pushed. His cheek rubbed up against the smell of piss and sap. The buck swung his head and tried to knock Paul away. Bared his teeth. Hee-hawed. Aimed a greenish antler at Paul's eye. Barely missed. Paul stepped back and proceeded to dig again, swearing at the animal. He paused finally to rest, and leaning on the shovel, said, "Go, you old fart." He took the shovel and swung it at the buck's rear. A crack and a snort and the buck fell sideways, his hooves suddenly loose. It flailed and found a footing and erupted from the hole Paul had dug, ploughing along the windbreak of poplars, down in through the ditch, up onto the road, and beyond to the next field where it foundered and carried on, eventually disappearing into the bush along the creek.

Later that afternoon, perhaps because of Lise's visit, or perhaps because of the stranded buck, Paul had tried to call Nicole. Wyatt answered and Paul was so surprised he lost his sense of direction. He finally asked about Nicole. She was gone. Where? Just gone. And Sky? Gone, too.

"Nicole ran," Wyatt said. "Everybody does that."

Paul didn't speak. His breathing was suddenly quicker. Wyatt's voice was clear, as if they were sitting in the same room. A tap dripped somewhere. "Are they all right?" Paul asked.

"I thought you were dead," Wyatt said. "I thought, Christ, I killed him. I didn't mean to, but there you have it." He laughed but it wasn't really a laugh and Paul imagined that this was Wyatt apologizing. Paul could hear him light a cigarette. "Anyways," Wyatt continued, "I thought of turning back, you know, finding you, but Sky was crying for Nicole and anyways, look, you made it. I told Nicole what a fine outdoorsman you were. A fucking survivor. She was upset." He paused. Said, "Angry." Then he said, "I'm glad I was right. Really. You there?"

"You didn't hurt them, did you?" Paul asked.

"I loved her. And Sky. I came home one day and they were gone. She'd left a note with that loopy handwriting of hers. An amazing gesture that. She didn't have to, did she?"

"Do you know where they went?"

"That's the thing. I don't. Do you?"

Paul thought of Wyatt sitting in his little house. The shrine of guns and knives in the next room. The TV going in the background. He saw the uselessness of this conversation but still he said, "What you told me about Sky not being my blood. Remember?"

"Wasn't true. Not at least as far as I know."

"Even though you said it."

"I lied. I was angry."

Paul didn't say anything. He listened to Wyatt breathe. Then, finally, Wyatt said, "You don't hate me?"

"No, I don't."

"You gonna forgive me then?"

"I could do that. Yeah."

"You're amazing, Paul. I'm sorry."

When Paul had hung up his hands were shaking and his breathing was ragged, though he wasn't sure why. He sat in that spot in the kitchen and took in the final bit of afternoon sun and he tried to think, but he couldn't conjure up anything solid other than that persistent image of Wyatt and him standing outside the Explorer and Wyatt handing him the mittens and hat and then the door shutting and then Sky's eyes and hands in the yellow light of the dash. He remembered walking and running and walking and falling several times and finally the truck coming up to meet him. Then he

woke from a shallow sleep and found himself on the floor of the
cab. His cheek rested on the rubber mat, a bent and soaked novel
looked him in the eye. He raised his head and listened to the truck
motor run. He was sweating. His fingers hurt; the tip of one thumb
would eventually fall off. He sat then and looked out the windshield at the road and the fields. The sun was shining. There was
no more wind. Snow was melting on the pavement. It looked like
a wonderful day. The clarity of the sun and the sky meeting the
earth. The snow crystals in the air. The wonder. All of that.

That winter he had dreamed again of Stephen. Long, involved
dreams. One time Stephen and he were walking on water and Paul
was talking but Stephen wouldn't answer. Paul turned to see his
face but couldn't, and every time he stopped talking Stephen began
to sink. So Paul continued talking. The lake was endless, as, it
seemed, was the dream, and when Paul finally woke he was breathless and thirsty and his throat was sore.

The dreams were not cathartic, though Paul wished they were.
Their madness and unpredictability unsettled him. He imagined
that until his own death he would dream of Stephen and he
wondered if this was normal. One night he dreamed of two boys,
neither of which was Stephen. They were strangers walking away
from him down a wide road. Paul watched them until they disappeared. He remembered this particular dream because it came back
to him the following day, a Saturday in late March. Paul drove to
Winnipeg to buy some bee supplies and just on the outskirts of
Furst he passed by two boys hitchhiking. First, he had continued
on without stopping, but then a mile further he slowed and took
the exit across the median and circled back to pick them up. They
climbed in and Paul drove them out to the Number 1. They were
young boys, fourteen and sixteen, and they were headed to Falcon
Lake where their mother lived. Paul eyed them and said, "Tell you
what, I'll drive you up to Richer. At least there's a gas station there
where you can warm up."

The younger boy nodded and said, "That'd be great. We know this corner up here. Lousy for rides. Nobody ever slows down."

Near the Richer turnoff Paul asked, "You dressed warm enough?"

Both boys nodded.

"Here," Paul said, and reached down under the seat. "I've got an extra hat here."

The younger boy looked at the toque sitting on Paul's thigh.

"Go ahead. You've got a long way to go."

The boy took the hat. Put it on his head.

Paul pulled onto the shoulder by the corner store. "Here," he said, "Good luck."

The boys climbed out. Paul waited for the door to close and then he crossed over the divided highway and turned back to Winnipeg.

Four hours later, returning home, his half-ton full of bee equipment, Paul passed by the Furst turn-off and continued on to Richer where he pulled into the corner store lot. Paul went into the store. A young girl was behind the counter. She was putting on nail polish. Paul asked, "Did you see two boys out on the highway? In their teens."

The girl looked at Paul. She held the little brush so it pointed at Paul's head. "Uh-uh," she went.

"No boys came in here either? To warm up? The older one had a black hat with a hornet on the front."

The girl's tongue curled as she leaned towards her hands. She blew and talked at her knuckles, "I didn't see any boys. No black hats either." She looked up. "Were they from around here?"

Paul shook his head.

The girl said, "Strange boys? I'd've noticed them then. They yours?"

"No. No. Just kids hitchhiking."

The girl nodded. Waved her orange nails at Paul as he left.

Paul sat in the half-ton and looked across the lot to the highway. He pulled out to the westbound lane and drove back to the Number 12. Figured the boys must have gotten a ride immediately, or they went up the road a bit, or hitchhiked home. Gone like the dream they had walked out of.

Paul knew some people at the social. Harry Kehler was there with Bunny. They were sitting at a table with Gladys Frohm. Harry was eating popcorn and drinking beer. His arm was around Bunny's shoulder; he leaned towards her once, then twice, to whisper some confidence. Bunny's eyes closed and opened as she listened.

Paul stuck with Sue and Chris. Bought them each a beer and ordered himself a double scotch. They sat and watched the crowd. The D.J. played mostly modern tunes. Paul said to Sue, "I haven't danced since your wedding."

"Do you want to?" She held out her hand.

"Maybe later. You go with Chris."

"Wanna?" Sue asked.

Chris stood and followed Sue out onto the floor. They were the only ones dancing and Paul watched Sue move, her hand going up once as if to touch Chris's shoulder but missing him and falling away. Chris, as he danced, looked at Sue's legs. She was wearing black pants that make little bells at her ankles, and shoes with big heels and a silky skimpy top.

Sue and Chris danced for two more songs, not talking, not touching. Paul fetched another drink. Bumped into Bunny who said, "Paul," and held his elbow.

"Hi, Bunny."

"What are you, a hermit?" she asked.

"Maybe I am," Paul said. He looked at her nose, her teeth, the bunny in her. Her real name was Elizabeth and then it became Lizzy and finally Bunny. Harry married her as Bunny. Paul said now, "How's Harry?"

"Harry's good." She went up on tiptoes. Tilted her head. Paul remembered her diving at him in Gladys's kitchen, her quick hiss as she rolled her ankle. This was a different woman standing here today.

Paul said, "I'm glad."

"He said just yesterday that we should invite Paul Unger over."

"He did? Well. There's a lot of stuff there."

"You wouldn't have to. I'd understand." She touched his elbow again.

Paul looked down at his drink, saw that he had finished most of it, and joined the line again behind Bunny. He said, "Looks like tonight'll be a merry-go-round."

Bunny smiled and appraised him and she nodded out at the dance floor and said, "Sue's beautiful."

"Yes, she is."

"New boyfriend?"

"I don't know. Isn't it strange that I don't know?"

"She likes him. I could tell right away when they walked in."

"Well, I hope it goes both ways. Not much fun otherwise."

Bunny looked at Paul as if he had said something profound. Then it was her turn and she ordered two beer. Paul stood beside her. He could see how her belly pushed against her dress, a small bulge. He liked that. Wondered if Harry found it endearing.

"You come talk. We're over there." Bunny pointed with a beer and then weaved her way through the tables towards Harry, her hips dodging chairs and shoulders, her little round chin pushing out towards Harry, who saw Paul and lifted a hand in greeting. Paul lifted a hand back.

Another double for himself, two more beer for the children, and Paul managed to wind his way back to his table. More people were dancing now. Sue and Chris kept going. An hour passed during which Paul watched the dancers and made frequent trips back to the bar. Sue and Chris finally joined him and hoisted warm bottles and drank deeply. Chris's face was red. Out on the floor, Julia Barndt, a girl Paul knew in high school, was line dancing with her husband. He was a tall thin man who sold cars at the local Nissan dealer.

"Line dancing's great," Sue said.

Chris shook his head. "It's weird," he said. "Like you can't think for yourself."

Paul nodded in agreement, though he admired the memory

required. All those steps, the claps, the turns. His head felt light. He needed to eat something or he would get sick, or just fall asleep and be lousy company.

"Julia's a poet." He said this to no one, simply stated that fact and then added, "I remember Lise reading me one of her poems. It was about Jesus."

"Are you drunk, Daddy?" Sue seemed concerned. She touched his shoulder.

"Close," Paul said. "Not there yet. I'm fine."

"You look so sad. Doesn't he look sad?" Sue asked this of Chris, who in his benevolence both nodded and shook his head.

Sue's head floated away and then reconnected. Paul stood, wobbled, excused himself, and pushed through the crowd to the washroom. He entered a stall, bent forward, and threw up into the toilet. He held on to the seat with his hands. His leather watch strap was splattered by vomit. He considered that fact but did nothing about it. He had drunk too fast on an empty stomach. Tried to remember what he had eaten for supper and recalled a bowl of cereal and a slice of raisin toast. He threw up again. Went down on his knees and hugged the toilet. Laid his head on his arm and perhaps slept, for the next moment someone was banging at the door. It was Chris, wondering if he could help.

"No, I'm fine. Just fine." Paul stood, flushed, and backed out of the stall. In the mirror, Paul watched Chris watch him clean his face and hands. Chris turned and left then and Paul followed him back into the hall, where the dance floor was full. He saw a flash of Lise, hair pulled back, being spun by a ponytailed man. A boy. They disappeared. Sue came off the floor and took Paul's arm. "You silly man," she said. She guided him back to the table, sat down beside him.

He said, "Lise is here."

Sue looked away. Turned back to him. Held his hand. Said, "You wanna go home."

"Yes." He stood, picked up his jacket, and walked out of the hall into the night where he leaned into a strong wind and heard the bark of geese overhead. He looked up. Found nothing.

Sue appeared at his side and said, "I'll take you home and come back."

Paul thought he should apologize but could not gather the words. Fatigue or some other weight rested on him. Sue believed she knew the source of his grief. She said, "I told her not to come. Not with him at least. It's mean."

"It's not that."

"Well, if you aren't upset, I am."

"Thank you, sweetie." Paul put a hand on her neck. Kept it there, felt her vertebrae, the shift of her tendons as she drove. He leaned his head back against the seat. Closed his eyes. Startled at one point, snapped to, only to discover Sue's hands and face caught in the glow of the dash. For a moment Sue resembled Nicole and this was a strange comfort. Paul watched carefully until his daughter came back into focus. His fingers, still on her neck, had discovered an artery.

"You have a neck like your mother's," he said.

Sue looked at him. She said, "Mum told me about Wyatt and Nicole. About Wyatt trying to kill you."

"That what she said?"

"Well, didn't he?"

"I suppose. Funny. All winter I've been amazed. It's like because I didn't die, I've climbed onto a different plane." He stopped, considered this, and said, "A person might ask why I didn't go back and get Sky again. Did I give up? I ask myself this. There is no good answer. Perhaps I was afraid."

"Sure you were. Nicole's evil, Daddy. I can see that now. She probably told Wyatt to kill you." The blip of blood going through the artery picked up speed as Sue talked. Paul waited. She said, "I hate her," and then, as if location were related to hatred, asked, "Where is she?"

"I don't know. Though last month I talked to her father and he said that Nicole was in Texas. With Sky. Everybody was fine. She was going to call me. Her father said that."

"And has she?"

"Not yet. Though she could. Any time. Or never. Sometimes I

believe she'll show up at my door again. Sky hanging on to her leg.
I love him."

"She's really selfish, Daddy. You know that."

"I don't expect much. I've got my life."

The car found the gravel shoulder, swayed and came back
straight. The rhythm of the road, the darkness outside the car, the
half-light inside, Paul's dream-like consciousness, the previous
conversation, these produced an intimacy that allowed Paul to say,
"You know that night Stephen left? He tried to come back, but I
locked him out. He tried all the doors, even kicked at the front
door, but I wouldn't let him in."

Paul stopped talking. This was like dropping a heavy stone off a
cliff. Paul waited to register its effect. He had the sense that he had
held his breath forever and now finally exhaled. He closed his eyes.
Gravel banged against the car chassis.

Sue touched his leg. His head. Played with his hair. "Oh,
Daddy," she said. Her hand on his head was a comfort and she left
it there until she slowed for Paul's driveway and turned in. She
stopped the car and then turned and pulled his head towards hers
and kissed his forehead. Her face was warm. Her neck smelled of
perfume and sweat. Her breast pressed his shoulder and he thought
of the intimacy and secrets of family. She held his head as if he were
a child, then released him. Paul said, "Bring Chris back here for the
night. Doesn't matter how late. I like him."

"Isn't he great? Thanks, Daddy." She kissed his ear.

He stood in his yard and watched her car disappear, the sound
of her tires on the gravel eventually blending with the wind. The
sky, the dark fallow fields beyond, the night. He went inside and
pulled off his clothes and showered. Towelled himself dry and lay
down naked beneath his blanket and closed his eyes to stop the
nausea from returning. He saw Lise dancing with Jeffrey, who was
too tall, almost bird-like, and he imagined Lise's small body working that young angular length. Jeffrey looked nothing like Stephen
and that was a small mercy. He saw Harry's hand going up in greeting, and then falling away to gather in Bunny as she sat down

beside him. He thought about Sue touching his neck and head and the smell and mystery of her. He wondered what she would think of him tomorrow, after she had had time to ponder his confession. He drifted at the edge of sleep and considered that none of this mattered and he felt a calm he had not known for a long time. He slept without dreaming, waking when Sue and Chris came in. Heard through his doziness their giggles, the clatter of cups and plates in the kitchen, the smell of toast, and then he slept again and woke late. He rose, made coffee, and surveyed the yard through the front window. Sue and Chris were still sleeping, tucked away in the far bedroom, the one Nicole and Sky used to share.

At the edge of the trees he could see the woodpile he cut and stacked one day last winter. A cord of maple, cut and split and piled, and measured, four by four by eight. It had been a dark day, just after Christmas. His mother had called to say that Mrs. Wish was pregnant, wasn't that wonderful, and then she had asked about Lise, and Paul had gleaned the first inklings of Lise and young Jeffrey. Concluding by Paul's silence that this was news, she sighed, "Oh, my, Paul, I don't know. I don't know." And she hung up, all unknowing.

Paul had gone out then, into a light snowfall, to accomplish something. He had enough wood to last the winter but decided to acquire more. He worked the maples at the edge of the clearing, using only an axe, and by nightfall he had achieved the perfect pile. Looking at it now, he believed he might never take wood from it. Simply let it stand.

Sue and Chris woke in the early afternoon. They appeared like two cats and sat at the kitchen table. Sue, in pyjamas, perched on Chris's lap, her bare feet overlapping. Paul served toast and coffee. Conversation was muted but easy. Paul asked about the rest of the social. All Sue could remember was the poet, Julia Barndt, falling over drunk and lying with her legs parted.

"I could see right up her skirt. She just lay there and nobody picked her up. Not even her husband who was dancing with Bunny. Yeah, and Harry was looking for you." She said nothing about Lise, and Paul didn't ask. Neither did they speak of the previous night's conversation.

After eating, Chris and Sue left for Winnipeg and Paul was alone again. He worked in the honey house. Hauled several hives into the out yard. The phone was ringing when he returned to the honey house but stopped before he could reach it. It rang again later that evening but he was in the bath and so once more missed it. Sue telephoned just before midnight to thank him for the wonderful time. "Chris liked you," she said. "Says you're too serious, though."

"Okay. Did you phone? Earlier?"

"No, this is the first," she said. Then she added, "I was thinking. You shouldn't torture yourself, Dad. Things are more complicated than you think."

"I know that."

"Do you? I mean, Stephen didn't die because you got mad at him."

"I know that, too," Paul said. A spring fly banged against the shade of the lamp. Buzzed at the base and aimed for the light. Bounced away. "It's okay," he said, as if it were important to comfort his daughter. Then he added, "Lise doesn't know. About me locking him out."

"What difference would it make? Besides, Mum doesn't have to know everything. People think they need to know everything but they don't. It's not fun, all that knowledge. You have to leave it alone, Dad. I love you, all right?"

Paul nodded at the phone. Asked again, "And you didn't call? Earlier?"

"I didn't."

That night he went to bed and considered again that confession was like falling. The solace came from finally hitting something solid. He thought he should be more at peace but if he was he couldn't tell. He imagined that Nicole phoned and she laughed in his ear and said, "Paul," and told him that she and Sky were coming home. "See?" she said. Paul harboured those thoughts, descended finally into dark layers of sleep that were dreamless. A knocking woke him during the night; it came down from above and pulled him up through the inky layers. He lay and listened to a brisk spring wind passing through the bare trees. Something banged, wood on wood, an aimless rhythm. He got up and stood in the porch and looked out onto the yard. He could see the ripples in the puddles, made by the wind. The honey house door swung open and banged shut. Again. Paul dressed and stepped outside and walked down the stairs and across the yard to the door, which swung out again and banged. The latch had broken. Paul found a hammer and nail, banged in the nail halfway. Bent it and secured the door. Walking back to the house he stopped and looked up at the sky. There were few stars and the wind was cool, yet it carried a faint warm smell, as if to say, Soon. A jet passed overhead. He thought that if he were to call out, the words would be caught by the wind and taken upwards and disappear.

He turned and went back inside. Sat on a chair and looked down at his hands folded in his lap. When he stopped crying the darkness hadn't gone away yet.